GW00707488

THE INTERLOPER

A NOVEL

THE INTERLOPER
A NOVEL

EILÍS DILLON

Hodder & Stoughton
LONDON SYDNEY AUCKLAND TORONTO

'A Dialogue of Self and Soul' is quoted from *The Collected Poems* of W. B. Yeats by permission of A. P. Watt Limited on behalf of Michael B. Yeats and Macmillan London Limited.

British Library Cataloguing in Publication Data
Dillon, Eilís
   The interloper.
   I. Title
   823'.914[F]   PR6054.I42
   ISBN 0-340-40669-0

I am content to follow to its source
Every event in action or in thought;
Measure the lot; forgive myself the lot!
When such as I cast out remorse
So great a sweetness flows into the breast
We must laugh and we must sing,
We are blest by everything,
Everything we look upon is blest.

W. B. Yeats
(A Dialogue of Self and Soul)

1

I've got to tell this story to someone. The beginning of it happened a long time ago, more than fifty years, when Ireland was a very different country from what it is now. I was quite bewildered when I came back. Nothing was as I remembered it, not even the faces of the people. Dublin was packed with cars and well-dressed citizens. No one was in rags. Of course there were poor people but they didn't have the look of desperation that they had when I was young. The most remarkable difference was the air of confidence everywhere, even though the question of Ulster and partition had arisen once more and one could hear it being discussed endlessly everywhere.

It was in September 1972 that my doctor, Bill Webber, told me: 'If there's anything special you want to do, the sooner the better. You haven't got much time.'

He is a neighbour of mine in the Berkshires, where I live all the year round and he comes for the summer to get away from the heat of New York. We've known each other so long that he didn't go through the motions of breaking it gently. He knows enough of my history to be able to say briskly: 'Use your time well. I can predict this and that but one can never be certain that any of it will happen.'

'How much time?'

'A year, perhaps longer. The tests show that it's there, all right, but at your age the cells renew themselves more slowly. No panic, but you may not be very comfortable at times.'

'Can I go to Ireland?'

'Of course. It's easier than going to New York, these days. I'll give you the name of a doctor there who will look after you if necessary.'

In a flash I had seen what I wanted to do but I couldn't give the details to him nor to anyone else. He had been to Ireland and he recommended Buswell's hotel, in the centre of the city. I could have afforded something more expensive but I liked the idea of mixing with the people who used the hotel bar. He said I would never be short of company in the evenings, and this was indeed true. I sat there by the hour, chatting with anyone and everyone, until the level of sound went above where I could hear what my companions were saying. Then I would slip away to bed and sleep to the hum of voices from below. I slept soundly in Dublin, better than I had done for years.

It was no more than a week before I found someone who put me on the track of Paul Dunne. I had already found that a good many of the men who frequented the hotel bar had heard of him, or had met and never forgotten him.

There was one man, named John MacDonagh, a civil servant near retiring age, who said: 'I haven't thought about Dunne for years. We heard he died in Germany during the war, in the 1940s, and then I discovered that he lives in a cottage in Wicklow. I'm in Social Welfare, and his name appeared on some list or other. Did you know him well?'

'Very well indeed, at one time. But I haven't been in touch with him for fifty years.'

MacDonagh said, looking at me strangely: 'He was one of the people who could never forget about the civil war and partition and all that. The rest of us had to bury it and get on with building up the country. I still don't know for certain which side was right. But you can't keep a war going forever.'

I could see that he was wondering if I was one of those elderly Americans who were running in guns for the I.R.A.

'I believe in avoiding war,' I said.

He relaxed and said: 'Then why not let sleeping dogs lie? Those old warriors have had their day. Why stir them up again?'

'Old times,' I said vaguely.

Dunne himself called me an interloper, even before he knew why I had come to look for him. Funny word to use. I think he meant something else – an interferer, a waker-up of sleeping dogs, as MacDonagh had said.

Of course I found people who knew where he lived. It was a broken-down cottage in the Dublin mountains, Rocky Valley to be exact. I got there on a misty afternoon in December, one of those days when the damp eats into your clothes and every move you make is a torment. At least that's how it is at my age, and with my poor health.

A track led up to the cottage, rutted with years of heavy rain, never repaired. I left my rented car at the foot of it, after I had taken one look, and walked – or rather climbed – up to the door. The cottage was set on a little platform of rock, quite stark, no attempt to make a garden or even to grow a rose-bush. It looked deserted, but for a trickle of smoke from the chimney. I began to doubt if I had come to the right place. I paused at the door. I was puffed, and if this was really where Dunne lived, I didn't want to appear too decrepit before him.

He opened the door within seconds of my knocking, and stood there staring at me. He was very thin, as thin as myself, and his eyes had sunk into his head, making them seem bigger. He looked weather-beaten. His hair was almost all gone, and what he had of it was a yellowish grey. His clothes were very old: a tweed jacket with one button missing, baggy flannel trousers that rambled around until they took the shape of his figure – a scarecrow, in utter contrast to what he had been when he was young. Instantly I remembered how he always managed to overawe me long ago. I don't know from Adam how he did it, but I actually began to feel self-conscious about my own appearance, my suit and tie, my smart overcoat and my tweed hat that I had bought at the airport after I had taken one look at the weather.

He recognised me almost at once but he played a game of pretending he didn't know who I was. I took a step forward, with my hand out, but he pulled back instinctively. It was only for a second. Then he said: 'Michael D'Arcy.'

He shook hands as if he hated doing it. The wind was nibbling at me and I gave a shiver. He missed nothing. He said: 'You'd better come in. I have a fire.'

The inside of the cottage was clean but the furnishings, such as as they were, seemed on the edge of extinction. A wood fire warmed it pleasantly. A door beside the fire presumably led into the bedroom. I could see a dingy kitchen through another doorway along the back wall. Wooden boxes of different sizes had been placed on their sides to serve as bookshelves. The covers of the books were a uniform dark brown, probably from the smoke of the fire. One armchair was half-turned towards the fire, its cretonne cover in shreds. An up-ended box served as a table beside it and held an untidy pile of books. An old wooden rocking-chair was set at the other side of the fireplace but it also had a pile of books on it. There was a kitchen table with one chair, and a dresser with chipped mugs and plates. Dunne said satirically: 'Take the armchair. You look under the weather.'

He was rolling from heel to toe now, sure that he was in better shape than I was. I must have looked quite shocked. I was angry with myself for having shown my feelings so clearly. He hadn't changed – never so happy as when he had someone at a disadvantage. But I hadn't come here to resume our old relationship, at least not if I could help it. I said: 'What about you?'

He indicated the chair at the table, pulled it out and sat on it, leaning one elbow on the litter of papers that lay on the table. I was beginning to recover. Dublin people had always kept cottages in the mountains for weekends and holidays, often as wretched as this one. It was his country retreat, that was all. I wondered if he had any neighbours, if anyone ever dropped in to visit him and have a chat in the evenings. I had seen no houses near. He frightened me by reading my thoughts: 'I don't have any visitors.

No one comes up here in winter. My nearest neighbour is nearly half a mile away. There are hikers in summer, sometimes.'

He sat and stared at me without speaking. It would have broken my nerve if I hadn't remembered that he had always had this trick. Some people thought it proved he had great wisdom. While the rest of us chattered like monkeys he would be perfectly silent, swinging his gaze from one face to another without changing his expression. Inscrutable. His height was an advantage, and long ago he was blocky rather than heavy, with sharp, dark-blue eyes. I've known other people with eyes like that who were only short-sighted. Before he spoke, you got an impression that Dunne was a special person, valuable, important, powerful in an effortless way. Some actors and musicians have this quality – worth its weight in gold to them.

I'll never forget the evening he came to Rabbit Island in Lough Corrib, a sunny cold day in late October, 1920. The island belonged to my father but he didn't know we were there. He had no sympathy with the Movement – that's what we all called it in those days. My mother was rather sympathetic; my father never. Towards evening Seán Kelly, the Corkman, was trying to light a fire of damp turf and addressing it savagely as if it were human: 'Come on, there, take a light. Lord God, man, aren't you the sacred soil of Ireland that we're fighting for?'

The singing Cork accent was part of Kelly. I could as soon forget his face, his round, hazel eyes and soft mouth, and his wild black hair.

It had rained the night before, a thin sprinkle but enough to dampen the twigs that we depended on for kindling. Kelly was an expert – he would get a fire going when no one else could. We were all hiding out from the Black-and-Tans for different reasons. We each had a gun of some sort, so that we could have put up a fight if necessary. Also, when we were leaving for the island, I had taken my father's three shot-guns that he kept for sport. My mother said she would tell him that they had been requisitioned by the I.R.A. I knew he would guess that this meant me, but he would not betray me.

I was twenty-one years old, a deserter from the Arts Faculty at University College, Dublin, where I had enlisted in this army. My father growled from time to time that if I had gone to Trinity College I would never have done it, but this was not true. My older brother Frederick had been at the National University too, until he went off to France with the British army. He was killed in 1917, with the rank of Captain.

I celebrated my twenty-first birthday on the island. My mother managed to send me a cake by one of the fishermen who lived along the shore and who all knew we were there. The five of us devoured it at one sitting. Then we settled back to playing cards, twenty-five, with pebbles for stakes. You would think they were golden guineas, to see the men slap their cards on the board we used for a table, when they were winning, or gather them up sullenly when they lost. No one in my family ever played cards, except bezique. I didn't dare mention that. I had to learn the rules of the game by trial and error. There was no cheating – it was all very serious.

We were never really hungry. We had a sack of potatoes and we ate them cold for breakfast and in the middle of the day, and cooked more in the evening. Sometimes we caught trout and baked them on stones heated in the fire. Rabbits too – they were everywhere, popping out of their burrows at dusk, easy to trap. We slept in the stone hut that the poteen-makers used and cooked in their hollow where the smoke was invisible against the grey rock that backed the fireplace. We were sheltered from the wind by a little grove of beech-trees.

There is a special tang in the late autumn days in Ireland. I've noticed it again since I've come home. The damp air brings out the smell of the withered leaves. They fell in drifts when the wind rose. We had gold sunsets and sharp, cold mornings. When I went down to the edge of the lake I dipped one foot in cautiously and pulled it out again more than once, before I had the courage to walk in. That daily bath was a standing joke with the others – they wouldn't have dreamed of swimming in the lake water. They swore the cold would be the death of me, or else the swallow-holes would get me. I had been taught some Spartan habits in my English school, where we were obliged to take a cold shower first thing every morning – quite a feat in the winter climate of Lancashire.

I often wonder whether the daily cold bath was a vestige of the Roman occupation of Britain. Since the Romans couldn't have existed without baths, it may even have been the reason they decided to go home to a better climate where it was easier to heat the water. Or it may have been a plot of the Jesuits to cool us down after a night of dangerous dreams. Anyway, my washing ensured that I never got what the men called the Republican Itch, an awful mixture of scabies and impetigo, brought on as much by bad food as by lack of washing. On my various travels, whenever I saw a stream of any size, no matter what the season, I made sure to get a dip in it.

I remember that we were very quiet on the island by day. I was the youngest. Mike Faherty was a year or two older. The other three were in their late twenties. One of them, Brown, was married and had small children, and we knew he worried about them constantly. Late at night we sang fierce songs about Ireland. Kelly had a beautiful baritone voice. He knew the gentle songs as well, 'Carrigdown' and 'The Banks of my own lovely Lee' and 'The Bantry Girls' Lament for Johnny' and a great many in Irish, most of them melancholy and bitter. Then there would be a long silence, until he would break out hilariously into an English comic song from the repertoire he had acquired off gramophone records. A fair sample was the one about the child who swallowed a shilling:

Punching the kid to get out the bob –
We've only got ninepence out of him yet
But we're getting it by degrees.

That afternoon, the twenty-first of October, the weather
began to get really cold. The evenings were already darkening early and the men were nervous. Brown and Cummins,
the two Galwaymen, had begun to talk about the night of
the ghosts, Hallowe'en, as if they seriously expected a visit
from some of them. I was more afraid of real men. I walked
down to the shore to get away from them and my stomach
gave an ugly twitch when I saw a boat making straight for
the island. I remembered the face of the big Black-and-Tan
who used to strut up and down the main street of Galway,
fondling the two revolvers that he always carried, and firing
a few shots when the fancy struck him. He seemed to be
permanently drunk. That face still haunts me, especially in
the helpless position of sleep.

I watched the boat for a few minutes, hiding behind a
thorn-bush a little back from the shore. A dozen swans went
paddling by, very fast, carried along by the current towards
the river. You could imagine the long swing and heave of
their feet. They were beginning to feel the cold, too, and
wanted to get down to the salt water at the mouth of the
river as quickly as possible.

I could see a solid, bare-headed man sitting in the stern
of the boat, somehow looking as if he were not used to the
water, perhaps clutching the gunwales nervously – I'm not
quite sure now how I sensed it. The rower was a little fellow,
wearing a tweed cap turned backwards and an old blue
serge jacket that had once been part of his Sunday suit.
Murty Connolly – I knew him by his hunched shoulders
and the way he dipped his oars very fast, lifting them high
out of the water. There was nothing to fear, and still I stayed
out of sight. When they were almost ashore I heard the big
man say: 'Are you sure they're here?'

An educated accent, and a superior tone that we never

used to the local people – a visiting officer. He couldn't be anything else. The boatman answered him with a contemptuous drawl: 'Ara, where else could they be?'

I was tempted to run and warn the others that the great man had arrived, but apart from the loss of dignity, I was inclined to take a hint from Murty's attitude. I walked out into the open and came towards them, deliberately using a strolling pace so as not to reveal that I had been drilled as a soldier. We had all learned this from Seán Kelly. I pulled the boat ashore, saying casually: 'Hello, Murty.'

'Hello, Mr. Michael.' He always called me Mr. Michael, or even Mr. D'Arcy in the company of strangers, though he had known me since I was a baby. In private I was Micilín. 'I've brought you a visitor, Commandant Dunne, from Dublin.'

Murty kept his head down as he gave me this information. The way he pronounced the word 'Dublin' must surely have shown Dunne what he thought of him. Dunne paid no attention. He looked me up and down, then said: 'Captain D'Arcy. Murty said you would be here. Where are the others?'

'At the camp.'

'We'll go there at once.' He turned to Murty with a complete change of tone. 'You can hide the boat, or better still take it back.'

'Are you staying the night, sir?' Murty asked.

'Probably not,' Dunne said impatiently, as if it were no one's business but his own.

Murty said: 'Then I'll wait. Mr. D'Arcy will know where to find me. I'll be in the cove beyond, doing a bit of fishing.'

He shoved off the boat and rowed away fast. Dunne looked after him, then asked me suspiciously: 'He doesn't call you Captain D'Arcy. Is he in the Movement?'

'He gets epileptic fits.'

'Why didn't he tell me?'

'He's ashamed of it.'

15

But I couldn't see why Murty should tell the story of his life to anyone and everyone.

Dunne said: 'A useful man, all the same.' Just within the cover of the trees he stopped me by holding my arm and said: 'Tell me about the others.'

'I should ask for your credentials,' I said, pulling his leg to see if he would relax. For a moment he glared at me furiously, so that I actually had a second of suspicion about him. Then he gave a short, barking laugh and said: 'Quite right. But you should remember me. We met in Galway in March, at the Forbes' house.'

I did remember him. He had been dressed smartly, almost theatrically, making even me feel countrified. I particularly recalled a spotted silk tie, dark blue and very wide. Now he was wearing a collection of ill-fitting garments, trousers several sizes too big, held up by too long a belt, a striped work-shirt like the ones the countrymen wore, a woollen pullover that might have been either blue or grey, full of runs and holes, a handwoven jacket of undyed tweed and battered brown shoes. You never saw such a scarecrow, and still he managed to keep his air of authority. He was the worst-dressed officer I had ever seen, even in our guerrilla army. His face and neck were burned by the sun, as if he had been out all summer – his hands too, like a hay-maker's hands, and they were none too clean. His hair looked as if it had been singed in a fire.

'You're thinking I could pass for a tramp,' he said. 'That's just what I'm hoping for.'

'There are five of us,' I said. 'We're all on the run for different reasons. Kelly was recognised at an ambush in Cork County. He was sent here to get as far away as possible – he would be shot at sight. The rest of us are well known hereabouts. We were told to wait for further orders. They're a long time coming.'

'You're due back at the university.'

'That can wait. I didn't get there much last year either.'

I knew he had brought our orders and I was burning to

know what they were. That island had become like a gaol – hell for hearty young men.

He asked: 'Who are the others?'

'Don't you know?'

'It should be Brown and Cummins from Galway, and someone called Flaherty.'

'Faherty,' I corrected him, 'from Mweenish, out beyond Carna. He set up an ambush out there in May and someone informed on him. They're all here.'

'Well, let's go and meet them.'

I made sure to go in front. Though he was my superior officer, I didn't want him prancing along as if he owned the island. There was something about him that brought ideas of this kind to the mind.

He followed me through the light beech wood. An ancestor of mine planted it a couple of hundred years ago, but the holly trees are as old as Ireland. Here and there they stick up, short, thick trunks and shiny leaves, glittering with health in the midst of all the decay around them. The dry beech leaves rattled down, yellow and red and orange. A heron crossed, high up, his ungainly legs dangling and his broad wings beating the air as if he had a long journey before him. Then suddenly he went down out of sight, to land somewhere quite close.

You may be surprised that I remember that scene so clearly. I've often thought of it, especially when I lived in the Middle West of America, probably because it came at one of those endings that one encounters from time to time in life. Sometimes the pain of exile was almost intolerable. The pull of this country is as mysterious as the love of a woman. I knew it already, from my English boarding-school. Though I had disliked him on sight, the fact that Dunne shared this feeling gave me a sense of fellowship with him, as we climbed between jutting rocks, thick with ivy, and looked down into the camp.

My four companions were sitting on the flat rock that we used as a bench, outside the open door of the hut. Each of us had a pallet in there, but we made sure not to spend more time inside than was strictly necessary. There was no window and mighty little other comfort. Our nights would have been uneasy even without Cummins' snoring and Kelly, calm and humorous by day, screaming with terror in his sleep.

Faherty and Cummins were doing something or other with a rabbit snare. Wire was scarce, and when it broke it had to be repaired by twisting it onto the next piece, with the loss of an inch or two. Brown and Kelly were leaning on their elbows, enjoying the last of the sunlight which fell full on the rock at this time of the evening. Cummins was saying: 'There's a roll of wire at home, if only I could go and get it. And a few pillows and a couple of blankets.'

Kelly said: 'Sounds as if you're planning to spend the winter here. I'm sick and tired of this place. By the time we get back into action we'll have gone soft.'

He settled himself against the rock and shifted his shoulders back and forth, restlessly scratching his back. Their voices carried clearly though they were speaking quietly – something about the way the hollow gathered the sounds and let them flow upwards. They hadn't heard us coming, as I realised when I made a deliberate shuffling noise to warn them. Brown leaped up, his gun in his hand like a flash. He had spent hours every day since we came, practising a quick draw. He let his arm fall when he saw me. They all looked suspiciously at Dunne, then Kelly said: 'Commandant Dunne. We met in Cork. You're welcome as the flowers of May.'

When Kelly used that bantering tone and one of those exaggerated phrases of his, I knew he was sceptical of his company. He had told me about that meeting, Dunne all business, with notebooks and pencils and guns strapped all over him under his jacket, asking to see records, wanting lists of officers.

Kelly had said: 'Lord God, man, if we kept records there wouldn't be one of us alive, nor a single farmer that would take us in when the column is on the march. I can tell you the name of every man in the Movement from here to Ballycotton but there's no one going to write them down.' And he said to me, when he described the incident: 'There's Dublin for you.' He added tolerantly: 'But I suppose they had to keep some kind of control.'

As he climbed down into the hollow Dunne said: 'I have orders to move for all of you.'

Cummins let out a shout of laughter, then said: 'I hope we'll be going where we'll get a bit of a dance. I'd give a lot now to get my arms around a fine soft lump of an Irish maiden.'

Cummins was always a joker. To hear him talk you would think he was a perennial danger to the women of Ireland. In fact, it was he who insisted that we risk our lives every Sunday to go to Mass in Oughterard Church. We had to row across to Glann and then walk with the Sunday crowds, any of whom might have betrayed us. With my Jesuit training I could have explained to them that they were not obliged to go to Mass at all, but they would have been shocked. I imagined how it would be to recount old Father Latimer's dry-voiced explanation: 'The Catholic Church doesn't care for fanatics. You are obliged to go to Mass frequently. How often is frequently? Three or four times a year is considered ample.' They would have thought I was a pagan.

Kelly and I saw at once that Dunne was offended, whether through prudishness or because of Cummins' lack of respect we couldn't have guessed. He had a schoolmasterly look about him, humourless, not our kind of comrade at all.

That was another word of Kelly's: comrade. An old-fashioned word, like so many he used quite naturally.

Dunne's news was more or less what we expected. We were all to leave the island. Our war, which had started four years ago with the Easter Rising of 1916, by now had the full support of the people. The excesses of the Black-and-Tans had discredited the British government, so

19

that public opinion even in England was on our side. A new push was about to begin and each one of us had a part to play. Brown and Faherty were to be sent to Donegal as organisers. Kelly, Cummins and I were to be judges in the new arbitration courts. It was the landed gentry, of all people, who had demanded that we set these up, since no one took their cases now to the old British courts of justice. The judges sat in state as usual. They turned up at the court-houses with a cavalry escort and great ceremony, but as the cases came up one by one, it was found that they had been settled out of court. That didn't mean the farmers had stopped quarrelling among themselves or that there was no crime.

We left the island that same evening. I felt unpleasantly excited, though I was not really afraid. To be windy was considered contemptible, though all of us had been privately terrified at one time or another. Murty rowed us ashore after dark and we separated outside Oughterard village, to the sound of flowing water and whistling curlews.

After that, Dunne and I travelled around Galway and Mayo for a few weeks, while he taught me the mysteries of being a judge. I couldn't make out why he had been chosen for this work. The people who appointed him presumably didn't know him very well. The fact that he was a Dublin-man may have had something to do with it. There were not quite enough of them to go round, people who knew something more than you could learn in a tiny village or even in a small town in those days. And there was his silence. When he was stumped in an argument, he preferred not to answer at all, but if you pressed him hard he would say wearily: 'There are two sides to most questions, don't you think? Let's agree to differ.'

Because he was older than I was, at first I used to assume that he had found some foolish loophole in my logic. His intransigence about politics was the most infuriating. He refused to talk about the day when we would have won this war and be left holding the baby we were fighting for. When

I pressed the argument, he became ironical and sarcastic, almost to the point of suggesting that I had lost my nerve. I couldn't make him out – I had never before met anyone with such a short view. I even thought it possible that it was he who had screwed himself to too high a pitch, and was afraid of cracking. It was a long time before I found out how wrong I was.

Dunne was quite effective as a judge, keeping his distance better than I could. We would arrive at a farmer's house, either out in the country or near a village. We would be given tea – tea and bread and butter and eggs was our diet most of the time, sometimes bacon and cabbage. Occasionally there would be a scrawny old hen, long past her prime, served with a heap of boiled potatoes. Not being a countryman, Dunne often had indigestion. I was better conditioned, from my school.

After tea we would go to the place where the court was being held, either in another room in the same house or at the school-house if it were not too far away. Most of the country school-houses were in remote places, on top of windy hills or in bleak valleys, thought to be convenient for everyone, but in fact inconvenient for all. Naturally we avoided the villages and little towns because they were regularly combed by the Black-and-Tans. Three of us would sit behind a table, myself and Dunne, with the local chairman, who was often the teacher, between us. Sometimes the chairman would be the parish priest or a curate, and the lying was always less outrageous then.

Such lies as they told! Sometimes we had to stop the whole business and explain that a court was not a place where you made up the best story you could think of. You had to tell the whole truth, in the sight of God, even if it was not in your own favour. Out on the coast near Leenane, where a long dark finger of water pokes in from the Atlantic, a furious man complained that his neighbour continually borrowed his boat, without leave, to go fishing. That man was of the seed and breed of thieves, said the plaintiff, and he was further known to chase the wives and daughters of the whole area, and he had been seen many a time with other people's property in his house, downfacing anyone who tried to get their things back. He milked neighbours' cows. He stole the new-born lambs on the mountain and put his own mark on them before the owner could find them. The priest said: 'You have no evidence for any of that, Johnny. The law only heeds crimes that can be proved.'

Johnny roared in astonishment: 'And is that rasper entitled to tell as many lies as he likes, on top of all his thieving?'

Dunne said: 'Of course not. He must tell the truth too.'

'You wouldn't get an ounce of truth out of that man if you shook him for a week,' Johnny said contemptuously.

Still Dunne was patient, explaining that if we found the defendant was lying we would send him to gaol. We had various gaols, mostly disused sheds in desolate places. Our criminals went off to them willingly enough, accepting their fate and instructing their relatives not to tell the regular police where they were, in case there might be an attempt to rescue them.

That case ended, like many another, with the two enemies shaking hands and promising to behave well in future. Often there was a dance afterwards – the musicians appeared as if by magic, just when embarrassment might have set in.

2

Even for me, the truths we uncovered were sometimes very disturbing. I have often thought that a bitter case near Tuam was a turning point in Dunne's life. It was lovely smooth country. The farmers raised sheep and cattle and horses. The houses were slated, dry and warm inside, with clean, old-fashioned parlours that were normally only used for weddings or wakes. At this time of the year the grass was grazed to the bone. Pale sunlight gleamed on the dry-stone walls. Everything was much more orderly and neat than in Connemara.

The house where the court was to be held was two-storeyed, with a red-painted door and windows. Through the open kitchen door we saw sides of bacon hanging from the rafters and a big turf fire on the hearth, with a kettle singing. We were told that the teacher, Pat O'Toole, would be the chairman of the court, and the parish priest was also expected to come. This was good news. Most of the priests were on our side by this time, but there were still some who tried to turn the people against us.

There was a fire in the parlour too. The farmer's wife gave us a hearty meal in there, with fried bacon and eggs and heavenly soda-bread. She had no sooner cleared the table than people began to arrive, men, women and half-grown boys, all rather quiet and obviously under strain. No young girls came into the parlour, though we could hear them giggling among themselves in the kitchen across the hall.

We had moved the table back and ranged chairs at one side of the parlour. The women sat on these. They tucked their long, dark-blue skirts in neatly around their ankles and threw back their brown shawls, then patted their hair and whispered to each other, taking no notice of the men who crowded in the doorway. After a while some of the men edged in and lined the wall opposite the women. They all took off their hats and held them firmly. No one looked frightened, not even the accused man. Pat O'Toole pointed him out to us. He was a tall, handsome fellow of about thirty-five, with strong black hair just turning grey, and bold, dark eyes. He stood to one side of the fire, staring around at the company. It seemed to me that everyone present avoided his eyes.

His name was Bartley Kane. The statement before us said that he was brought to court by his neighbour, Patrick Cahill. They had adjoining farms a few miles away, in a poorer part. Cahill declared that Kane was putting spells on his land and using black magic to injure him and to draw his wife away from him. The wife was there, sitting close to us with her back to her neighbours. She was a slight, red-haired young woman with delicate pale skin. When she looked up at us suddenly, I saw that she had extraordinarily bright green eyes. Her skirt was not long enough to cover her slender ankles. She had delicate wrists too, and fine, long hands. Her expression was perfectly blank – there was no telling what was in her mind. Her husband, Cahill, was about sixty. He was bald on top, with a fringe of scanty white hair above the ears. He kept muttering angrily to himself and had to be restrained by his friends from crossing the floor to attack Kane.

It was my last court with Dunne. He was leaving next day for Dublin and I would have to play the great man on my own. You can imagine how anxious this made me – I watched and listened with desperate attention, so as to learn as much as possible.

The first evidence was given by Cahill. He had become aware that something was wrong when he found that cows he left in a big field adjoining Kane's were aborting their calves. He searched around by the bounds ditch and found a dead calf buried close to it. Dunne asked: 'Was it in your field, or in the defendant's?'

'In mine, of course. Isn't that what I'm telling you? And I came up another evening, and didn't I find a clutch of eggs – thirteen of them – they were in a hole in the ground, and a small scatter of clay over them.'

O'Toole asked: 'Couldn't it be a hen laying out, if there was a hollow in the ground?'

'I never saw a hen to cover her eggs with clay,' Cahill said contemptuously. 'I know who done it, all right.'

An old woman who had been sitting quietly next to Mrs. Cahill suddenly shouted: 'And he got the eggs from me, the blackguard, intending harm to my own daughter.'

O'Toole said: 'You'll get your turn to speak, Mrs. Brennan. You must not interrupt the witness.'

She hitched her shawl up around her ears and subsided, watching Cahill fiercely as if she didn't think he was capable of telling his story properly. I couldn't help wondering what would be the feelings of an English magistrate faced with this tale of spells and magic. Of course it exists in England too, as it does in every country, but I thought it wouldn't often find its way into a court of law.

Cahill said: 'When I found the eggs, I knew who was at the back of it – that *stall* over there, that's been after my wife ever since I took her home with me, and after my land and my sheep and cattle too. He ought to be transported to Van Diemen's Land, out of the sight of decent people –'

There was a peculiar hissing sound, as if all the people had drawn in their breath at the same moment. Cahill had lost his temper and was shouting: 'Get him out of the country – that was the old way with the likes of him – get them across the water – emigrate them so they can't come home no more – there's many a better man found shot for less –'

Dunne said: 'That day is over. You'll be in trouble yourself if you threaten the defendant. We haven't yet proved that Bartley Kane is responsible.'

Cahill said furiously: 'How can you prove a thing like that? What will he do but deny it? Look at him there, laughing at the whole lot of us, and more divilment planned as sure as there's a tail in a cat.'

Kane was not laughing. He was gazing at Cahill with hatred. His mouth was clamped shut and his big broad hands were locked together as if to keep them from going for Cahill's throat.

Cahill said mockingly: 'Ask him – go on – ask him did he bury that calf to bring misfortune on my cows – and the eggs to do the same to my wife. Ask him does he be meeting her in quiet places when I'm away at a fair. Ask him does he know it's a sin to lay a hand or an eye on another man's wife.'

There were shocked moans and gasps from the listeners. They were like people watching a fire, fascinated, absorbed, determined to miss nothing, but at the same time detached from any need to intervene. Only the people directly involved showed their feelings. I had seen the same in Connemara once, when a man was drowning from his boat, too far offshore to be rescued. He might as well have been a fish.

Mrs. Brennan turned again to glare at Kane. Her daughter still stared straight ahead as if she had heard nothing. Dunne said quietly: 'We'll ask a lot of questions. Is that all you have to say?'

'Isn't it enough?'

We went outside to confer with our chairman. There was such dead silence in the parlour that it would have been impossible to speak freely there. The men by the door made way for us. Even in the hall we couldn't have had our conference, since the audience spilled out there. It was a fine moonlight night with a sharp frost, but I was glad of the cold air after the fug inside. We moved a few yards away and stood huddled together, speaking in whispers though no one was near.

O'Toole didn't come from this part of the county but he

26

had heard all the stories at one time or another. Cahill's mother had been the owner of the farm until her death at the age of ninety-one, two years ago. As soon as Cahill inherited the farm, he asked Mrs. Brennan for her daughter, though it would have been more suitable to have asked for herself. It was considered a good match, in spite of a difference of at least thirty-five years between their ages. I asked: 'Was the daughter willing? Was she forced in any way?'

O'Toole said: 'She was quite willing. There was no need to force her. I was surprised – she had been going with Kane for several years and I took it for granted they would get married some day.'

Dunne asked: 'What were they waiting for?'

O'Toole gave him an odd look, as much as to say he was an innocent abroad, then said: 'In these parts no one gets married young for fear of having a big family of children to feed. They wait until the woman is too old to have more than four or five.'

'Is this the men's idea, or the women's?'

'More often the men's. They're afraid of responsibility.'

'The women have more courage?'

'Usually, yes. When they're kept waiting too long, they get embarrassed. They feel they look foolish, that everyone is watching them. And so they are.'

'What about the mother? Would she have wanted her daughter to marry Kane?'

'She was always against it.'

'But it was all right to marry Cahill?'

'Yes. His land is better, for one thing. Kane's land is poor, though it runs next to Cahill's – too much bog, and there's a stream that floods every couple of years and destroys his best fields. He has a bit of rocky hillside where even the sheep don't get much grazing. The mothers around here are prudent – they have to be. I've heard that Mrs. Brennan's mother made the same kind of match for her when she was young.'

'So the mother was pleased?' I asked.

'Delighted,' the priest said. 'She came over to my house specially to tell me about it. I didn't argue. I'm used to it, and it's not my business. A lot of them make matches like that. It seems to work as well or better than so-called love matches.'

There was no bitterness in this statement. It was simply a fact he had learned in the course of his work. He and God were watching calmly while human beings destroyed themselves with petty passions. He was interested, but never involved, like the people who had come to listen at the court. In the parlour I had noticed that his frock-coat was faded to a colour that was almost bottle-green. It must have been at least fifteen years old. His clerical collar was yellow with age. The farmer's wife had already told me that he was a holy man who spent hours every day in his church praying. While she admired him for this, her tone suggested that she would have been better pleased if he had followed the common custom of his cloth and bred cattle and greyhounds. I was surprised to hear that Mrs. Brennan had confided in him at all.

Dunne said: 'Do you think Cahill is telling the truth?'

'The truth as he sees it,' the priest said. 'Around here they believe in magic as much as they believe in God.'

When we got back to the parlour, the people were whispering among themselves but were still very quiet. They watched us politely as we settled ourselves at the table. Dunne seemed agitated, and I thought the priest's last remark had upset him. He said abruptly: 'Let's get on with it, then. Call Mrs. Cahill.'

The red-haired woman didn't stand up. There was no swearing, just question and answer. Dunne asked: 'Mrs. Cahill, did you know about the dead calf?'

She said softly: 'I did when my husband told me about it.'

'Why did you think it was there?'

28

'To do harm to my husband's land, to make his cows go wrong.'

'Do you believe that that would happen?'

'It's an old story, sir. Some say it does harm, that it brings a curse on the ground.'

'Who did you think was wanting such a thing?' O'Toole asked.

'My husband said it was Bartley Kane.'

At last she turned her head and looked directly at Kane, and he stared back at her. I felt uneasy, as if this were not a court but that we were eavesdropping on the most intimate affairs of these people. Dunne must be my model in this or I would be useless when I was left alone. He asked: 'And what did you think?'

She paused for a split second before answering. I was hoping she would refuse, since surely her opinion had no legal value. Then she said: 'I thought it was likely Bartley Kane.'

'Why?'

'Because he do be after me still, the same as if I was never married. He would like to do harm to my husband.'

Her voice was barely a whisper as she said this. I saw Kane squeeze his hands together. Dunne went on to his next question: 'Did you try to stop him?'

'I never spoke to him at all but the once since I was married. It was after that my husband found the calf.'

O'Toole said in a low voice: 'A diseased calf can carry contagious abortion. It's a real injury. The eggs are just devilment.'

I was glad he had intervened. I didn't want Dunne to question her about her conversation with Kane. That moment had passed, and Dunne called on Mrs. Brennan.

'When did Bartley Kane ask you for the eggs?'

She stood up with a jerk and said in a loud, harsh tone: 'In the spring, clocking time. I was glad. I thought it was a sign he was getting his mind on other things and rearing

29

a few chickens for himself. But sure, he never put a clocking hen on them at all, only waited until they were gluggered and then went and buried them on old Cahill's land – the blackguard.'

Her voice had begun to sound hysterical. Dunne said: 'You must not say that, Mrs. Brennan. The court hasn't taken all the evidence yet.' But once she had said it, she had to be asked: 'And why should he bury eggs on Mr. Cahill's land?'

The priest put his head down and stared at his shoes. Mrs. Brennan said loudly: 'So that Nora would never have a son of Cahill's. He wanted to keep her for himself, God forgive him. He wouldn't wait until his turn came. He'd rather destroy her altogether than see her with a son of Cahill's. But sure, even if 'twas born in Cahill's house, isn't it all the same who's the father –'

Suddenly realising that she had given herself away, she clapped both hands over her mouth and glanced quickly around the room, her eyes wide open, with a strange glare in them as if she had suddenly lost her reason. No one moved. The old woman stood stock still, as if she were waiting for God to strike her. Kane looked at her directly and said very quietly: 'That's what was in your mind. You would have been contented then. I wouldn't do it for all the land in Ireland. Jesus Christ knows I'll never touch her now, not if I live for a hundred years.' He turned to Cahill and said almost humorously: 'They'll take good care of you now, you may be sure, the both of them. You have two fine women, a good bargain. You won't be seeing much of me from now on.'

He walked out of the room. The men by the door parted to make way for him, almost as if they were afraid to touch him. With a look of desperation, Mrs. Brennan watched him go. Suddenly she turned on Dunne, shouting raucously: 'Look now, what you done, with your court and your law, a fine man gone forever from us, Nora left – left –'

Dunne should probably have said nothing, but he must

30

have thought his position made it necessary. He went into a kind of summing-up, saying that neighbours must live together in peace, and that from now on in Ireland the rule of law would have to be upheld, and that Mrs. Brennan was partly responsible for what had happened, that once her daughter was married to Cahill she should have kept out of their affairs. She listened to him for a minute or two, then hitched her shawl up around her ears and stood up, saying with the utmost contempt: 'There you are, talking away like a ha'penny book, and you nothing but a Dublin jackeen. What do you or your likes know about Ireland?'

She marched out, and a moment later Cahill and his wife followed more quietly. There was dead silence, into which the incredible sound of music crept, a fiddle and a concertina playing in the kitchen. Little murmurs of conversation began, and then everyone began to shuffle out of the parlour. Relieved that it was over, I looked at Dunne. The change in him was shocking. He was pale as death, and he was sitting rigidly, gazing at the backs of the departing crowd, reduced utterly by the old woman's words. All his authority seemed to have evaporated. The priest said: 'I wish I didn't know as much about Ireland as I do. The old people arrange most of the matches – I had no idea the girl was in the plot. I thought she was simply obeying her mother, like the rest of them. No harm for the truth to come out.'

'I wasn't sure she knew there was a plot,' I said. 'Perhaps it was just the mother's idea.'

'Perhaps. It's as clear as daylight that she planned for Kane to marry Nora when Cahill would die of old age, whatever about fathering a child for her before that.'

O'Toole said: 'Cahill looks very healthy to me. I won't be surprised if they produce a big family.'

Dunne had recovered himself, and was perhaps aware that the others were talking to give him time. None of us had stood up, though I'm sure they all felt the need of fresh air as much as I did. Then Dunne said bitterly: 'Those

31

women – peasants – predators – the morals of animals – stamping out their territory – eating their mates – like spiders –'

The priest said calmly: 'They're the backbone of Ireland, all the same. They survive better than the men.'

Dunne glared at him. 'Does that excuse their conduct?'

'Nonsense – of course not. I'll tell you something, young man. You and your revolution, or whatever it is, may change the face of Ireland, but you won't change the people. They've been burying eggs for five thousand years. They're not going to stop because you tell them to. They certainly won't stop for me. I can imagine that Saint Patrick was a very tired man by the time he died.'

Dunne said with great restraint: 'I'm sorry.'

'That's all right. They're not as bad as you think. A lot of it is instinct. The Church's business is to keep instinctive behaviour within bounds, not to squeeze it out of existence. I'm glad you made your speech. You said things that can only be said by an outsider – even from me they wouldn't tolerate the homily you gave just now. Don't look so dispirited. Well, I must be off home.'

'A philosopher,' Dunne said bitterly, when he had gone.

'It's part and parcel of living in the country,' O'Toole said. 'We all have to learn it eventually.'

The music was louder since the door had been opened. It was drawing me forcibly out of the parlour – nothing I loved so much as a dance in those days. And Dunne's gloom seemed overdone. I had to get away from him. I said: 'They'll expect us to appear at the dance.'

O'Toole and Dunne came in and stood politely for a while, then went away to sleep, leaving me whirling around the kitchen in sets and half-sets and long dances and waltzes with the local girls until I was ready to drop.

Dunne went back to Dublin immediately after that court and I had to carry on by myself. It was more than a year before I saw him again, and in the meantime I had learned a great many things. One was that the air of authority and command that I had picked up in the Officers' Training Corps in my English school was more of a liability than an asset. I knew better than to lecture the country people about their morals, as Dunne had. The fact that I spoke Irish so well was a mark in my favour, but I could never shake off the atmosphere of the big house I had grown up in, nor put on the soft, apologetic manner that was characteristic of Western men, even the most hard-bitten and determined of them. Nor could I cover my English accent, except by speaking Irish.

The last months of that year were a nightmare for all of us. Terence MacSwiney died on hunger strike in London and was buried in his native Cork on the first of November. I heard that Kelly had ventured to go home for the occasion and had had a narrow escape from arrest. On that same day Kevin Barry, a boy of seventeen that I had seen at the university, was hanged like a common murderer in Dublin. A huge crowd prayed outside Mountjoy gaol until it was over. Later in November, one Sunday morning, eleven British Intelligence officers were shot dead by men of the Dublin Brigade. The same afternoon the Black-and-Tans fired into a crowd at a football match and killed fourteen people, some of them children, and wounded about sixty, before horrified British officers intervened and did what they could to save British honour. And in December the Black-and-Tans took petrol from the military depots in Cork and poured it into buildings, then set it alight with Verey pistols, afterwards rampaging through the city in a drunken frenzy. The burning was in retaliation for a military operation, the Kilmichael ambush, in which sixteen Black-and-Tans had been killed.

Old, unhappy, far-off things – but they were the things that drove us wild in those days. We were always gunmen, killers, murderers: they were brave soldiers doing their duty. But the burnings and killings were causing anxiety in London, as I knew they would. Winston Churchill, always a good psychologist, saw that it was a mistake to allow policemen such a free hand. Any reprisals should be conducted in an orderly way, by army officers. Churchill appreciated the motives of his opponents even when he detested them. He would never have said, as Lloyd George did, that he had murder by the throat. War on the grand scale was what Churchill preferred, never skirmishes like the ones we had in Ireland.

For me, that winter was the lowest in all of that dreadful campaign which we fought like rats, below and above ground, rarely knowing whether or not we were succeeding. I sustained myself with the hope that British public opinion would come to our aid before our supplies of guns and ammunition ran out. This is exactly what happened – members of the Cabinet said that the people of Ireland were becoming increasingly hostile and that soon it would be impossible to govern the island at all. Prophetic words – too late, as it turned out. Hatred built up during the winter and spring of 1921. Our plans were made for the next two, three, four years, when the fighting would have to move into the mountains and lonely valleys, where we fancied we could stand siege forever. Martyrs, saints or just plain pig-headed – whatever it was, it poisoned us. We fed on hatred, let it carry us along so that we would never have to think. Without this attitude, I believe we couldn't have endured the cold and hunger and dirt of our wandering lives.

We had very little communication with Dublin, and I often wondered about Dunne. I knew he was there, associated with headquarters in some capacity. Since my weeks with him I had reluctantly developed confidence in his integrity. We didn't use that word then. Everything was either black or white. Either you were a good Irishman or you were not. Photographs of young revolutionaries all over the world have the same expression as my companions had, the same fierce stare, the same tight jaw, the same look of invincible certainty. We all looked hungry, not only for food but for action.

Then, without warning, I began to have misgivings. It

had nothing to do with the absurdity of a handful of virtually unarmed men on the outer rim of Europe undertaking to fight the British Empire to a standstill. I never doubted that what we were trying to do was right. What happened was that I began to see that guerillas become professionals, in time.

The first stories of atrocities by the Black-and-Tans had aroused disgust for two reasons – firstly that they should be condoned by the prime minister of a civilised country, and secondly that human beings were capable of such inhuman behaviour. As time passed, our men were trained to be as ruthless as the enemy. I saw that they had learned the lesson all too well.

I was staying in a house in County Clare when the shock of recognition happened. The men I was with were rejoicing – that's the only word I can use – in the lingering death inflicted on a resident magistrate, buried in the sand and left to drown in the rising tide on a desolate shore.

I walked out of the house and wandered all night around the fields and lanes, scarcely knowing what I was doing. Nothing could justify this. Then what was war? Ritual killing? I could never have joined in that. The British had rules which they had broken. Did that mean we could break the rules we had made for ourselves? Once we did this, it seemed to me that we had lost the war. I knew it was not my business to think, once I was committed to the cause, but this was more than I could ever stomach. The men I was with were countrymen. They could kill a pig or a sheep without a thought. Now they could kill a man. I was too squeamish. I was no longer fit for their company. I decided to get out, find Dunne and consult with him.

Two days later, the first of June, I had got myself to Galway to catch the train for Dublin. It was a heavenly day, not a breath of wind. The herons were reflected full length in the waters of the canal that runs by the railway. They seemed quite undisturbed by the rattle of the train.

35

To look at the grey stone houses of the villages, trailing off into the quiet fields, one would never have believed that the inhabitants were living in terror of their lives. The summer of 1921 was a specially warm one, long sunny days and balmy nights. I had scarcely noticed it until now.

I was told that Dunne was staying in Terenure, in a house that was mostly let in single rooms to old people. The short street backed onto some fields. The couple who owned the house lived in the basement. I went down there and rang the bell and was directed upstairs to a room at the back of the house.

I can't make out now why I took my scruples to Dunne. I think I must have imagined he would understand them because he knew the West of Ireland well, and had seen how poor the people were. They had always administered rough justice among themselves, but there was another law, the British law of the land, which they had respected even while they hated it. Soon they would be like jungle animals. They would accept no jurisdiction of any kind. It would be every man for himself. Scarcely any of the men I saw had ideas about reconstruction. They could only think as far as striking the next blow. It was clear to me that the sooner this war was over, the better for all concerned.

I poured this out within minutes of my arrival. Dunne had aged, and he was thinner. He didn't get up when I came into the room, just looked at me as if we had been meeting every day. He was sitting at a desk in a high-backed chair. The curtains were drawn almost fully but he had an electric lamp on the desk in front of him. He leaned back, with that expressionless gaze that I remembered. It was neither condescending nor amused, yet I began to wish I had my words back. The blank, animal look had come into his eyes. Have you ever been stared at by a dog, just before he makes for a bite? It should have been enough for me. He's angry, I thought. He hasn't understood me at all.

I began to explain further: 'Since you left me I've been all over Connacht, and up into Derry and Donegal, in Cork

36

and Kerry as well. It's the same everywhere. They're all heroes now. In another year they'll all be generals. They'll take no orders. It's beginning to happen already. They're saying that Dublin doesn't understand the needs of the country – well, you've heard that too, I'm sure. They know there will be peace talks and they say Dublin will sell out to the Orangemen. They say Dublin will agree to partition. If that happens, they'll refuse to obey orders. I see no end to it – already they're prophesying that in fifty years' time, everything will still be the same.'

Dunne said: 'You're tired. You've been out on the circuit too long.'

'This has nothing to do with being tired. The whole feel of the country has changed. Every man is his own politician.'

I don't know how long I would have gone on protesting, repeating myself, but I noticed that Dunne was looking towards the door behind me. I turned my head and saw her for the first time – Pamela. She stood in the doorway, her back to the light, her face in shadow and her untidy red hair glowing as if it carried a hidden light of its own. She was tall, and the curves of her figure had a careless elegance in spite of a shabby green skirt and a blouse that looked several sizes too big for her.

Dunne said impatiently: 'Come in, Pamela. It's only Michael D'Arcy. And he has good news.'

3

Before I could splutter a contradiction of Dunne's statement, Pamela was advancing towards me with her hand out. I took it, and gazed for the first time into those splendid eyes, like green lamps, with a fleck of brown, set off perfectly by arched, dark-brown eyebrows. The image of Mrs. Cahill in the court came back to me, the calm beauty lost in the flat farmland of east Galway. The two visions came together and resulted in a real *coup de foudre*, love at first sight, insane, unreasoning love for a complete stranger. Don't tell me it doesn't happen. I've checked all over the world. I've brought the conversation around casually from time to time, and everywhere I've met men and women who have had the same experience. It's like being shot in the back. You can do nothing about it, not even run.

I was glad of the dimness, to hide my goggle-eyed stare, though I scarcely knew what was happening to me. It seemed that Dunne had to keep the curtains drawn even by day, because of the possibility of being seen from the field behind the house. He was on the run, and had been for several months, but his assignment kept him in and around Dublin all the same.

Pamela went to sit beside him, gazing at him anxiously as if to check that he was in good health, then said: 'What is the good news?'

Her voice was sweet and rather high, her accent unmistakably upper-class English. Surely she couldn't be London Irish, even with that heavenly red hair. Such an accent takes generations to develop. I knew it well, from visiting my friends' houses in England. There my own accent, hopelessly British in Ireland, sounded hilariously Irish to them.

Instead of answering her question, Dunne said: 'If what he says is true, the whole country will be behind us.'

I said in astonishment: 'Excuse me – I thought I was saying the opposite.'

'I know you thought so, but you're wrong. What you have told me is that the people won't accept partition. They'll want to fight on if there's a sell-out.'

I said, almost shouting in my fury at not being understood: 'What I said was that if Collins and Griffith and de Valera agree to partition of the country, the people I've been with for the last few months will refuse to accept it. They'll take nothing less than total freedom at this point. They say that's what they've been fighting for. They know the northern Protestants were promised partition years ago, but they say the World War has changed everything. They say small nations will get a hearing from the League of Nations and they'll all have to be treated better from now on. It's no use talking to them. This war has gone on too long. The people's judgment is gone. They think they have nothing to lose.'

'Yes, you explained it very well. I wish I could go down the country myself and hear it at first hand. I may do that. This is the best news you could possibly have brought us – don't you agree, Pamela?'

'Of course. We've been longing to hear it. I'm so glad for you.'

And she laid her head for a long moment on his knee. He made no response, no move towards her. He didn't stroke her hair. His knee didn't go on fire. He just sat there, half-turned in his chair, saying to me: 'Where did you come from today?'

'From Galway. It's not a fair sample – you know how uncertain they always are in Connacht, but plenty of them will follow the Cork and Kerry men. I crossed the Shannon last month and went to Listowel and Tralee. Everything

39

has changed. Nothing is organised, so there's still hope, if peace is made quickly.'

'Talks haven't started yet. If we had another three months it would make all the difference.'

'Three months of what? I tell you, we're on the very edge of civil war.'

'Three months of fighting, of course. If Collins were any good he'd be glad of this – he's always saying the northern Orangemen will break us in the end. The men should be stiffened in this attitude, if what you say is really true.'

'It's true all right. I've covered the whole coast.'

I could see what he was getting at, but I could scarcely believe it. I looked more closely around the room. It had a settled air. There was a pile of books beside the bed and more on some small shelves by the fireplace. Nothing like books to make a room seem lived in. The bad air – the window was tightly closed though it was such a warm day – gave me a feeling of claustrophobia, as if it were a prison. I asked: 'How long have you been living here?'

'Almost since I saw you last,' he said. 'It has never been raided, for some reason. I come and go quite a lot, but so far I haven't been followed.'

I began to wonder if the headquarters' staff was well aware of what was happening and had reckoned with it in their plans for peace. They might even think I was guilty of insubordination, if they heard of my scruples. In search of some comfort, I let my eyes rest on Pamela. Dunne noticed it, and misinterpreted my reasons. He said: 'Don't worry about Pamela. She's one of us.'

'Is it safe for her?'

'Oh, yes. She'll be all right.' His careless tone infuriated me. 'If anyone has noticed her they probably think she's the charwoman.'

'You've never been arrested?'

'I've been stopped, but they didn't know who I was. I mightn't be so lucky the next time.'

'How much are they offering for you?'

It was one of our standard jokes, in bad taste like most young men's jokes. I guessed that Dunne had not heard it before, but he seemed to take it in good part as soon as it sank in. Pamela's reaction was different. She gave him an anxious look, as if she were afraid he would burst out in temper at me. She relaxed when he said: 'Nothing at the moment. They don't seem to know about me. They have strange gaps in their information. There's Michael Collins, walking around Dublin every day, though there's a price of ten thousand pounds on his head. He doesn't look the part – he looks more like a stockbroker than a soldier.'

'So do you,' I said. 'And you know, he was a stockbroker, after he left the Post Office.'

Dunne seemed pleased. A bit of an actor? His dark-grey suit fitted perfectly and he was wearing a silk tie. A hat and a cane were laid on the bed, since his last outing. The trench coat and tweed cap which were almost the uniform of the I.R.A. down the country, were a long way from this. So was the collection of rags in which I had seen him last. I asked: 'What about the Igo gang?'

This was a carefully selected corps of policemen from all parts of the country, who waited at the railway stations and paraded the city in pairs to identify countrymen who had come up for the day, seeking instructions from headquarters. They had wrought havoc since they had been in action. They could also identify suburban Dubliners, since the corps contained a number of Dublin policemen.

Dunne said: 'They don't know Collins, probably because he lived in London until recently.'

'And yourself?'

'I've always lived in the town. No one out here would know me.'

To Dublin people, suburban Rathmines and Terenure were not part of the city at all. I couldn't help admiring Dunne's courage in braving the city streets. But it was hard to think of him deciding the fate of the nation. I had had no idea that he had become such an important figure. I

41

didn't know what to make of it. I still found him slightly ridiculous, and I couldn't think of him as a leader.

In spite of everything I felt that I had to continue with the mission that had brought me here. Speaking loudly and forcefully I said: 'When you see Collins you can tell him that things are very bad in Sligo and Donegal. The people are saying it's a new Plantation of Ulster. They're furious at the pogroms – the Protestants are murdering the Catholics and driving them out of their homes and jobs, just as they did three hundred years ago. The Donegal and Derry people say it will never change until the Catholics begin to fight back. And the oath of allegiance to the king – they will never stomach that. No one has anything against the king himself. They know he has been trying to make peace. They just say he's not the king of Ireland. These are simple issues to them.'

By the end of this I was chattering desperately, not understanding why he made no comment. He just sat there staring blankly at me – the trick I had seen him use before. I wasn't taken in by it. But I knew I couldn't afford to get angry. I was preaching restraint – I had better learn to practise it myself. I even held in when he said at last: 'So they have come that far. We've been hearing that we can rely on a good deal of support – now it comes straight from the horse's mouth.'

He revealed his teeth as if he were smiling, but to me it looked more like the snarl of a dog. I always thought of dogs when I was with Dunne.

Though I despaired of making any impression on him I said: 'A split in our ranks now would be a disaster. I came to tell you two things. One is that the men are almost out of hand as far as military discipline goes; the other is that their political views are dangerous. Can't you see?'

'I can see it worries you, with your background. It doesn't worry me at all. You're too sensitive, as you've noticed yourself. We're not playing a game.'

I was speechless at this string of insults. It would have

42

taken a week to answer them. In those days we hadn't got around to using the words 'civil war', because in a sense that was what we had already. My background, as he called it, dated back to 1172 when the Normans came to Ireland. My family's loyalties had usually been to England, but I was as Irish as you can be. The Dublin Metropolitan Police, the Royal Irish Constabulary, even some of the Black-and-Tans were Irish. Many of the Tommies who guarded prisoners in gaol were Irish. In Galway, the Connacht Rangers were in barracks in Renmore and were expected to help out with police raids from time to time. What was all that but civil war? The pogroms in Belfast were carried out by Carson's army, the Ulster Volunteer Force. Carson himself was born in Dublin. Is it any wonder Dunne couldn't see that he was proposing a new kind of war? I could see it only dimly myself, and the prospect appalled me.

I was knocked completely off balance by his reaction. I made no attempt to explain further, even when he seemed to want to discuss the issues with me. He made a long speech, beginning with a garbled version of the opening words of the Proclamation of the Republic: 'In the name of the dead generations that went before us, we must fight to the very end now. This must be the last war on Irish soil –'

My point was that if we didn't stop the fighting now, we would never be able to stop it at all. His words buzzed around my head like swarming bees. After the first sentence or two I could no longer follow what he was saying. My mind was fully occupied elsewhere. At that moment I would have given the whole of Ireland and all its fighting men to hold Pamela in my arms.

Dunne ran out of steam after a while. Perhaps he imagined he had converted me. He looked as if he might say: 'Now that's settled, you can run out and play.' He had certainly given me a lot to think about, but my convictions had not changed in the slightest. He had managed to suggest that

43

my sympathies for the drowned resident magistrate were based on the fact that we came from the same class. I could have killed him for that. I knew he would misuse the information I had brought him, but I didn't regret having come to see him – how could I, when it brought me into the company of Pamela?

You may think I should have left the Movement when I saw the way it was going. The answer is that I didn't see it, because it was not visible. These were all conjectures. I couldn't value my juvenile opinions above those of an older, more experienced man.

One certain result of my visit was that Dunne made sure I stayed in Dublin with him, instead of going back to the West. He said I was obviously good at getting the feel of the country, but that he had other work for me. The phrase had brought me back to the island – Kelly constantly teasing Cummins about his alleged womanising, saying in his lovely soft voice: 'Cummins has the feel of the West – hasn't he had his arms around every girl in it?' Everything was different now. There were no more jokes, at least wherever I had been lately. Where had that spirit gone? Perhaps Kelly hadn't changed. He was back with the First Cork Brigade, still surviving, or so I had heard.

I was glad to stay in Dublin. While I was on the court circuit I had retained my rank of Captain and had taken part in various engagements. As I've said, my brother and I had been in the Officers' Training Corps at school and had been taken to camp at Salisbury Plain, so I knew something of what to expect from the British army. I had kept a firm hold on my men, because I could never think of them in any other way than that they were under my command. In private they christened me the General, and joked me about my accent, but I knew it was done from affection.

Part of my training had consisted in learning not to show fear, but in fact my nerves were in ruins. I had been close to death too often. There was an incident in a district west of Lough Mask, on the side of the Partry Mountains, when the school-house was raided just as I had sentenced a tramp called Grey Dan to a week in Sing-Sing. We were all chuckling at his consternation at being sent off to America for stealing a roll of wire netting, and someone was explainig to him that Sing-Sing was Mike Morrissey's booley on the mountainside, when the lorries drove up. Grey Dan hustled me out by the back way, and hid me in a dugout in the nearby bog. From our refuge we could hear the screams in the school-house as the others were tortured. When all was silent we emerged, and saw – things I dare not dream of. Then Grey Dan took me to the same booley – Mike Morrissey's hut on the mountainside – where we served his sentence together before it was safe for me to emerge.

The last occasion was in Galway. We knew it was dangerous for us to stay in the town, especially in the house where we were sent to sleep. I was with two officers from the Connemara brigade – Mullins and Walsh, heavy, hearty men who could run all day on the mountains, then eat a stone of potatoes at a sitting and start all over again. We had been travelling from north Mayo since early morning. The local intelligence officer, named Hynes, met us at the railway station and took us at once to a tall house in a back street off Eyre Square. I said: 'Aren't we too near the barracks? Eglinton Street is only fifty yards away.'

'That's one reason you can't pass through,' Hynes said. 'They're on the rampage tonight. They don't come through this street at night if they can help it. Eyre Square and William Street are their spots after dark.'

'But it's not dark yet.'

'Sorry,' he said. 'Nothing to be done. You'd never make it.'

There was a glow in the sky after a long sunny day. Crossing Bohermore was a nightmare. This was the street that led uphill out of Eyre Square, very broad, lined with houses, never a lane or a yard door in sight that would have served as a bolt-hole. The army lorries came roaring down here from the barracks at all hours, so that we were sand-wiched between them and the police barracks where the Black-and-Tans were stationed.

We crossed singly, trying to stroll, then followed Hynes through an alleyway into a somewhat wider street which curved back into the Square. I noted the two exits and said jokingly to Hynes: 'At least we have a back door.'

'I think you'll be all right,' he said, looking worried. 'A pity you didn't come yesterday. I'd have got you a boat across the river then, but I can't do it tonight.'

He took a key and opened the door of a tall house, and led us straight through to the yard at the back. I saw that it was the store of a public house, with open-fronted sheds full of barrels on two sides. The third side, at right-angles to the house, had a door that led into a little room, furnished with three iron beds, lit by a tiny window. Hynes said: 'You'll be snug as three bugs in there. The girl will bring out some supper in a while. I'll come for you early in the morning. Don't stir outside – there's a jacks there in the corner if you want it.'

There was. It also opened into the yard, but since the room was probably often used as a hiding-place, a door had been broken inside as well. We sat on the beds and talked sleepily about the men we were to see next day. All our reports had to be given by word of mouth, and we went over our information to make sure we had it straight. A quiet knock on the door announced the girl with supper, bread and butter and hard-boiled eggs which we ate quickly out of newspaper wrappings. She had not brought any plates. Almost at once we began to think of sleep. We could see that it was still daylight, though the grimy window let in very little of it. We lay on the beds in our clothes, placing our revolvers beside us so that they could be reached in a second. Almost at once I heard the other two begin to breathe rhythmically as they were overcome with sleep.

I don't know how I heard the lorry draw up. I felt rather than heard a sort of vibration in the air, then nothing. At the risk of making a fool of myself I sprang off my bed and shook the others awake, saying: 'They're here – the Tans – I heard the lorry stop outside.'

They didn't think I was foolish. Mullins said: 'Outside, into the sheds. That's our only chance. They'll have closed off the pub.'

He led the way out. A curtain moved in one of the upstairs windows that overlooked the yard, not of our house, but of one that faced the Square. Mullins and Walsh darted into one of the sheds, which contained some sacks as well as barrels. I scurried into the one beside it, pressing my long, thin body into the space between three barrels which were just tall enough to conceal me. Through a tiny space I could see a piece of the yard.

The waiting time was endless. For a few minutes I thought that they had gone, or else that I had been mistaken. Then I heard shouts, a drunken laugh and the voice of the girl who had brought our supper, wailing in terror, saying over and over: 'There's no one, I tell you; there's no one.'

They were at the door of our room, ripping it open. A voice said: 'Gone like rats. Three empty beds.'

Another said: 'Worth a try though.'

They glanced into the open sheds. I've never lived a moment of my life like that one, the great shadow cutting off the light, the face I couldn't see peering into the darkness. Then he was gone and the voices moved away towards the back door of the house.

Before they reached it, I heard a window-sill being pushed up, and a woman's voice called out: 'They're there, all right, in the shed.'

One of the Tans shouted: 'Where?'

'The shed, behind you! Two of them. They went in a few minutes ago.'

There was no escape for my two friends. The Tans hauled them out with shouts of delight and began their usual game with them, perhaps not knowing they were armed. Then there were several pistol-shots, a howl of pain and rage and a further series of shots, followed by pounding, hurrying boots and finally complete silence.

I crouched, frozen, in my tiny refuge. I would have been glad to die, but the young don't die so easily. I stayed there for about an hour, until complete darkness had fallen. At last, from the open back door a long triangle of lamplight crossed the yard. I heard soft movements nearby, and voices of women talking quietly. Still I didn't move, until the girl came into the shed and whispered: 'Young man – are you there yet?'

I was barely able to answer her. She heaved at one of the barrels until she moved it slightly and I was able to get out. I walked like a drunkard out into the yard, the girl holding my arm and keeping me in the darkness until we reached the door. The bodies of my two companions still lay where they had fallen, one across the other. I made an instinctive movement towards them, but the girl hurried me inside. Hynes was there, ready to take me away.

'We lost two fine men tonight,' he said, his voice shaking with anger. 'That bitch upstairs – I thought she had left town. Thank God she missed you.'

I was a long way from thanking God for my escape. I seemed incapable of feeling anything at all from then onwards. These things would have aroused most of my comrades to a higher fighting pitch, but my temperament was different. I knew that I was finished.

Dunne knew nothing of this. He instructed me to take lodgings in Dublin and come to his room every day where I would help him to keep records. Later we would go to Tipperary, and it would be my business to tell the men how strong the fighting spirit was in the West. I said nothing, though I hoped to get out of the assignment when the time came.

I went back to my old lodgings in a terrace house near the canal bridge at Rathmines. My landlady, Mrs. Malone, was a nationalist, and she knew why I was back in Dublin. She was afraid I was too near the military barracks for safety, and she gave me a room in the return, at the back, with a window through which I could escape if the house were raided. She had several students staying, but I didn't know any of them. She said they were all engrossed in the prospect of their examinations, which were due in less than a week, and that it would be easy to avoid them. My father had cut off my allowance, reasonably enough, since I was no longer a student, but Dunne said he would pay me three pounds a week, more than enough for my needs.

I walked to Terenure every afternoon and helped him with his notes, most of them concerned with the various organisations all over the country and the men in charge of them. As Kelly had said, they were enough to hang half of our army if they were ever discovered. They were kept in file covers, labelled by counties, and put into the chest beside his bed at night. He spent most mornings in the city, and he always came back with a bundle of hand-written notes in his pocket. It was my job to sort these out and record their contents in the various files.

No one came to the house, except myself and Pamela. She arrived soon after I did, with a basket covered in napkins, dishes of food that she brought for Dunne. She would lay them out on the desk: a meat stew in a casserole, or half a roast chicken, a baked potato or two and some stewed fruit or a piece of pie. He ate absent-mindedly, while she coaxed him as if he were a sick child. The first time I saw that performance I could scarcely believe it. He went through a long pantomime of being too busy to attend to his meal, until she had called his attention to it several times. At last he threw down his pen and turned impatiently, saying: 'Well, we must eat to stay alive.'

And he set to and finished the lot. There was never anything for me – not that I wanted it. I made sure to keep out of all that by having a bite in Bewley's in town before I came, or else joining Mrs. Malone in the kitchen. She wouldn't allow me to eat with the students, in case one of them might try to augment his income by informing on me. After thirty years as a landlady, she wouldn't trust them as far as she could throw them, she said.

One day I arrived a little late in Terenure, to find Pamela already there. She was sitting beside the desk, where she had laid out her dishes. There was no sign of Dunne. She was crying, big tears running down her cheeks, which she brushed away every now and then like a two-year-old child. She sprang up the moment I came in but collapsed, bawling, when she saw who it was. Then she wailed: 'He should have been back half an hour ago. Where is he?' She grabbed me by the lapels of my jacket. 'Have you seen him? He's so careless. I'm sure he's been arrested. I keep warning him but he doesn't listen.'

In those times, if someone didn't come home, the chances were that they had indeed been arrested. I should have been alarmed too, but I must confess that my first reaction was pure delight. She was close enough for me to see into the depths of her magnificent eyes, swimming in tears, burning with fear and anguish. It was a golden opportunity for me to wrap my arms around her and comfort her. I said that half an hour was nothing, that it was much too soon to get anxious, that he would probably arrive at any moment and that she shouldn't show signs of distress or he might think she was lacking in courage.

I got her to sit on the bed and find her handkerchief, and then I asked her questions about herself. This was for my own satisfaction but it helped to take her mind off Dunne's possible fate as well. She told me that her father was a high-ranking officer in the British navy, retired and living in Yorkshire when the war broke out. He was recalled, and went down with his ship in 1916, at the battle of Jutland. Her mother was left penniless but was given a grace-and-favour apartment in Hampton Court. Pamela had come into some money of her own three years ago, when she was eighteen. When the war was over she came to Ireland to stay with her aunt, a Mrs. Sanders, her father's sister, who owned a big estate called Mount Sanders in County Meath. I said: 'Then your father was Irish?'

'Not at all. He came from Northumberland. The family always went into the navy. They lost their money long ago. Mine came from my godmother. Mount Sanders belonged to my aunt's husband. He's dead too, killed at the second battle of the Marne. My aunt says that if he hadn't been a damned fool he would be alive today. She says the officers should always stay back and let the men do the dying.'

'She sounds a terror,' I said, not knowing how to receive this.

Pamela said: 'She's strong, that's all. The Sanders are all dead now, and she's there by herself. That's why she was glad to have me. She runs the estate better than any man could do. She can get people to work for her when they won't do a tap for anyone else. The women in my father's family are all like that. I wish I were.'

'You're not doing badly. Where did you meet Paul Dunne?'

'He came to Mount Sanders to collect the guns. There were three men in the party. My aunt gave them dinner.'

'And the guns?'

'Those too. She told them that if the Irish want to own Ireland they'll have to fight for it. She didn't want the guns anyway – she doesn't like blood sports. Neither do I. Paul promised they won't burn down Mount Sanders. He said he would give instructions himself.'

And everyone would jump to obey. That was what she thought of him, to judge by her tone whenever she said his name.

As I sat beside her, I was drinking in the movement of her mouth, the way she lifted her hand to brush back her soft, untidy hair, how she crossed her little narrow feet and arranged the preposterous skirt over them. Surely she should have known my condition by telepathy. She didn't. Her whole attention was concentrated on Dunne and his place in history. That was what she called it. Just to be associated with such a person, she said, made her own existence worthwhile.

I moved a little away from her, for my own safety, and said: 'So you came with him, to Dublin.'

'Not at first. He came several times to Mount Sanders.' For the dinners, I thought nastily. She was looking abstracted now, remembering the great decision she had taken. 'My aunt couldn't have stopped me from coming, but in fact, she didn't want to. She thinks we should all be in this together, all the people who intend to live in Ireland, so she said it was quite right that I should do my bit. That's what she called it. I had to be near Paul. Did you know he reads Blake? And he writes poetry.'

I sprang off the bed, suddenly unable to sit so near her without touching her. Fortunately she misunderstood my reasons. She said apologetically: 'I know you love him too. He told me about you, how you travelled around together, in Galway. I'm afraid I've upset you.'

'Not at all.'

What I was burning to know, she would never tell me, and I would never ask: was Dunne equally besotted with her? I believed he was not, but I knew I was a bad judge. My own experience so far was confined to hugging nice girls at parties – the Jesuits had seen to that. But now I had bigger ideas, and it was unbearable that I should be bested by a man I had dismissed as a rigid Irish bachelor.

A bitter, haunting, inescapable pain was already coursing through my whole body so that I would have been glad to do what Pamela was doing again, weeping with sheer misery. I found it impossible to endure. I went back to her where she lay prostrate on the bed. I lifted her up, and for one marvellous moment she clung to me while I murmured consolations into her angelic little pink ear. Then I said: 'You should go home now and rest. I'll stay here and wait for him. I'll bring you news as soon as I hear anything.'

She was living ten minutes' walk away, in Rathgar, she

said. She gave me the address, a lodging house inhabited mostly by bank clerks. The landlady cooked extra food for Paul's meals every day. This put me in a panic. I said: 'Isn't she curious about where you go, with your basket?'

'She would hardly think of asking,' Pamela said, with the air of Hampton Court.

'You'd better have a story ready,' I said, 'a sick friend, anything at all. You could be followed here at any time.'

'Paul says people probably think I'm the charwoman, with these clothes.' He had made that remark in my presence, as I well remembered. 'Of course, I could dress much better, but I'm practising to be poor. Paul says he will always be poor, because he will devote his whole life to the cause of Ireland.'

Her eyes shone with ecstasy. Would they be married, then? Still I couldn't bring myself to ask, though it would have been reasonable and appropriate. In a panic I said: 'The Tans don't treat women much better than men. For God's sake be careful. They haven't hung any women up by the thumbs yet but they have broken teeth and ribs and jaws.'

She burst into howls of anguish. 'Is that what they'll do to him, if they arrest him?'

'Didn't you know?'

'I know it's dangerous, but I hadn't seen it – I hadn't imagined it – as you said –' She stopped suddenly and dried her eyes with the corner of the bedspread, having failed to find the handkerchief she had been using before. She said firmly: 'If I fall into their hands, I'll think of my aunt. Then – if they do those things – I'll just have to bear it.'

If Dunne had come in at that moment, I'd probably have punched his nose. She had no idea what she was risking. There was no question of 'bearing it' when one fell into the hands of those limbs of Satan. Some people were strong; others were not. There was no way of discovering in advance which you were. The weak ones were reduced to a state of dithering terror; the strong ones held on to their wits until

53

they were unconscious or dead. I couldn't speak to her of these things, but I was not sorry I had warned her.

Before she left, she made me promise to see that Dunne ate his meal when he came in.

I went to work on my files as usual. Notes from the various officers showed that there was no falling-off in our numbers, though we might have expected it, with the prospect of peace in the air. If anything the numbers had gone up. It seemed that I had read the signs correctly – the brutality that had alarmed me was a symptom of stiffening resistance. The latest reports showed that the successful burning of the Custom House, which had virtually paralysed the Civil Service machine, and the attempted rescue of Commandant Sean MacEoin from Mountjoy gaol had put new heart into the country brigades. But MacEoin had been sentenced to be hanged for the murder of District Inspector MacGrath in Ballinalee. MacGrath might easily have killed MacEoin, since he had set out with a party to catch him at home. The dead man's relatives sent in a plea to spare MacEoin, who had always treated his captives as prisoners of war, but the implacable military court condemned him to death. A military court that condemned a man to be hanged was only one of the anomalies of that very peculiar war. If they carried out the sentence, there would be reprisals and everything would be worse than ever.

I laboured on until well after five, when Dunne came in. He glanced at the dishes, long gone cold, and said: 'Poor Pamela. I see she was here as usual.'

'Yes. I made her go home to rest. She was afraid you had been arrested.'

'I almost was. There are raids all over town. Collins is in a desperate state over MacEoin. I almost think he's losing his nerve.'

'Collins losing his nerve!' I burst out laughing, then saw the look of rage that he turned on me.

He answered calmly enough: 'I hope you're right. He goes on and on about MacEoin as if we hadn't lost many a better man. Today he's like a lunatic. That loud manner of his is disgusting.'

'He's a countryman.'

'And I'm a Dublin jackeen.'

So it still rankled. I turned away, silenced. Collins was our god in those days: the bravest soldier, the cleverest tactician, and still the most careful and caring friend. He never lost sight of the personal side of our lives, and spared us as many as possible of the thousands of heartbreaking things that went with our situation. When he talked of the North, it was never in terms of territorial ambition, always of the sufferings of the Catholic workers who lived in their ghettos in daily fear of brutal raids, burned houses, destruction and even death, without the protection of the police. If I sound sententious, I can't help it. I could talk about that side of Collins for an hour and never come near the truth. Why try it? The heroes of one country are the enemies of another; sometimes even the enemies of the next generation in their own. One thing is certain, that everyone remembers where he was when Collins died.

That point was still ahead of us. What I had just learned was that Dunne and probably a great many more had gone very far in their dislike of Collins' command. The split in the ranks which I feared began to seem inevitable.

4

The summer dragged on. There were various signs that the
British were as sick of the war as we were. Commandant
MacEoin was still in prison, and Lloyd George refused to
consider letting him go, though all the other prisoners were
to be released. De Valera as President replied by refusing
to negotiate further and MacEoin was released forthwith.
The effect of this on de Valera's prestige was tremendous.
When the truce was signed on the eleventh of July, almost
overnight the whole atmosphere of the country changed.
For ordinary people, the war was finally and decisively over.

Dunne was furious. He came back from the city after a
meeting with some of the country officers at G.H.Q. and
burst into the room in Terenure, where I was quietly getting
on with my work.

'Rats. Cowards. Scoundrels.' He marched back and forth,
three steps with each word, glaring at me venomously.
'They want to go home and celebrate their victory. They're
useless, gutless.'

I said cautiously: 'Perhaps it is a victory. They've certainly worked hard enough for it.'

'So you're on that side, are you? Let me tell you that there
is no hope whatever that we'll get what we're fighting for.
We're going to be cheated again, you'll see.'

He turned away, as if he couldn't bear to look at me, but
suddenly he gave a kind of twitch and strode across the
room to stand in front of me. He stared at me for a moment
and then said, with venomous intensity: 'This weakness
must be kicked out of the people. They must learn. They
must be taught a lesson.'

I closed my eyes. The upstairs room seemed to have

shrunk. I said desperately: 'I wish you would stop marching up and down. There's nothing we can do. Can't you wait and see what happens next?'

'No.' His voice had taken on a hard sound, like a barking dog. 'We can't wait. We must re-form the brigades and get ready for the next phase. We have a breathing space. It would be criminal not to make use of it.'

'Have you had orders to do this?'

'Of course. Do you think I'd go ahead without them? I take it that you'll be with me?'

'I suppose so.'

I know now that my judgment was distorted. I should have stated my position clearly, but I was bone tired and I scarcely knew myself what my reasons were. I had certainly lost my political sense, so far as any of us ever had one.

And there was Pamela. She was sitting on the bed watching Dunne in his rage, like an anxious child watching its father. I couldn't bear to quarrel with him in her presence. She would take his part against me and I would lose her forever. I still had hopes of detaching her from Dunne. I had never accepted her relationship with him, it was so absurd. Surely she saw how he glanced at her sometimes, as if to make sure that she was appreciating his fine temperament.

Would anyone believe that such a collection of mixed motives would land a man into the trap where I found myself from that day onwards? Dunne assumed I was converted to his ideas, since I hadn't said I was not, and I hadn't the nerve to explain myself. Gutless, indeed. He was right about that much.

He calmed down after a while and told me what his orders were. He and I were to take charge of a training camp for senior officers in the West. Dunne had just been with Commandant Emmet Dalton, who had chosen me to go along as adjutant because of my experience with the Western column. I was thought to be an expert on moving by night and using cover, and I had a reputation as a drill sergeant from my school days. Another reason was that I knew the area where we were going.

So it was that once more, in September, I was on my way to the West, shut into a railway carriage with Dunne. A friendly porter had arranged that we had it to ourselves. Dunne was playing the stockbroker again, in a neat suit of fine tweed. He looked old enough to be my uncle, and anyone glancing at us would probably think that was our relationship. He can hardly have addressed me as 'my boy', but the words were somewhere around in the air.

I kept my distance in my corner, reading Edgar Wallace. Dunne had a volume of Blake's poems, which it seemed to me that he held ostentatiously high. All the way to Galway I hated him as only the very young can hate. It never occurred to me that he might feel it. My pain for Pamela was as intense as a toothache, but he appeared quite unconcerned. With his privileges he could have kissed her on the platform at the Broadstone station, but he had barely touched her hand.

At Galway we changed to the Clifden line, and as the train crossed the high, white-painted bridge over the Corrib I felt a sudden lift of pure joy, as I used to do when I was coming home for summer holidays. The smooth-flowing river, the little varnished boats, the houses clustered at the waterside were always the first sign of forthcoming freedom, it seemed forever, even though I knew I would be condemned again to school in the autumn.

Dunne was watching me. He said: 'Coming home, aren't you?'

'Yes.'

'You haven't been home for a long time.'

'A year.'

'Do you write?'

'To my mother. My father is out of sympathy with the Movement.'

'Still? How do you know?'

'I don't, but I doubt if he'll change.'

58

'Pamela tells me that a great many of his kind have.'

Now that he had mentioned her name, I would have given anything to get him to talk about her more, but he was looking out of the window, across the river to the burned-out ruins of Menlo Castle. He asked: 'When did that happen?'

'A few years ago. Two women died in the fire before they could be rescued.'

'It was an accident?'

'Yes.'

'You can visit your family, you know. Commandant Dalton said to tell you.'

'Thank you. I was going to.'

My ironical tone certainly reached him, as I could see by the way he turned away. It was dangerous to assume that he was thick-skinned.

At Oughterard we were met by one of the local officers, an old friend of mine named Peter Hynes, who took us to a small hotel in the town, where we were to be lodged for the two weeks of our stay. That same evening we were taken to a hall where Dunne gave his first lecture.

It was on the organisation of intelligence units, a subject he had at his fingers' ends, and he delivered it with complete authority. The officers were deeply impressed, and after their initial shyness had worn off, they asked a great many questions. Dunne answered carefully, keeping exactly to the point and getting the questioner to discuss the topic further until he was sure the answer was satisfactory. He was at his best: relaxed, courteous, attentive, at ease.

Everyone assumed that we were close friends as well as colleagues, and I could see his stock go up by the minute. They admired his certainty, and took it for granted that he was an expert on all aspects of the war. Back in the hotel bar at the end of the evening, Hynes said: 'The men are wondering why we're doing this course now. Isn't the fighting over and done with?'

'You must get that idea out of their heads,' Dunne said.

'A truce is not peace. We may have to begin again any day.'

'The men are sick of it. They want to go home and get on with their work. And anyway we have hardly any guns.'

'I've heard that kind of talk in several places. You must persuade them that the time has not come yet. What's the use of throwing away all the years we've been fighting? We must go on until we have everything we wanted at the beginning. Pearse's ideal –'

Patiently. Slowly. Not a word about cowards, rats, scoundrels, kicking things out of people. I listened in silence, seeing why they liked and admired him, but quite unable to feel the same. An excellent man, I told myself – I was the worm. But it was no use.

They had given us a room together, partly for safety in case the house were raided, though in theory all such raids had ceased. I had to endure him day and night throughout the course. I couldn't help wondering whether he felt the same repugnance towards me, but it seemed not to be so. He was always extremely courteous, and would discuss the day's activities with me as if I were exactly on his level.

This was why I thought it would be bad manners to leave him behind when I went to visit my parents at the end of the course. Until then there had not been a moment to spare, day or night, and though he knew this very well, Dunne had asked me more than once when I was going to go home. If he was curious about my family he didn't show it. He seemed merely concerned that I shouldn't go back to Dublin without paying them a visit.

We went on the last day, in the afternoon. There was to be a party in our honour at Peter Hynes' house and we promised to be back for that. Peter managed to get a car, and he drove us there himself. As we passed between the D'Arcy stone lions on either pillar of the gateway I said: 'Do you remember how we used to climb up and ride on them when we were small?'

Peter said easily: 'I do, well. There's a great view from up there.'

But he would not come into the house. Nothing I could say would persuade him, and I soon gave up the effort. I knew the reason very well, and I didn't want Dunne to discover it. Hynes' father was a linesman on the railway, and neither father nor son would ever in normal circumstances pay a social visit to our house, though he would cheerfully have gone there on business.

The grass at either side of the avenue was nibbled down by my father's Border Leicesters so that it looked clean and neat. Nothing like sheep as lawn-mowers, he always said when people admired it. Wire netting, surprisingly intact, kept them out of the woods beyond, though it must have been a temptation at times to our neighbours.

The woods hid the house for a minute or two. Then we rounded a curve and there it was, a stone façade with oval windows under the roof and oblong Georgian ones below, wide shallow steps that bridged the ground-level area where the kitchens were and a great circle of gravel before the door. A typical eighteenth-century house, when labour was cheap and the gentry had big ideas.

Peter pulled up in front of the door to let us out, then drove off around the corner in the direction of the stable-yard. He knew the place well, from his childhood. By now I suppose all the I.R.A. men did. His school friends worked in our yard and gardens, and an uncle of his was my father's head groom.

Standing on the steps, I was glad I had asked Dunne to come with me, if only because his presence would put a brake on the conversation. I glanced at him for reassurance and found that it was he who was looking uneasy, perhaps taking his cue from Peter. He said in a low voice: 'Do you really want me to come in with you? Don't you want to be alone with them?'

'For God's sake don't desert me,' I said. 'You'll see.'

A girl I didn't know opened the door. She was wearing a parlour-maid's uniform, neat as a new pin, as my mother always taught them to do. Her face was vaguely familiar, but I knew she hadn't been in the household when I left. She looked us over suspiciously, then asked: 'Were you wanting someone?'

'Just tell Mrs. D'Arcy there are two visitors,' I said.

As I made for the drawing-room she said: 'Sure, you must be Micilín. I heard you were over in the town drilling. My brother Tommy was there at all the classes.'

'What's your name?'

'Maggie Molloy. We're from Recess. I have an aunt in Oughterard. I remember you coming into her shop when you were a little lad. I'll get your mother quick.'

Through the open drawing-room door we heard her running upstairs. I could feel my heart beating quickly and my hands sweating with excitement. It was unpleasant to wait like a stranger in my own house, but I had long ago decided that this was the only way I would come back.

The moment I saw them, I had qualms of conscience. My father seemed smaller and thinner than ever, and a great deal older. They came into the room together. They had been holding hands, and they dropped them on the threshold. That and my father's almost derelict appearance cut me to the heart. I had never before seen him dressed carelessly, though it was almost a fashion among some of our neighbours to look seedy.

My mother had changed terribly too. She had always been the more confident of the two, but now she kept glancing at my father as if she hoped for a lead from him. She said: 'We heard you were in Oughterard. We hoped you would come.'

Other than that, no sign of affection. That was never her way. One had to assume it was there. My father in his familiar sarcastic tone said: 'Won't you introduce your friend?'

'Commandant Dunne, my parents.'

He came forward politely and they shook hands with him and my mother said: 'Please sit down.'

We all went to sit by the empty hearth, the long, deep

sofa on one side and two armchairs at the other, under our feet the Persian rug that I used to lie on when I first learned to read, over the mantel the gilt-framed Waterford looking-glass. There was an awkward silence, until my father said: 'How long are you staying?'

'We're going back to Dublin tomorrow,' I said.

'Do you want to go back to the University?'

'Later, perhaps. Not yet.'

'Surely it's all over?'

'We don't know. This is only a truce.'

It was no use. In this house I could never be anything but a disappointing child, but it no longer mattered. I pitied the old people from the bottom of my heart. The last three years had changed me into a different person, one they had never known and wouldn't like any better than the old one. As if he guessed my thoughts my father said: 'Things will never be the same again. Not just in Ireland but everywhere, all over the world. Well, that's obvious. Why should we expect anything else? My older son was killed in France, Mr. Dunne. We've had a lot of the war in this house.'

'I'm sorry.'

'Thank you. It's happened to everyone. We're trying to change, but it doesn't come easily.'

The querulous tone was not intended to be pathetic, I knew, but that was how it affected me. I wondered if I would have done better without Dunne. If I had come alone, I might have appealed for sympathy myself by pouring out the tale of my experiences, the nights on the march, sleeping in ditches, the ambushes, never knowing whether or not I would live until the next day, the longing for home and for a sight of these silent, withdrawn people who meant so much to me.

But I wouldn't have done it. I had never spoken freely to either of them in all my life. I had no way of knowing what I meant to them. I hadn't even the faintest clue of their relationship with each other, until today for the first time I saw them holding hands. Of course I had seen them angry, but never with each other. Possibly they had a private arrangement to have their quarrels *in camera*.

For me, reality was in the kitchen and the stables – *nostalgie de la boue*, my father called it. School was supposed to cure me of it, but just when the miracle might have happened, I joined the Irish Republican Brotherhood, and was sworn in by Peter Hynes.

Maggie brought a tray of tea, and served it like a professional, until the moment when I caught her eye and she winked at me. Fortunately my mother's attention was on the tea things. I returned the wink, and she went off smiling to herself.

A rush of memory brought me inevitably back to my last meeting with my father. It was in the hall, as I was about to set out for Rabbit Island. Though I had not said that I was leaving for good, he sensed it and asked: 'Something new going on? Do I deserve the courtesy of being told what it is?'

This typical way of addressing me always brought out the worst in me. I mumbled: 'I'm sorry, I can't tell you.'

He stared at me with loathing and said: 'Why did it have to be your brother who died?'

Then he turned and went back to his work-room. I had no doubt that he was remembering the same thing now, while we drank tea politely out of the best cups and ate cucumber sandwiches. The difference was that then he was bitterly sure of himself. Now he looked lost and hurt.

I asked about the farm, and he brightened for a few minutes while he talked about the Friesian cattle that he was trying. He said, again in that querulous tone: 'Tuberculosis in cattle is killing off the population of this country. When your lot gets in I hope you'll do something about it. They tell me it's the damp climate that gives it to the cows, but Friesland must be one of the dampest inhabited spots in the world, after Connemara. Lazy-minded thieves.'

It was not clear who these were. I was glad to see him a little more energetic, even though it was only for a moment.

We left soon afterwards, and they came out onto the steps with us. Neither of them asked me when I would come back, and when I turned to wave to them from the car I found that they had already gone inside.

On the way back to Oughterard Dunne was quite silent. I was glad of it – I had no wish to hear his thoughts on our visit. Peter had no inhibitions. He said: 'Your father has failed a lot, Micilín. He has no interest in things the way he used to. It's natural, I suppose, with the two of you gone and all the fighting. He says he doesn't know who he's talking to these days.'

'Do you think he's frightened?'

'More dispirited, I'd say. It's hard on the gentry to see the end of their day.' After a pause he said: 'My uncle and myself were thinking we might get him interested in breeding a few good-class horses. And he has some grand sheep. He knows a queer lot about breeding animals. It might put a bit of heart back into him. We're going to need the like of him, in the new Ireland.'

Peter was the first person I heard using that expression, which became common currency in the following years.

I enjoyed the party that night to the full. We danced sixteen-hand reels and long dances, and were entertained by solo step-dancers and singers. The men danced with long swinging steps, springing around the room, delighted with the murmurs of admiration on all sides. The songs were patriotic ones – 'Down by the Glenside', and 'The Croppy Boy', and 'Óró, Sé do Bheatha Abhaile', which Peter Hynes sang himself with great energy. I often think now that this was the kind of thing the men were fighting for – the right to enjoy themselves in their own way, without apology. They couldn't have expressed it, but Peter Hynes said later: 'With God's help we'll have many another evening like that when the good times come.'

We went back to Dublin the next day and I tried to pick up daily life again. Like a patient lackey I followed Dunne about. I must simply have suspended judgment, probably in an unhealthy defence against making up my mind too soon about the things that were happening. He seemed so certain of what he was doing. I may have thought I had no need to think it out for myself.

The idea of dividing the country into two states terrified me. I couldn't believe that this would happen, that the Northern Protestants would desert their brethren in the South and accept an arrangement that would virtually emasculate both of them. I waited daily for both sides to see that this was what they were being forced to do, but scarcely anyone else seemed to see it that way. I thought that sectarianism, obscurantism – whatever you call it – on either side, was a disaster. But very few people spoke of politics in those days. I kept silent, since I believed no one would listen to me.

Just before the truce was signed, fifteen Catholics were murdered in Belfast and a hundred and sixty of their houses burned. Pamela wept for the poor people turned out into the streets, trying to escape their pursuers by flight to the South, and she said to me: 'Don't you see that you must fight against partition? If you don't, you're condoning that kind of persecution? It must not be allowed to happen.'

'I know,' I said. 'But we simply can't fight any longer. We haven't the means.'

'Coward!' she said. 'White feather! Fight to the death. You must. You can't give in now.'

We were in Bewley's café, eating sticky buns and drinking thin coffee. If she had asked me to climb Mount Everest then, I would have consented. I had her to myself while Dunne was at a meeting, and I hated wasting my time talking about politics. I gazed into her eyes, full of excitement as she attacked me, and saw amazement dawn there, as she realised my feelings about her. She put her hand up to her mouth, then said: 'Oh, no. Not that.'

'Why not? Pamela, I never stop thinking about you, day or night. It has nothing to do with Ireland, or the future of the country or anything else that everyone talks about.

Don't tell me now that I haven't a chance,' I said in a panic. 'I can wait. I've waited a long time, after all. I haven't hurried you.'

'But I belong to Paul. You know that.'

'Do you?'

She brushed that aside.

'There are too many important things happening. We can't think of ourselves.'

'Have you said the same to Dunne?'

'Of course not. There's no need. He has other things on his mind; we understand each other.'

I couldn't believe this. She had told me once that she was practising to be a poor man's wife. I should have accepted that, I suppose, but I had almost come to believe there was nothing between them. Dunne never showed her the smallest sign of affection, and he rarely spoke of her to me. I had often observed that lovers can't forbear from mentioning each other's names – if that was any test, the interest was all on her side.

She was saying: 'Paul can't look ahead now because he's in such danger all the time. He told me once that a dedicated revolutionary has no past and no future.'

'Then where do you come in?'

'I'll find out some day. Look, Michael, I'm sorry if I've hurt you in any way. I didn't think you would bother with me.'

'Bother with you!'

'Yes. I'm untidy and inefficient and not much to look at –'

'Who told you that?'

'I know it myself. That's why I'm useful. No one notices me.'

She seemed really to believe this. Surely anyone who ever saw that head of glorious red hair could never forget it. I said: 'How are you useful?'

'All kinds of ways.'

She would give no details, but I guessed that she was

being used as a messenger, a dangerous business, as I had already warned her.

Suddenly I blurted out: 'Come away with me. Let's forget all this. It's finished. They can do without us. Dunne thinks of nothing but the war. He'll never have time for you.'

She gave me a heavy, pained look, then tried to answer kindly. 'I know you don't understand what you're saying. You have no idea what it is for me to be associated with a truly great man, and with great events. Ireland now is the most exciting, marvellous place in the world. It's like Russia a few years ago, or like America during the War of Independence. The whole world is shaken by people like Paul. It's a privilege I couldn't give up. You don't notice it so much because you're a man, and because you're part of it. Nothing in the world will ever be the same again.'

There was no answer to this. Her mind was like an impenetrable wall. She paid no more attention to me than she would to the twittering of the birds.

For the next few months I lived in a state of near despair. Anticlimax had something to do with it, and also the fact that, though I disagreed completely with Dunne's position, still I couldn't break with him. But for Pamela, I might have gone home, or back to the University. I certainly would never have gone on with the comedy of preparing to continue the war. We hadn't enough guns to arm a quarter of the men we would need. We had lost the support of the country. The ordinary people didn't want another moment of war. The sooner we found a compromise, the better. Those were my own ideas, but I kept them very much to myself. I would have found no one in Dunne's circles to agree with me. De Valera would see us through – that was the general view of the future, among the dedicated and long-suffering Republicans.

The leaders went back and forth to London, Collins and Griffith and Barton and Duggan and the rest of them, all so high in the councils that they were only names to people like me. When the treaty negotiations were coming to an end, and the outcome seemed to me certain, I asked Dunne: 'What will we do if the terms are not acceptable?'

'Fight on,' he said, his chin stuck out and with that dogged look in his eyes. 'We can't stop now. You'll see, there will be no choice. The Cork and Kerry men will never agree to partition. It will be the same in the West. We'll be organised in advance. That will be our strength.'

His narrowed eyes and portentous tone of voice told me more about what was going on in his head than anything he had said. Still I didn't interpret it as well as I might have done. I still thought it was determination, rather than arrogance.

I know I was suspicious of his new air of authority, which I had first noticed in Oughterard, and which now took the form of giving me a set of instructions every morning as if I were his adjutant, responsible to no one but himself. I carried them out, since no one else had told me what to do. Besides, in deciding not to go back to the University yet, I had virtually committed myself to the Movement.

I now discovered that Dunne had evolved a highly organised intelligence system of his own. Using my files, he worked on it with me by the hour, until we knew the name and rank of every officer throughout the whole country. He also knew, or said he knew, which way these people would go when the terms of the treaty became known. He dictated dozens of letters to me, about the care and safety of the arms dumps that existed all over the country and the need to keep up the drilling.

Every few days I accompanied him to a meeting in an upstairs room of a public house in Parnell Street, where contingency plans were discussed. Though the longed-for treaty was in sight, the officers were as nervous as cats. Not one of them seemed to me to have a sense of victory. They could hardly sit still for more than a few minutes at a time. Men began sentences and didn't finish them:

'If they insist on partition –'

'The Tans are still here and we can't –'

'The British army – idle now the war is over –'

'Money and land –'

'Guns – what will we do –'

'My people will never take the oath of allegiance,' one positive Corkman said.

A Dublin officer said bitterly: 'They may find they have to swallow it.'

The Corkman looked at him with hatred, then turned away with a sneer of contempt.

When the rest of the men were from the country, Dunne was in his element, full if ideas and instructions about the procedures to be followed in the event of a breakdown of the treaty negotiations. When Dublin men were present, he hardly spoke at all. I noticed that they paid very little attention to him, though they listened to him politely when he had anything to say.

On the evening of the sixth of December, the first real news of the terms of the treaty was brought to Dublin by Mr. Duggan, one of the delegates. Dunne had information immediately, however he got it. When I came to Terenure the next morning he was fidgeting around the room. He turned to stare out of the window, as if he couldn't trust himself to speak, then whirled around saying: 'They've done it. They've sold out. I knew they would.'

'They can't have. They were to come home with the terms and it's to be discussed in the Dáil.'

'They didn't do that. They went their own way. They've signed.'

I couldn't believe it. I knew nothing then of the pressures that had forced the delegates to exceed their instructions, nor of their own certainty that they were in fact the only men fit to take the momentous decision. At least that's how I worked it out afterwards. They knew there would be violent disagreement at home when the outcome was known, but they were prepared to suffer that. Almost at once we heard that on the night he signed, half past two in the

70

morning, Collins said to the others: 'I have just signed my own death warrant.'

'I always knew Collins was an arrogant fool,' said Dunne that morning. 'He has pushed us into civil war. A Free State, so called, with partition of North and South, the sorest point of all. And the ports will still be full of British warships. Ireland will be responsible for the cost of the war – try to imagine how the people will feel when they hear that they have to pay for the pensions of the Black-and-Tans. And we're to pay land annuities to the tune of five million a year. There's an oath of allegiance to the king – all the things we've been fighting to get rid of. You'll see, the people won't stand it.'

'You know this is not what Collins wanted,' I said. 'The people may have no choice, any more than he did.'

He didn't answer, and I didn't continue the argument. I was sickened by his condemnation of Collins. Apart from his record as a soldier, which was streets ahead of Dunne's, it seemed outrageous to blame one of the youngest members for the folly of the whole delegation. I had to listen to a great deal more of it during that day and the following ones, while Dunne worked himself up to be worthy of the destiny that he saw before him.

5

That destiny included me. It never occurred to him that I wouldn't follow him. We went together to listen to the debate on the treaty, a futile exercise I thought, since it had already been signed. Scarcely anyone knew me, though Dunne was recognised on all sides. To my great embarrassment I had grown still taller in the last few months. I was always very thin, and I still had the typical boy's face that runs in my family. Dunne was tall too, but he was bulky, and looked older than his years. Neither of us said a word, but we arrived and left at the same time, which made me feel ridiculous.

Dunne's seriousness was oppressive. I couldn't help thinking he was deliberately creating the image, as they say nowadays, which would be most useful to him in achieving his purpose.

'You can see the men are looking for leaders,' he said to me after one of these meetings. 'They need people with vision, people who can take responsibility for the conscience of the nation.'

It was a moment before I realised that he saw himself as one of those dedicated leaders. I was about to say that it's manners to wait until you're asked, but I stopped in time. Dunne never had much sense of humour, especially in matters concerning himself.

The Free State was to have a National Army, and commissions were being offered to men of our ranks who had proved themselves good soldiers. Both Dunne and I were offered them. As the British troops would soon be evacuated, it was natural that the I.R.A. should take their place. I wondered if he would be tempted, but still with that solemn

72

air he said: 'I have my oath to the I.R.B. If I take a commission I would give up my right to disagree with the policies of the government.'

This splendid excuse was just what I needed, and I said I would also refuse. I had had enough of fighting, and besides, it seemed to me that Ireland was too small a country to have an army of any significance. Ours had been a guerrilla war. You don't make soldiers that way. I knew this was not Collins' idea, but even my adoration of him couldn't make me agree on that point.

Dunne saw at once that my hero was somewhat out of favour with me and he didn't lose the opportunity to condemn Collins.

'"Absolute power corrupts absolutely",' he quoted solemnly. 'Now that the army is split he would be a disaster as commander in chief. We're facing a worse fight than ever before –'

On and on it went until my head was in a whirl. When the vote on the treaty was taken on the seventh of January, sixty-four deputies voted for it, fifty-seven against. As the leader of the opposing side, de Valera resigned as president of the parliament, and a day or two later Arthur Griffith was elected in his stead.

Still there was no open breach in the army. The British, having made what they saw as very generous terms, were certain that these would be accepted without much difficulty. They began to move their troops out of the country. I remember wondering if they had any idea of the struggle for power that was going on among their former enemies. Most of the British army officers that I encountered seemed to take no interest whatever in the convolutions of Irish politics.

Dunne was sent to Kilkenny to take over the barracks there. His orders came from Emmet Dalton, now a general in the new army. I was surprised that he accepted, in view of his wholesale condemnation of the pro-treaty members of the I.R.A. I didn't even try to question him about it. At first I was delighted to hear he would be leaving Dublin, since I would have Pamela to myself, but I soon found that he took it for granted I would go with him.

It was Pamela herself who inadvertently rescued me from yet another *tête-à-tête* with him. She came in rather later than usual one morning, looking agitated, and said at once: 'The guns will be brought in on Tuesday. You won't be here?'

Dunne said: 'How can I? I've got to go to Kilkenny.'

'Then what should I do? They won't like it if they find only me to receive them.'

'You can have Michael. I wanted him to be with me, but this means he'll have to stay at home.'

'Can't he go instead of you?'

'Dalton wouldn't agree. He'd be suspicious at once.'

'How will I know the men when they come?'

'Michael knows them. You can give him a list of names. You know some of them yourself.'

'Yes, I suppose so,' she said, looking at me as if she had never seen me before.

I said furiously: 'What is all this about? What are these guns? Why are you keeping secrets from me, talking about me as if I weren't here?'

'It's all right,' Dunne said soothingly, as if he were talking to a child. 'We're simply making sure that all the guns don't fall into the hands of the pro-treaty men. You'll see, the convention that we asked for will never be allowed to take place.'

'Is that certain?'

I knew that this convention was planned for the twenty-sixth of March, and all of my own hopes for peace between the pro- and anti-treaty sides were based on the prospect of civilised discussion there. Such innocence! I should have known how the propaganda was going, from the Sunday sermons at every Mass, where the priests thundered out condemnation of anyone who didn't seize the chance of making peace at any price.

Though I was all in favour of making peace, those sermons almost turned me in the other direction. Their whole tone was bullying and bitter. The Republicans were condemned outright, even named as instruments of Satan. It was almost laughable. One would think the Irish priests had never heard of the difference between the things that are Caesar's and the things that are their business. They're at it still, from what I can hear. They seem to have no faith in the people of Ireland. But I must not get warm on that subject. I sometimes wonder if I'm turning into an old crank. Nothing more likely, at my age.

In the city, there was a great deal of ugly gossip, some of which my landlady Mrs. Malone had retailed to me over breakfast in the kitchen. She said: 'We're back to the real nature of the people now. A crowd of begrudgers – that's all they ever were in Ireland. They're saying up in Rathmines that you're all communists. Did you hear that de Valera is a Spanish bastard and doesn't give a tinker's dam for Ireland? That's the kind of talk that's going around. And that Madame Markievicz is a loose woman.'

'People are sick of the war. They never wanted it in Rathmines anyway.'

'No one in their right mind wants a war, but you'd think they'd have a bit of gratitude to the boys that fought it. Gratitude! They say we'll be ruined now, when the British are gone. Do you think we'll have a civil war on our hands?'

I thought of Dunne. I said: 'Some people won't give an inch. I loathe the terms of the treaty, but I hope there will be some kind of agreement.'

She looked at me sadly. 'You've had enough of it. You look like an old man, and you talk like one too. It's time you got back to college. Down in my place they're saying they won't give up until we have the Republic, but I said this treaty is a step towards it.' 'Her place' was the village in County Meath that she had left when she was very young to marry in Dublin, and where she still had a brother and sister living on the family farm. 'They said I was gone soft

75

from city living. They're always fighting mad in the country. Easy for them, and they having the ditches and hedges to hide in.'

I remembered this conversation now, while Dunne was watching me. He said: 'The convention hasn't been dropped yet, but you'll see, it will be. Collins and Griffith will never let it happen.'

He seemed so sure of this that I didn't ask him where he got his information. The whole city was alive with gossip, as Mrs. Malone had said. I had already noticed a curious thing: spying, informing, call it what you will, seemed to have no further significance as a crime once the opposite sides were both Irish. I have no other explanation for the change that took place in people's attitude towards what would so recently have been regarded as military secrets. If people noticed anything, they were likely to chat about it to all their neighbours. Why shouldn't they, if the war was over? Some of the men had even begun to boast of their exploits as if the whole affair was past history. A few who had done little or nothing for their country did this, and I wondered now and then how they were planning to retrieve themselves if negotiations broke down and the war went on again.

I asked sardonically: 'Do you want to keep this business of the guns secret?'

'Of course. That's the whole point.'

'Where are they now? Where are they being taken? You can't expect me to work blindfold.'

He was staring at me with that opaque look. After a moment he said: 'Pamela knows all about them. She'll tell you.'

That satisfied me. I made no objections, lest he might change his mind. He would be away for two weeks, and I was determined to make full use of my time. Such an opportunity might never occur again.

When I look back on it, I still marvel at my simplicity. The project was to move two hundred rifles and several boxes of ammunition from a dump whose whereabouts were well known to Dalton and Collins and a great many others. They were to be taken by night to a place designated by Dunne and some of his trusted associates on the Republican side. This could only mean that the split between the Free Staters and the Republicans was already irrevocable, but I somehow managed to remain blind.

I had been with Dunne to several meetings in Parnell Square, where the hungry, anxious faces of the young Republican officers had shown how much they longed to avoid a break with their old friends. But there was something else there too – despair, loss, pain, bitterness, memory, or a combination of all these – that made it impossible for them to face the truth of their defeat. That was how they saw it, no matter how it was expressed. They had fought like tigers for the Republic and had imagined that it would come at last. Now they were ashamed of their leaders, who, they believed, had been duped into accepting a dishonourable settlement. They didn't blame them for their initial mistake, but now they wanted them to recant and start up the war again. This was impossible. To continue the peace, everything hinged on healing the split in the army and there was no longer any hope of this. It's proverbially easier to start a war than to stop it. We had a classic case.

And I was in it up to my neck. I could still have changed sides, as a great many did, but I was too weary to be logical. And there was Pamela. Waking and sleeping she was in my mind. I lived in a state of dream, in which I could have reached out and touched her even when she was physically absent. Her voice sang in my ears, long after she was gone, as it does still. I can hear her saying my name casually, over all the years, warmly, full of friendship and trust.

During that time when we were first alone together, I remember feeling as if part of my body had been missing and I had somehow found it again. The fact that she didn't love me was not so important. I simply knew that she was mine, as an arm or a leg belongs to its body. If it never

77

occurred to me that I might injure her I can only say that one doesn't fear to injure oneself.

I began to find out extraordinary things. A week before Dunne went to Kilkenny, Pamela had rented a ramshackle house in the hills above Rathfarnham and had moved there to live, though I had thought she was still in her lodgings in Rathgar. The guns were to be transferred to a newly constructed dugout in the grounds of this house. She took me there on a soft April afternoon, the Tuesday after Dunne left.

We walked uphill for what seemed like an hour from the tram stop, before we reached some rusted iron gates. They were stuck fast in grass and weeds so that they couldn't be opened, but we climbed around by the side and started up the avenue. It was pitted with ruts and pot-holes, overflowing from the recent rain. The house was buried among tall trees, which hadn't been cut back for years. Ferns and ivy crawled over what had once been a croquet lawn. Jackdaws were nesting in the chimneys and in the trees, and a scatter of empty snail-shells on the steps showed where the thrushes had found a choice spot for cracking them open. Blackbirds whistled their evening call, a cheerful, friendly sound.

Pamela had seen the dugout being made and she led me to it at once, laughing at my caution. 'No one comes up here,' she said. 'If anyone did, we'd hear them a mile off.'

It was in a small overgrown wood beyond the walled garden. The entrance was by a short ladder, and the square-shaped opening was covered with an old piece of plywood. Four biscuit-tins supported a bed-spring, as if it was intended to be used sometimes as a hiding-place. I had sheltered in more than one of these dugouts from the Black-and-Tans, and could see that the pattern was the same. Pamela was as proud of it as if she had built it herself, climbing down the ladder like a child and calling to me to come and look. I did, to please her, and it almost gave me the horrors.

We went back to the house to wait for the men, who were

not expected until ten o'clock at the earliest. They were to load up the arms after dark in the city, and then drive out with them to the new dump. Pamela didn't know where the old dump was, but Dunne had told her that it was in the grounds of a somewhat similar house in the suburbs. And he had instructed her to rent one like it.

'I had great fun finding it,' she said. 'I went to Prim's and said I wanted a house with character, that I could redecorate gradually, so I got it on a repairing lease. I had never heard of such a thing, but they told me you can sometimes get an old house that way. Aunt Molly gave me references – isn't it amazing? Just like a parlour-maid. And here I am. I've paid three months' rent in advance. They told me that no one has lived here for years.'

Darkness was falling and the close-growing trees were losing their colour. The grass was a heavy grey. She opened the door with a big iron key and we walked into the hall. She said: 'It's not damp, though it feels so cold. There's no smell of dry rot.' She turned up her nose and sniffed the air like a dog. 'Come and look at it, while we still have some daylight. There's a drum of paraffin oil. I found lots of lamps, but the good ones are too heavy to carry.'

She ran ahead of me into the rooms: a long one with windows on two walls, to the left of the hall, and a smaller one to the right, with a window only to the front of the house. They were furnished with pale, old carpets and tattered cretonne-covered sofas and chairs. At the back of the hall there was a small library, and beside its door the stairs began their upward curve.

We followed a passage off which there was a dining-room with a dark mahogany table and chairs, and went into a stone-floored kitchen. Dust lay everywhere. She said: 'I haven't lit the fire for days, though I did in the beginning. There's wood and coal in the shed.'

We brought in some of both and got the stove going with paraffin oil and newspaper. The chimney didn't smoke because the agent had had it cleaned for her, she said, and the drawing-room chimney too. The flames instantly made the squalid room more inviting. I took a cloth from the scullery, ran it under the tap and wiped the dust off the table and the chairs. Pamela said admiringly: 'You're quite a housekeeper. Come and see the rest of it.'

Upstairs there were several bedrooms, one of which she was using for herself. I asked: 'Weren't you afraid, all alone in this creepy place?'

'I'm never afraid to be alone. Anyway it's not creepy. It's a friendly house. The owners went off to England during the war but the man at Prim's said they may want to come back when things have quieted down again.'

The idea that they might come back made me furiously angry. Already I had settled into this heavenly, remote place with Pamela, and was living the life of paradise, cut off from the whole world. There was a dog, perhaps two, several cats, tame birds, perhaps some horses – I must have been slightly crazy – and no human being but ourselves, Pamela and I, eternally in each other's arms. But I didn't dare to touch her. I stood looking at her, my hands behind my back, while the light faded moment by moment around us.

She moved quietly out of the room, and I could hear her at the top of the stairs saying: 'Let's go down, Michael. It's time to light the lamps.'

In the kitchen I found that her mood had changed. She scarcely spoke as we filled two small brass lamps and placed them on the table, one at either end. We stood and stared at them, as one always wants to do with oil-lamps after they are lit. The worn, unpolished brass shone with a dull, secretive glow. After a moment she said: 'Are you able to cook? I have bacon and eggs and bread and tea. I'm hungry.'

'So am I.'

It was heaven to be hungry with her. I remember that the dry voice of Father Latimer came back to me: 'The man who know nothing of love knows nothing of God. God is love. That was Saint John, boys. Keep those words in mind always.' Had he ever loved? Perhaps he had had loving parents, which was more than I could be sure of. And I remember that I felt a surge of bitterness against the war that had eaten up my youth and made me, as Mrs. Malone said, like an old man.

How can people complain of domesticity, that rare privilege in this world? I could count the moments I have had of it, like this one in the shadowy kitchen, cooking on the hot stove, hearing Pamela behind me laying out plates and knives and forks, and cutting bread. The bacon and eggs were the food of the gods.

After we had eaten she sat opposite me, so that we could both feel the warmth of the fire. The coals glowed red through the bars of the range and combined with the soft orange light of the lamp behind her, so that her hair became a shadowy halo. Now and then she put up her hand to push it away from her face. I became possessed with a violent wish to brush her hair, to smooth it out with long, careful strokes until it shone, then to coil it or plait it into a crown as some girls still did. I asked suddenly: 'Have you thought of cutting your hair?'

'No. What a splendid idea. Let's do it now.'

I was appalled. Everything I had been through seemed to coalesce into this new horror. I began to shout, my voice shaking with rage: 'No – no – don't touch it – don't touch it –'

She stared at me with amazement, then came running around to the back of my chair, putting her hands on my shoulders, soothing me as if I were a nervous horse, rubbing me down gently, saying softly: 'Of course I won't, if you don't want it. I thought you were suggesting it, because you like tidy people and I'm never tidy. I've seen you looking at my hair – you've been doing it all evening, since we came into the house. I never think of it. That's why it's always in a mess.'

'Will you let me brush it for you?'

'Of course, later on, when the men have gone. Now please be calm. I've never seen you like this before. I thought you

81

were always so strong and clear headed, and now you make a fuss over such a little thing.'

'It's not a little thing.' I was shaking again. With an immense effort I controlled my voice. 'Yes, we'll do it later on.'

We took the plates out to the scullery and pulled up our chairs to the range to wait for the men. We left one lamp on the table and moved the other to the dresser, where I had to clear a place among the clutter of cups and dishes. Darkness shone malevolently on the curtainless window, where a thousand enemies could peer in. The wind moved the branches of the trees so that they creaked and swung. I said: 'Those trees should be pruned or they will die.'

'I thought one only pruned fruit trees. Anyway, it's better not to have them cut back as long as the dump is here. Paul says I'm not to have any workmen in, unless he recommends them.'

'Has he been here?'

'Not yet. He would have come if he hadn't been sent away just now. Of course, I've described it to him. He thinks it's ideal.'

'For what?'

'A hideout, a dump, all that kind of thing, when the new war begins.'

'Is he sure there will be a new war?'

'Oh, yes. Paul says there's no way out of it now. He says the country won't settle for anything less than a Republic.'

'But that's out of the question.'

'Paul says the British are bluffing.'

I didn't think there was much bluff about what was going on in the North. Everything was suddenly far worse there. Sir Henry Wilson was their new military adviser, and since the treaty had been signed, terrorism had increased, particularly in Belfast. The B-Specials and the Orange Order made it plain that they were determined to get the Catholics out of that part of Ireland, and they organised periodic raids which had sent thousands of refugees south in fear of their lives, as we all knew.

The terrorists were supported by thirteen battalions of British soldiers and their police-force was well armed. Only a month before, the new Northern Parliament had enacted a Special Powers Bill which imposed the death penalty for possession of arms, flogging for some offences, the suspension of trial by jury and even of coroner's inquests. This left the police with a very free hand. They were organised in three classes, full-time, part-time and a civilian intelligence auxiliary, to which one had to belong in order to obtain a licence for a gun. Not much room for Republicans there. It was said that this police force numbered more than twenty-five thousand men.

Dunne knew these things as well as I did. If I had been arguing with him I could have pointed out that in the beginning no one hoped for military success. The idea was to make a massive protest. As things had turned out it would be madness not to take what we could get and run. It's easier to fight to the death when there is no other option. The smallest hope of survival changes the whole picture and gives one different responsibilities. It seemed to me that the Republicans were opting for genocide.

Even argument was useless with Dunne now, in the emotional heat that surrounded the whole controversy. Two points in the terms of the treaty stood out as the worst stumbling blocks. Partition had already led to civil war in the northern part of the country, and in the South the oath of allegiance to a foreign king seemed to the Republicans to add insult to injury. I have often wondered why this strange survival was included in the document – surely it was not out of malice. Tradition, probably. At the meetings I had attended with Dunne, mention of either of these subjects raised the temperature to boiling point.

I couldn't bear to speak of such things to Pamela, especially as I knew she would continue to quote Dunne against me. The awed adoration with which she pronounced his name drove me wild. Any one of my thoughts was a condemnation of his logic, if not of his intelligence.

To change the subject I asked: 'Has this house a name?'

'Yes – Ferney, after Voltaire's house I suppose, but it reminds me of ferns. If the owners will sell it I could change the name, but I wouldn't want to. It's on the old maps as Ferney. It has a stream, almost a river, with a wooden bridge. That's one of the things that will have to be repaired. I might get a little stone bridge built instead. Wood will always rot in this climate.'

'Then you mean to stay?'

'Of course. What else would I do? Go back to England?'

'To Mount Sanders, I thought.'

'Much better to have a place of my own. I like to be independent, and I like Dublin. Of course, one can't look ahead, until we see what's going to happen. Paul told me your house in the West is beautiful. I'd like to see it some day. You must miss it.'

I presumed that Dunne had described my parents too, and I would have liked to find out what he had made of our visit to them. Naturally I couldn't ask her. I said: 'Yes, I'm ready for some home life now, but it's a few years off, if I go back to college.'

'Do you want to?'

'I know I should, but I can't keep my mind on it.'

'I'll have to see to the repairs. Where do you think I should begin?'

'On the outside, with the avenue and the front lawn, so that you can see the house properly. There could be some ground damp – you'll only find that by clearing all the outside drains. The overhanging trees would have to be cut back. The roof is probably leaking here and there. You can see stains on the walls in some of the rooms. Then the rooms could be painted one by one.'

'How wise you sound. How do you know those things?'

'From watching my father. He keeps the place in very good order.'

A sharp knock on the window brought me leaping to my feet in fright. It was exactly like the crack of a rifle – a sound that will be with me until the day I die, I suppose. Then I saw a disembodied face peering through the glass and a hand came up to a salute. Pamela said: 'It's Pat Corby – let him in.'

I took one of the lamps and went to the front door, feeling a moment of blind panic before I opened it. There he was, of course, a man from the Dublin Brigade that I knew well, from meeting him with Dunne. He was a plumber by trade, short and squat, with a rabbity look – something about his round, soft eyes and the way he wore his cap flattened down at either side.

He was very cheerful and talked very fast, with a strong Dublin accent: 'Captain D'Arcy – Private Corby on duty. I followed the light and saw the two of yez through the window, and I gave it a crack without thinking. Sure, I knew you were expecting us. We couldn't get the gate open. I had to leave the car outside. Then I couldn't find the front door. Only for your light I'd never have seen the house. It's black as the pit, but thank God it's not raining.'

He followed me into the kitchen and went to shake hands with Pamela. She said: 'Is the stuff safe? Have you got it all?'

'Sure. I left the rest of them minding it.'

'Who are they?'

'Fitzer and Cooney and Murphy. It'll take a while to carry it in. The back avenue is worse than the front or I'd have gone around that way.'

I went with him to the shelter, beating our way through the long grass to the wood and then fumbling around until we found it. I asked: 'Did you have a hand in digging this?'

'Sure,' he said easily. 'We're getting better at it every time. The side of a hill is the best, when we can find one in the right place. Less fear of seepage. The big estates are great – no one ever sets foot in them. It's a different story with the farmers. They know every blade of grass on their land.'

The car was a huge old seven-seater Ansaldo with the capacity of a small truck. It took more than two hours to carry the guns over the rough ground to the dugout, and to stack them in there against the walls. I did my share of the carrying but avoided going down into the dugout again. The other three ran up and down the ladder cheerfully and seemed not to question their orders too much. Once I began to ask them what they thought the future held for us, and Fitzpatrick said: 'Unless we get the Republic we'll never get what Connolly wanted. I'm a Citizen Army man. If Connolly was here now, he'd tell us to keep the fight going.'

If Connolly – if Pearse – if Clarke – who knows what they would have said? What these men needed was a leader to tell them what to do next. The loss of Collins to the treaty side had cut them to the bone. They needed someone like him. Dunne's inflexibility must have looked like strength. I dropped the question. Above all things I didn't want a political argument then.

Back in the warm kitchen Pamela had a pot of tea for us, and the last of the bread. She said: 'I'm afraid I haven't much to give you – the shops are so far away.'

I could see that the men admired her, and it warmed my heart towards them. Soon after they had eaten, they went away.

Immediately the wind intruded again, and then rain began to tap softly against the window. I felt a current of excitement run through me. I was no longer afraid. I began to make up the fire, shovelling the coal in carefully and tapping it down, my back to the room. After a moment I said: 'Now I can brush your hair.'

She took one of the lamps and went to fetch a brush from her room. It was backed with ivory and had carved initials, her grandmother's, she said. She handed it to me without a word, then sat in the chair I had placed for her in front of the fire. For the next hour I was in paradise. I took up handfuls of her hair and stroked it to the very end with the brush, then laid each smooth, long piece down on her shoulders. When all the tangles were out – and there were a great many of them – I went on and on brushing until it was glossy, shining with health, in a hundred different shades of colour, ranging from orange to dark brown.

She sat with her head bent forward, to give me room. The soft light of the fire touched the curve of her cheek, and I saw that her eyes were closed. For a moment I thought she was alseep, and the notion of her sleep made me unbearably sad, as if she had already left me.

I put down the brush and began to plait her hair into a thick rope, which I tied at the end with strands of hair that I took from the brush, as I had seen my mother do. When it was done I knelt on the floor beside her and laid my head on her lap. A moment later I felt her lean down and kiss the back of my neck.

No, we didn't make love, that night nor any other night during the next ten days. No one of this generation could possibly understand how pure we were then, nor how we managed to survive without sex. We lived on hopes, I suppose, and the magic and the mystery were certainly there – perhaps more so than now. The darkened house surrounded by trees produced a sense of fairytale, for me at least. I don't know what Pamela was thinking, except that she let me brush her hair last thing every night, in front of the kitchen fire. We found blankets and made up a bed for me in a small room next to hers, and I never once tried to visit her there.

By day we cleaned the house and tidied the gravel sweep and the old flower-beds in front. We found rusted tools in the coal-shed and oiled them so that they were fit to be used. We walked down to Rathfarnham for our groceries, to a small shop run by an old woman named Mrs. O'Grady. Pamela got milk every morning from a farmer half a mile away, but I stayed out of his sight.

No one came near us. We might as well have been on a

desert island. We discussed plans for the house and garden, most of them suggested by me. I knew it would soon be all over, and still I continued to pretend to myself that we could have a long future together.

As the day for Dunne's return home approached, I became more and more depressed, and Pamela more cheerful. Not an hour passed that she didn't mention his name, always with that same soft awe-struck note in her voice, as if she were talking about God. I had stoical patience because I had no alternative.

At last we had to go down. Pamela was full of excitement, longing to hear what had happened since we left the city. I said: 'I prefer no news.'

'Holidays can't go on forever.'

How could she call it a holiday? In all our time together she seemed to have given me nothing of herself. Silently I helped her to lock up the house and we set out to walk down to the city.

6

It was hard to believe that the desiccated, ragged old man who sat with his bony knees crossed at the other side of the fire had once caused me so much pain and anxiety. Now that he was so skinny, a flare at the sides of his nostrils was visible, giving the appearance of a perpetual sneer, and his skull showed its true elongated form. The general effect was of a kind of elegance, far from my old conception of Dunne, and it made me uneasy in a new way.

I found that I had suddenly lost my tongue. Surely he was wondering why I had sought him out. He might even have diagnosed the gun in my pocket – but I dismissed that thought as absurd.

The gun was a piece of bravado, in a way, quite unreal and out of key with the rest of me, and still I had gone to endless trouble to have it. I had had to smuggle it into the country, since no one in Ireland is allowed to carry a gun nowadays. You can get a licence, to be sure, but you have to prove that you need it. Like everyone else, I had several guns in America. I'm not telling how I got it in with my baggage – security wasn't so strict before the era of hijacking. Anyway, there it was, quite unknown to Dunne, making a dent in the skin of my leg as it pressed through my trouser-pocket.

He began to talk quietly, kindly, as if he saw the need to put me at my ease. Such confidence! This was what had impressed Pamela, his certainty and assurance – a side of him that I had no sympathy with. I've always had the greatest contempt for people of inferior intelligence who assume airs above their mental capacity. I believe that envy is at the root of it, and that they should come to terms with

89

their limitations. One of Seán Kelly's Cork proverbs puts it in a nutshell: 'Small boats should hug the shore.' Now as Dunne talked I began to see that such people have no alternative, that without this air of confidence they would collapse into nothing. He said: 'I never thought we would meet again. Stranger still that we ever met in the first place. I used to wonder how you got into the Movement. When we went on that training course during the truce, the other Western officers told me you were always friendly with them – one of their own, they said, not like a boy from the Big House at all.'

I knew he had questioned them about me. Peter Hynes had told me at the time. He had called Dunne a jackeen too, like the woman at the Republican court. Hynes had resented the questions. He thought it a breach of friendship, as indeed it was. Dunne was saying: 'We went to your house and I met your parents. Do you remember that?'

'Yes, I remember.'

'Have you been down there?'

'Not yet.'

'It was disgraceful that the house was burned, but it was too late by the time I heard about it. It was an independent action. I would have defended you. And your father – they had to force him to leave it in time. He loved that place. You could see it in everything he said. It was a beautiful house.'

'You know why they did it?'

'Of course, so far as anyone knows.' His voice dropped, and I noticed that his hands were clenched tightly together, the first real sign of his uneasiness. 'That was my district. I had to have a report on the whole operation. I remember it particularly because it was the first of a series of actions that were taken without proper orders.'

The gun – now might I do it, pat. I wasn't ready. Was he trying to conciliate me? That would be a bad sign, for him. My resolve wasn't weakened, but in spite of his disclaimer I was still not sure whether or not he was responsible. I was inclined to believe the official report I had received much later. Action – operation – the military terms seemed silly, at this stage.

I said: 'It's all so long ago.'

'Yes, ancient history. But it's still very much alive in Ireland. How long have you been in the country?'

'A couple of weeks. I've heard plenty of talk.' I didn't want to make him more nervous. It was always a mistake to underestimate Dunne. 'Things have changed a great deal on the outside. People are more comfortable, they take comfort for granted.'

'Too comfortable.'

For the first time I heard the old tone, the one that went with his remark that complacency must be kicked out of the people. I know now that the principle was the one that Marx and Lenin recommended, to keep the revolution going at all costs. Long ago I had no idea where Dunne got his ideas. I thought they were original. He never said where he had learned them, though naturally he had some that were common to all of us, mostly learned from the Fenians. I wondered too if he still went daily to Mass. It would be difficult, if he lived the year round in this remote place.

I said drily: 'That was Pearse's dream: comfort for all, the welfare state. Ireland has got what we were fighting for.'

'I heard that you got rich in America. Something to do with telephones.'

'Yes. I got a job with an engineering firm that manufactured them, and I invented a part for a telephone instrument. In a capitalist country you can get rich like that.'

'Had you any idea of rebuilding the house?'

'I haven't seen it yet.'

'I'm afraid it's only a shell. It would cost a fortune to rebuild.'

I crushed down my anger and said coolly: 'Then I doubt if it would be worth it.'

But this talk of his diminished the nightmare that had followed me since my return to Ireland. Of course I would have to go to the West. Of course I would have to see the ruins of my house and of my heart, where I had dreamed of placing Pamela and my children some crazy day when there would be peace again, the place where my father finally lost hope.

Dunne said: 'If you go to the West, you might look up Henry Gould's widow – remember her?'

'No. I knew he married a poor girl from Galway. I didn't know he's dead.'

'Long ago. He tried to murder her but something went wrong, and he was drowned himself. It was a nine days' wonder at the time. It seems he had succeeded in doing the same thing with his first wife and he imagined that he could bring it off the second time. She's still there, as lively as a cricket. She doesn't pretend to mourn him, but she seems to miss him all the same. You know he was a spy, of course.'

It was a long time since I had heard that word, common currency in our day, pronounced now by Dunne in the same special, contemptuous tone. I said carefully: 'I had heard it.'

'When do you think you will go?'

'I don't know. I have so many people to see.' Abruptly I decided to stop beating about the bush. I said flatly: 'You know they held a court-martial on me?'

He shot me a sidelong look. 'Must we go into that?'

'Why not?'

'Yes, it's true. They needed a reason for having burned the house. They had some story that you had informed on someone. It was all very vague. Peter Hynes stood up for you, and some of your other friends. The main accuser was a man from Recess.'

'I was told the motive was land hunger.'

'The people didn't know you. They were in a bad mood. Some of them thought the land would be divided among them as soon as the war was over. Court-martials were held everywhere, mostly without authorisation.'

'They condemned me to death.'

'Yes, but it was ridiculous.'

'It was enough to make me leave the country.'

'There really was no need. They wouldn't have done it.'

'You seem very sure.'

'Peter Hynes made them reverse the verdict.'

'I didn't wait for that. I had to think of my parents.'

Peter Hynes, Henry Gould, names from anywhere and everywhere but no mention of the one name that was pounding in my head: Pamela. Surely he must know that I wanted to hear about her. In my conversations with various people, no one had mentioned her. Could he be so aged and frail that she mean nothing to him now? I couldn't believe it. The greatest experiences of our lives were in that time when the three of us were together, first in the Four Courts when they were occupied by the Republican section of the army, and later in O'Connell Street, as it's called now, when the battle for the possession of Dublin was in full swing. Even for Dunne, nothing that happened later could blot out the memory of those events.

I remember exactly how it began, on a cold, dry morning in March when Pamela and I came down from Ferney, not knowing what to expect. In Terenure we found a note from Dunne telling us that the forbidden Army Convention was being held that very day, and that I should meet him at the Mansion House in Dawson Street as soon as possible. Pamela was filled with excitement. She said: 'You see, there are enough men with courage after all. Of course you'll go.'

'Yes, I'll go, but I don't like leaving you.'

'I'll be all right.'

She threw her arms around my neck and kissed me heartily on the mouth. After that I couldn't refuse her anything. Besides, to stay away would have been a declaration that I favoured accepting the treaty. That was a fair sample of my incapacity to think straight at that time. I soon found out that a great many of my comrades were equally confused.

I walked all the way into town, carried along on a bubble

of air. My legs seemed to have grown longer, like the legs one grows in a dream, where a single, floating leap can take you to a mountain-top. I felt neither wind nor cold, and was still absorbed in my visions when I arrived at the Mansion House.

The meeting was just over and Dunne was waiting for me by the door. He gave me a sharp look and said: 'You look very cheerful, almost as if you've just had a holiday.'

I took the hint instantly and tried to look more like the men who were coming out of the meeting-room. The younger ones seemed elated, but any of the Dublin officers that I knew were obviously worried and depressed. I soon found that the Convention had appointed an Army Executive of its own. Though no one said so, this could only be at war with the one already existing.

I date the civil war from that meeting in March, though for a long time there were apparent attempts to let time heal the differences. In fact, they were irreconcilable. Griffith, the president, had always said we should have the king, Lords and Commons for Ireland. I think he meant we should start from there. Republicanism meant anarchy to him. Military dictatorship was the alternative for some – it wasn't a dirty expression in those days, though a great many people were rightly suspicious of the idea – but in the last analysis it was partition and the oath of allegiance that set the two sides at each other's throats.

Still it was a long time before the shooting began. In the middle of April we Republicans took over the Four Courts as our general headquarters. Our leaders made several demands. The main one was that no elections on the question of accepting or rejecting the treaty should be held while the threat of war continued. They pointed out that in the present state of the country, and with the priests and bishops continuing to condemn the Republicans, there could not be a fair decision.

The Free State Army, as we had begun to call them, had

established themselves in Beggar's Bush Barracks and a joint Army Council was set up to try to preserve peace between the two factions and decide how the various posts which were being evacuated by the British would be allocated.

Having declined a commission in the army, Dunne was not in uniform, but he was elegantly dressed, as he had been when first I saw him in Galway. He had an office in the Four Courts and was once more busy with records, but I noticed that he didn't tell me to bring in the lists of names that he had in his room in Terenure. I worked for him as usual every day. As I had very little to do, there was plenty of time for Pamela. She came daily also, and helped the Cumann na mBan women who were doing the cooking in the Officers' Mess.

The food was fine when it came in, fresh fruit and vegetables and lots of good meat, but as Pamela was about the best cook among the girls, it was all ruined by the time we got it. Not one of them was able to cook a decent meal.

It was a few days before I discovered where all the things were coming from. I found that a couple of men went to the market every morning and picked what they wanted, paying the traders with chits. The traders were losing patience and sometimes had to be threatened. This made me horribly uneasy; but there was worse to come.

One morning a raiding party went out, instructed by Rory O'Connor, the director of engineering, to demand money from the Bank of Ireland. They came back with seventy thousand pounds, a huge sum in those days. I said to Pamela: 'This is robbery.'

She gave me a peculiar look and said: 'It's war.'

'I don't like these methods.'

'Can you think of a better way?'

'No.'

'Then you should keep quiet. If you talk like this to anyone else, they'll think you're turning traitor.'

I realised that I would have to learn not to speak my

95

mind, not even to Pamela. Besides, I soon found out that O'Connor, who gave the orders to demand money from the Bank, detested the method too. All would be paid back when we won – if we did.

No one knew what would happen next. Among our officers, an air of euphoria alternated with depression and anxiety. Our chief of staff, the Corkman Liam Lynch, was the gloomiest of the lot. We seemed to have no policy to put up against the one proposed by the Free Staters, which consisted simply in trying to make the treaty work. Everyone but Griffith disliked that treaty, so far as I could hear. I never heard anyone speak of the distant future, nor of the ideals that had once been our inspiration.

We had a fair amount of arms and ammunition in stock in the Four Courts, but for a while it seemed unlikely that we would ever use them. Before the end of April, both the Archbishop of Dublin and the Lord Mayor tried to bring the two sides together, but neither side would given an inch. Griffith refused to have anything to do with the men in the Four Courts. Still we heard that Collins was reluctant to give orders to shoot at his old comrades in arms.

When I reported this gossip to Dunne he said: 'I'm surprised that Collins' conscience is so delicate. Have you noticed the exchange of guns that's going on?'

I had indeed noticed it, and wondered what was the reason. Rifles and ammunition were sent to us at the Four Courts from Beggar's Bush Barracks, and we sent an equal quantity of ours in exchange. Now Dunne told me that the Beggar's Bush rifles were British army stock and would be identifiable as such if they were captured in any future engagement, whereas ours had come from here, there and everywhere. Our rifles were being collected for use by the Army of the North. It was the first time I had heard of this army, which Collins was planning to send to the relief of persecuted Northern Catholics.

'And if that army goes to the North, the blame will fall on those hot-headed Republicans, not on the reasonable

Free Staters who are doing everything in their power to get the treaty accepted.'

That story was soon all over the building, and it created bitter feelings against Collins. He became the focal point of everyone's growing hatred of the Staters, though surely the Republicans should have admired him for continuing the fight in any way that came to his hand.

Though battle was not yet joined in Dublin, comrades were shooting at each other soon enough. An election had been arranged in spite of the Republicans' protests, and the campaign began early in May. There were confrontations here and there as the Republicans tried to prevent election speeches being made. Sligo town was the scene of a few hours of shooting between Republicans and Free Staters led by the hero of Ballinalee, Collins' friend, General MacEoin.

Anyone could see that the war was by no means. over. Our little dump of arms at Ferney was only one of dozens. Even as the various barracks were being handed over to the Provisional Government, Republicans were making raids on other barracks and providing themselves with arms. Naturally the British were becoming more and more exasperated and demanding that the rule of law be restored, but by now things were almost out of control.

It was at that time that Dunne showed me an extraordinary document which he had been given when he was in Kilkenny. It was nothing less than a new Proclamation of the Republic of Ireland, and it was signed on behalf of the Council of the South Tipperary Brigade by twelve members of the Brigade whose names I knew well – Seámus Robinson, Denis Lacey, and Seán Fitzpatrick were the first three. They were all frequent visitors to Dublin and had been to all the meetings.

The document was couched in legal language, beginning with a number of whereases, in which the Free State Government was accused of having forfeited the allegiance of the people of Ireland by supporting the Articles of Agreement for the treaty. The signatories pledged themselves to 'rouse the nation from its lethargy' and to band together the army and the people to resist this treacherous attempt to usurp the national authority and destroy the independence of Ireland.

'You see,' Dunne said. 'We have the support of the country people, even if Dublin has lost its nerve.'

'It doesn't sound too hopeful,' I said after I had read it through. 'That piece about the lethargy of the nation –'

By now I was unmoved by documents of this kind. I saw it as a silly attempt to turn back the pages of history. The day for Proclamations of the Republic was over. One was quite enough, and it had said all that was to be said. This document was a declaration of war. I said as much, and Dunne said: 'Yes, that's what it is.'

'You sound pleased.'

'Once we know it's bound to happen, the sooner the better. In fact it has already begun. What do you call the battle for Kilkenny town? What do you think Collins and Griffith are planning with their new constitution? We're betrayed on all sides. The only honourable thing now is to go down fighting.'

I knew better than to say I'd rather not go down at all, no more than I would have commented on the yellow-brown cabbage and grey potatoes and half-cooked meat that were our diet. My policy was to keep my thoughts to myself and not have to suffer any more lectures from Dunne.

The assassination of Sir Henry Wilson in London was what sparked off the final show-down. We Republicans were blamed for it, naturally, but we were all pretty sure that Collins himself had ordered it. Wilson was an efficient soldier, and he had done a good job of arming the Orangemen in the North and protecting them against prosecution for their atrocities. Collins must have had some idea that with Wilson out of the way, there would be an improvement of the situation in the North.

Who knows what Collins thought, at that stage? He was said to be drinking heavily, and to have become morose and silent, obsessed with the sufferings of the Catholics in Belfast. I never saw him during that period. Those who did said that he was no longer the hearty, spontaneous, cheerful young man that he had once been.

Naturally the British were furious at Wilson's death. They captured the two assassins easily, since neither of them tried to escape. Collins made several attempts to have them rescued, but they were hanged in due course, adding another pair of martyrs to the canon. And Winston Churchill demanded that Collins should put his house in order, since it was now his responsibility, and flush us out of the Four Courts.

Things happened very quickly after that. Our garrison had continued to requisition goods from stores and pay for some of them with money removed from banks. Receipts were given for the rest, and repayment promised for some distant date when all would be peaceful again. The National Army never intervened in these actions. Now suddenly, when a party went out from the Four Courts to requisition cars from a garage, to transport some of our men to the North, they were prevented by a detachment of Free State soldiers. Leo Henderson, the officer in charge of our raiding party, was arrested. Our garrison retaliated by kidnapping General O'Connell, the deputy chief of staff of the National Army, and sending a message that he would be held hostage until Henderson was released.

By this time most of the daily visitors and office staff had been ordered to move into the Four Courts. When I broke this news to Mrs. Malone, she said: 'God protect you. I'll be praying for you.'

She gave me a bag of apples to take with me, and said: 'Try to get your sleep. Come back to me when you can.'

The other Republican points were strengthened at once – the Ballast Office on the corner of Westmoreland Street, Lever Brothers' buildings on Essex Quay, the Masonic Hall in Molesworth Street and the Kildare Street Club, a good corner position. One morning Dunne and I were instructed to inspect them all and to tell their officers that action seemed near.

The officer in charge at the Club asked: 'When?'

'Any moment,' Dunne said. 'Show me your guns.'

They had managed to accumulate an amazing collection, a rifle for every man as well as a good supply of Webleys, and plenty of ammunition, stored in the cellars with the wine.

Dunne looked them over, then said: 'You could hold the street for several days. We may not be able to get messengers with information across the river from the Four Courts – you'll have to make your own decisions.'

'We didn't think we'd be left sitting in here so long,' the man said. 'About time something happened.'

We had never been in much doubt that we would have to retain these buildings by force. Like ourselves, the men in the various positions were all set for battle. In the Four Courts we even had several nurses who were members of Cumann na mBan. Two Franciscan priests had been with us from the start, and others paid regular visits to the various posts.

The Four Courts building was beautiful: a grand central dome supported by twenty-four columns, with the courts and their chambers leading off it. It was also a perfect fortress, and the feeling of isolation perversely gave a boost to my ebbing morale. Being young, and in danger along with my comrades – Pamela and the other girls included – all of them single-minded and unquestioning, produced in me an unexpected euphoria. I slept soundly whenever I was off duty and became one of the crowd the rest of the time, as I hadn't been for months.

A few days after General Wilson's death, at midnight, I was passing through the central hall under the great dome on my way to our sleeping quarters. I saw Rory O'Connor come out of the court-room where he had established his office. As he did so, a man named Tom O'Reilly ran in from the gate and handed him a note. He took it and glanced through it, then went quickly back into the office.

We crowded around the messenger asking: 'What's up? What's that about?'

O'Reilly said: 'Chap on a motor-bike brought it. He's from Beggar's Bush. He's outside, waiting for an answer. Beautiful bike he has. Funny time of night to come. Must be something stirring.'

We didn't have to wait long. O'Connor came back after a moment or two and said: 'Just tell him there's no reply.'

As O'Reilly left with this message, several other officers came out of the room. We all stood watching them, and after a moment O'Connor said sombrely: 'They've given us until four o'clock to get ready for the attack.'

Mellows, the cheerful little commandant from the West, said: 'What they asked for was surrender by four o'clock.'

O'Connor said: 'It's the same thing. We've been expecting it. They've been borrowing artillery from the British. We think the building will hold out.' He looked us over slowly and without raising his voice said: 'We expect every man to fight for the Republic to the end. Remember that we stand for Ireland alone.'

I never forgot those words, and the resonant, dramatic tone he used, quite different from his usual one. No one seemed to think he was overdoing it – in fact the men seemed to be inspired by the old-fashioned phrases and to feel that they suited the occasion.

We stayed talking excitedly in the hall for a while. Then one of the men said: 'I wish they hadn't given us four hours. What are they waiting for?'

No one answered, but it seemed like a signal to us to disperse. The senior officers went hurrying about their business, supervising their special responsibilities. Dunne came through the hall, saw me and sent me to make sure that our prisoner General O'Connell was safe. I went down to the cellar, to the store-room where he was held.

General O'Connell was a cheerful-looking, red-haired

man. He was happily engaged in a game of bridge with some of his friends from the Dublin Brigade. They had up-ended a packing-case and placed four chairs around it. Racks of files lined the walls. An improvised bed had been made up in one corner.

None of the men were as relaxed as they seemed at first sight. O'Connell looked up quickly, like a startled fox, and said: 'Something's happening?'

I saw no reason for secrecy. 'An attack, at four o'clock.'

Instantly the others put down their cards and stood up. One of them said: 'Sorry, Ginger. We've got to leave you. Michael here will take care of you.'

So I sat down, nervously fingering my revolver and wondering what I would do if he made a dash for it. He was too intelligent for that. I had always admired him for his fight against the Black-and-Tans when he worked with Brugha at G.H.Q., and I felt ridiculous in my present position. He made it easy for me, talking about everything under the sun. He loved the South of Ireland and wanted to go back to West Cork as soon as possible after this was over, he said, to do some fishing. Gougane Barra was the most beautiful spot in all Ireland – had I ever been there? I said no, that I didn't know that part of the country well, and he continued to chat about the joys of fishing.

At last I was relieved by two privates and I was able to go and find Pamela. She was down in the cellars with some of the other girls, setting up a hospital room. I stood at the door and looked at them sadly. They were going about their work seriously, full of tensely controlled excitement. A uniformed hospital nurse that I hadn't seen before was directing the others.

Pamela came over as soon as she saw me and said: 'Paul told me you'll be with him. He's just been here. For God's sake –'

I thought she was going to ask me to take care of him, but instead she leaned up and kissed me gently. I held her close to me, feeling her heart beat against mine. This was the third time she had kissed me, and I was overcome with delight in her warm, almost childish confidence. When I released her and looked into her eyes, I saw that they were full of tears – she always cried easily.

I dried them with the clean handkerchief which had somehow survived in my breast pocket and said: 'I'll come to see you whenever I can. We don't know what's going to happen. Keep your heart up.'

At half past four the action began. I had never before heard big guns, and the sound was horrifying. I raced up the stairs and joined Dunne and the others in the hall. He took me at once to the roof of the dome, where three men were in position, partly sheltered by the parapet. They were all Dublinmen: Davis and Roche and Byrne. Byrne had an aunt in Wexford and had learned the local ballads from her, which he used to sing in the evenings during our weeks of waiting. He was singing softly now:

> We are the boys of Wexford who fought with heart and
> hand
> To burst in twain the galling chain and free our native
> land.

He turned quickly when we came up the stairs and said: 'Look at that view. Isn't it beautiful?'

We could see the river below, strictly enclosed between its stone walls at first, then rambling off towards Chapelizod and Islandbridge. The thin moonlight lit up the water, glittering with a pale light that contrasted with the soft, dull glow of the gaslit street lamps. High clouds trailed across the sky.

Dunne said: 'Never mind the view. Look there.'

Across the narrow street, below the level of the dome, the windows at the top of a house had been smashed out and several rifles were pointed at us. While we ducked under the shelter of the parapet, bullets spattered against the copper dome behind us. Byrne let out a growl of rage and went crawling along under the wall. As we left them we could see him kneel and aim carefully.

Dunne said: 'Find Curran and tell him to send up half a dozen more snipers and some ammunition. That lot must be cleared out.'

I did as I was told, then rejoined Dunne who was making the rounds of the machine-gunners at their posts at the upper windows. They were raking the entrance to Wine-tavern Street where the Staters' gun crews were scurrying around. Shells were being fired at five-minute intervals and had already hit the walls but had done very little damage. Their noise was nerve-wracking, but our men seemed more excited than frightened.

As we watched, several cars drove into the street in front of the guns, to screen them from our fire. Our men sprayed them with machine-gun bullets but it was impossible to estimate the effect. Soon afterwards the guns were moved to Bridgefoot Street and the bombardment continued.

Dunne said: 'Get the snipers to try for the gun crew. They should be able to spot them from up there.'

I climbed to the parapet again and passed on the instruction to a man named Conroy from the Dublin Brigade. He joked: 'Tell them to stop that noise out there. I can't concentrate.'

Shells were coming again at the rate of one every five minutes or so. Sometimes one came whining through a window and wrecked everything in its path, then exploded. Up there on the dome I saw that the sky had clouded over. The moon was gone, the river black as lead. Soon it would begin to rain.

7

Have you ever found yourself at a point in your life when only the next five minutes were important? That's how it was with us while we went through the pantomime of defending the Four Courts. Very few of us had been under fire in this way, though we had all had our share of guerrilla warfare. The worst part of it, for me at least, was the sensation of being trapped. This aroused an irrational anger against our attackers, especially as we felt we hadn't invited the situation ourselves.

Quite soon I saw that O'Connor's statement that the building would hold out was ridiculous. It was true that we were not suffering many losses. Several of the men were slightly wounded by flying pieces of masonry, but the snipers on the roof seemed invulnerable behind their parapet. Still, if the bombardment continued at its present rate, the building must inevitably be reduced to rubble eventually. Long before that, surely, the enemy would decide to breach the walls. There was no possibility that we would be saved by their ignorance. General Dalton had fought in the British army in France, and knew exactly what to do.

We had a day of intermittent shelling and sniper fire before a massive bombardment of the building was mounted, with the object of making a breach. Until they heard the shells pounding against the walls at ever shortening intervals, our men had been getting quite cocky, almost as if they thought we might win this battle. Dunne was everywhere, encouraging them, suggesting new positions and tactics to the snipers, who were his special charge, sending me on messages up and down through the building, keeping me reporting back to him constantly, so that I had very little chance of having even a few words with Pamela. I ached all over with longing for her, and almost envied the men who had to go down to the cellar to be bandaged.

As night fell on the second day, we became aware of tremendous activity all around the building. The snipers had a good view outside, and when I was up there on the parapet with them I could see troops massing in all the streets around us. The guns were still at the far side of the river.

As the noise of machine-gun and rifle fire got louder, on my peregrinations around the building I came upon our Franciscans again and again, always huddled in corners with frightened young men, hearing their confessions. To me that was the most sinister sight of all, a symptom that everyone felt the trap closing in. The detachment of the priests was astonishing, and their courage too. They were in as much danger as we were but they did their duty without comment, and seemed scarcely to notice the appalling racket all around them. They were not as young as the rest of us, and their beards gave them a fatherly, almost medieval look.

When the final assault came, suddenly the building was full of struggling bodies, men attacking each other with rifle and bayonet in hand-to-hand fighting such as I had never seen in all my life and hope never to see again. We were totally overwhelmed. The Staters swarmed into the building and took over the central hall and the library by sheer weight of numbers. They took about thirty prisoners while we retreated farther and farther back, though we knew very well that we were making a last stand. No amount of courage or skill could save us now.

I was sorry for O'Connor and Mellowes. Both of them looked utterly worn out. O'Connor's old tweed coat seemed about to fall off his shoulders. None of us had slept for forty-eight hours, though we sent the men off for a short doze when they looked as if they would fall asleep on their feet.

Dunne, the dedicated man, seemed indestructible. His suit was stained in many places, but it was not rumpled. It almost looked like an army uniform. His boots were the only ones that were not dusty. He must have given them a quick wipe from time to time. Mine looked as if I had walked over a mountain in them, and the sleeve of my jacket was badly torn where a piece of flying stone had narrowly missed breaking my arm.

Early next morning there was a temporary truce while doctors from the city arrived – twenty of them riding on a dray – and took away the wounded to hospital. Dunne sent me down, in a borrowed jacket, to supervise the transfer. I could scarcely believe my luck. She was there, her hair wisping down as usual, stuffed untidily into a nurse's cap, her arms bare to the elbow, tucking blankets around the men on the stretchers, fixing bandaged limbs as comfortably as possible, warning the stretcher-bearers to be careful as they carried them out over the rubble. Her clear, high, cultivated British voice rang out over the others so that she seemed to be in charge of the operation, though this was far from being the case. I stood watching her, as I was entitled to do since I had no business there other than as an observer, until one of the Free State officers said: 'Do you want a lift to the hospital, doctor?'

All I had to do was accept and I would have been out of that hell-hole within minutes. I might have been recognised, but in the excitement I would probably be safe enough. Still I didn't dream of taking the opportunity. I said: 'Thank you, I'll just see this lot out and come along later.'

He went off, and Pamela came over to me saying: 'I heard that. I think you're splendid. You could have got out and walked away.'

'Yes. Did you think I might?'

'Of course not.'

She gazed at me with shining admiration, so that I became slightly drunk, swaying towards her as if I would throw my whole weight on her shoulders. She stepped quickly out of the way and said: 'Have you been hurt? You seem dizzy.'

'No, not at all. I'm all right.'

'And Paul?'

'Not a scratch. I'm with him all the time. Hasn't he been down to see you?'

'Once, just for a moment. He brought a man down yesterday, that's all.'

No weakness there. In his position I would have been with her several times a day, with or without an excuse.

She said: 'What will happen now?'

'We're to fight on,' I said, and I might have added that it wouldn't be for long. Then, as she made no move to follow the stretcher-bearers, I asked: 'Aren't you going to the hospital with the men?'

'No. They'll be in good hands. I'm still needed here.'

The last of the stretchers went out, and I hurried back to find Dunne and tell him that Pamela was still downstairs. He said: 'That's what I expected. I sent her a message to say that she could go, but I knew it wouldn't be any use.'

'You could have ordered her to go.'

'Why should I? She doesn't want to be an exception. We need the women.'

'Of course. But you'd better get someone to order them out now, unless you want them all to be killed with the rest of us.'

Dunne was preoccupied with directing the machine-gunners towards their next target: the windows of the main building from which rifle fire was once more beginning to rattle and whine. It was impossible to pinpoint the shots. There was something hysterical in the way the men aimed and let fly, darting from one objective to another, consulting eagerly with the officers, ignoring their danger as if they were only being harassed by a pack of flies. Dunne detached himself long enough from this to say that I should ask O'Connor to get the women out of the building at once. You may be sure that I wasted no time in carrying out this order. They left reluctantly, saying they wouldn't be far away if they were needed.

Soon afterwards, the thing that I had most feared happened at last. It was almost noon when a man came running up the stairs shouting that the other end of the building was on fire. It was so far from us that some of the men hoped it would drive the Staters out and leave us in possession, but that was out of the question. Besides, we knew it was inevitable now that our dump of explosives would blow up.

Off in our dark rat-hole retreat – store-rooms mostly, I think – we huddled, waiting. When it came, we were shocked into a state of utter numbness. We had plugged our ears with cotton wool from our field dressings, but it was hopeless to try to resist that sound. It beat on the ears and into the brain so that I thought I would never function normally again. For one ghastly moment it seemed that all my companions had died, sucked out of life in one great godlike handful, leaving only empty bodies behind.

When we recovered, it was to move slowly and carefully away from each other, as if each of us feared the others were no longer real. Dunne was the only one of us who showed any sign of life. He couldn't utter a word, no more than the rest of us, but he managed to put out his hand and touch the shoulder of one of the men – Cullen, I think – with what was clearly meant to be a sympathetic smile.

Then we went in our dazed condition, rambling like sleep-walkers, to find the rest of the garrison who were in one of the huge offices on the ground floor. They were no better than we were: surprised to find themselves still alive, seeing their condition reflected in ours, not one of them able to say what we might do next. We knew that the gateway was mined, and the flick of a switch would blow up the Staters in their armoured cars at the gate. O'Malley had made this suggestion earlier, and had said that we could make a run for it, but the idea looked ludicrous now. He didn't repeat it.

A Cork boy named Paddy Horgan said half-heartedly: 'We're not finished yet. They'll be in from the country in their thousands any minute now . . .'

No one answered. We knew that even if those thousands came they wouldn't be able to fight their way through to us. Still I felt certain that death was not yet. I can't remember exactly why, but it may have been a form of acceptance, or fatalism. It was very like the thing called resignation, that comes when you know your death is inevitable, as I do now.

Daylight streamed down on us through the broken building as we went off to look for further bolt-holes. A cloud of smoke hung high in the air and bursts of flame went flashing intermittently upward as the east wing burned more fiercely. Paper ash and whole sheets of unburned paper floated around us. We dragged our rifles, too tired to lift them. In any case it seemed pointless. Better to wait for the finish.

I found a high room whose floor was heaped with a confusion of files and books, covered with dust from the caved-in ceiling. When I looked down, I could see the scurrying figures below. The armoured cars looked like feeding rats, their noses together, nuzzling their prey. The uniformed soldiers made an easy target, but I had lost the will to kill them, if I had ever had it.

The young Corkman, Horgan, who had come with me, aimed with his rifle, saying: 'Even if we're finished, one bastard less.'

I was too late to stop him. I saw a man fall and lie writhing on the pavement. Horgan said with intense bitterness: 'It's the same enemy, only a different uniform.'

Before he could aim again, on a lower level of the roof we saw one of our garrison run out and wave a white cloth on the end of a stick, swinging it rhythmically to and fro.

Horgan said furiously: 'I could shoot down that flag.'

He half lifted his rifle, then dropped it, turning a miserable face to me, saying: 'Traitors. Another few hours and we'd have them on the run.' He let the butt of his rifle drop on the floor. 'I'm so hungry now, I could eat a dead Christian Brother.'

I exploded with laughter, but he remained quite serious. I said: 'We'd better go down.'

He followed me slowly down to the hall, where the handful of us that was left stood around, waiting for we knew not what. Even Dunne looked haggard, though he stood perfectly erect as usual. O'Connor and Mellowes and O'Malley were in conference with the Free State officers in their clean uniforms, angry faces and raised voices showing clearly that we need expect no quarter. One man kept barking: 'Unconditional surrender! Unconditional surrender!'

Another was trying to calm him down, pulling at his sleeve to keep his attention.

General O'Connell remained apart from the rest, looking at us curiously, but saying nothing. Our men pretended to ignore him, and after a minute or two he turned his head away as if he were examining the damage to the building. There was plenty to look at. The roof was like a sieve and great holes gapped the thick walls, so that one wondered how they remained standing.

Our officers turned to face us and O'Malley said: 'It was a grand fight, lads.'

I saw tears running down Horgan's cheeks, unashamed. Most of the others kept their eyes on the ground, as if they couldn't bear to see defeat in the faces of their friends. One or two held on to each other, silently.

With no military orders, O'Connor led us out of the building. The men tried not to shamble, but it was impossible. At this point I doubt if any of us cared what happened next. I was amazed to see that a crowd of people had assembled to see the end of our drama, among them a knot of pressmen with their notebooks at the ready.

We shuffled into a line against the quay wall and an officer went down with a couple of soldiers, collecting our guns. No one spoke. When they reached O'Malley, he pulled out his revolver and made to hand it over, then suddenly chucked it backward over his head into the river. The officer's eyes lit up with an appreciative grin, quickly suppressed. Then he turned to one of the privates and said: 'Here, get them some cigarettes. That will keep them going.'

The private went off, clutching the handful of coins the officer had given him. The men in our line looked after him hopelessly.

I think that friendly officer probably saved our lives. A moment later, a noisy car drove up and another officer leaped out. The pressmen moved forward in a body and one said: 'General Daly, sir.'

I remembered him. There was no sign of sympathy there. He shouldered the man aside and marched over to us, blazing fury in every move, saying sharply to our officer: 'What are you waiting for? Shoot the lot of them.'

'Nonsense. Are you mad?'

'Shoot them all. You'll never get a better chance. They're lined up and ready. I'll take responsibility.'

'So will I. It would be crazy. The world is watching us.'

'Get it done before the world knows what we're doing. The sooner that lot is out of the way, the better. It's my business, not yours. Take your orders.'

I hadn't heard anyone talk like that since the Black-and-Tans. Daly whirled around, as if to give the order for our destruction. God knows what would have happened if the other officer had not said quickly: 'See that bunch watching us? That man that spoke to you just now? Those are journalists from several countries – the world knows already. You'll disgrace us all, with your talk of shooting them.'

Daly shouted: 'I told you, that's my business.'

'Then you can damned well take the surrender too, if you're such a great man for taking responsibility. I only lined them up. If you give orders to shoot them now, you'll never hear the last of it. And it mightn't stop at shooting – look at that pack of wild animals you have to deal with. Are you going to be able to control them?'

The Free State soldiers were certainly in an ugly mood, after what they had suffered from us. A lot of their mates had been badly injured by the big explosion, and it seemed to me a matter of minutes before they would go for us.

Daly said: 'Why haven't you taken the surrender?'

'Did I get a chance? Get on with it yourself.'

'Very well.'

As Daly approached O'Connor and O'Malley, our officer beckoned to the pressmen to come nearer, then said: 'If you want the great moment, here it is. General Daly is taking the surrender.'

Daly's aide had the document ready, and O'Malley signed it. The pressmen took photographs and asked questions, but O'Malley just stood there grinning and would say nothing. Daly snatched the paper and stumped away, seeing that nothing but orthodox behaviour was possible now. Some of the pressmen followed him, calling out questions. Those who stayed behind got better results from General O'Connell, who was still standing with us, as if he had some hopes of parting friends. Even he would only say: 'I didn't like the noise – all those bombs and things. And the food was getting scarce. Glad to be out, like everyone else.'

In those days, it was a common sight to see a herd of bewildered cattle or sheep being driven through the streets of Dublin towards the markets near the Phoenix Park. I thought of this as we walked along in an untidy group, faces smutty, clothes in tatters, the countrymen with their tweed caps slanting backward and their eyes red-rimmed from lack of sleep. Neither Dunne nor I had ever been arrested before. He walked close beside me, without speaking, but probably feeling some sensation of support from me. I disliked the notion of captivity extremely and particularly loathed the officers who ran beside us, barking like dogs in their eagerness to get us locked up as quickly as possible.

We were halted at Jameson's distillery, which had been taken over by the Staters and had a convenient room on the ground floor. It was obviously some kind of disused store, with barred windows onto a corridor and none to the outside world. Our short spell in the fresh air was finished. Our guards slammed the door shut and we heard the key turned in the lock and the men walk away.

A tightly packed room full of unwashed men is a great trial to the nerves. Still I think we all felt safer in there, for a few minutes at least. Then Skinner O'Reilly went over to the window and began to fiddle with the bars. He gripped two of them in his fists and tugged at them with all his weight, separating them into two curves. Another man, named Griffin, joined him and succeeded in pulling out both bars. We could scarcely believe it.

Skinner said: 'This is great, lads. We'll be out of here in two shakes. I'm going for a look-see.'

He leaped onto the narrow sill like a cat and hung there for a second, then pushed one shoulder through the opening. The rest of him followed without much difficulty, and he dropped into the corridor. Everyone kept perfectly silent. We heard him move cautiously away.

In a moment he came sliding back, whispering: 'Come on, anyone that will fit. There's a bunch of women outside, but they're busy blathering to each other. They won't mind us. Come on.'

O'Malley was the first out, then Lemass and Griffin and O'Reilly, then Horgan and one or two others – I can't remember now. Dunne and I looked at each other. He said: 'You first. I might get stuck.'

I got my lanky body through without any trouble, but Dunne almost failed to make it. I waited for him, and we followed the rest out into the street.

We were barely in time. The women had stopped blathering and had started yelling, and the soldiers were running along the street towards us. We turned tail, into an alleyway, over a wall, along another alleyway, across a busy street, through a shop and out at the back, Dunne leading the way as if he knew every inch of it. We had no idea whether we were being followed, but at last it seemed ridiculous to continue to flee any further. We leaned against the wall of a lane somewhere off the Coombe, and listened. There were no shouts, no running feet. Dunne said: 'We'll do better to walk quietly from now on.'

If I had been alone, heaven knows what I would have done – sneaked back to my lodgings, perhaps, and waited for things to quiet down. Dunne never doubted me. I saw no sign whatever that he was wavering. On the contrary, his confidence as a leader seemed to have increased, even though he had no one but me to lead. I followed him like a sheep. There is a world of difference between the sheep and the shepherd, as I have often observed since then. A sheep could have led me, I was so weary from loss of sleep, and hunger, and horror at our recent experience.

Then, in spite of my fatigue, or perhaps because of it, the thought ran into my mind that I could have killed him in the Four Courts. That must have been the first time it occurred to me that I would do it some day. I may have been capable of it then, because I remember feeling a sense of relief that our guns had been taken away from us by the Staters. Might I have done it? In a fit of madness or anger, perhaps, not in cold blood as I could do it later.

Dunne said: 'We must sleep. We're no use to anyone in our present condition.'

'Where?'

'Not too far from here. We'd better not try to cross the canal – we might not be able to get back.'

'Get back – why should we want to get back? It's all over.'

'It's not over. It will never be over. We'll never give in to a Free State – it's out of the question.'

His energy astonished me. I couldn't have made such an impassioned statement to save my life. I said: 'All right, let's sleep, here in the street if you like.'

'You're spun out,' he said kindly. 'Come along. We don't have to sleep in the street. We'll go to my father's house.'

I knew that he must have had a father, like everyone else, but he had never mentioned him, nor spoken of his family at all, that I had ever heard.

'Where does your father live?'

'Baggot Street, not far. It's after six. He walks home. He may not be there yet. I don't want to run into him. Come on – the sooner we get into bed, the sooner we can get back into action. We're no use to anyone like this.'

I didn't ask what he was planning. Any kind of action was beyond me at that moment, but before we set out for Baggot Street Dunne insisted on calling at the Kildare Street Club, which was still occupied by our forces. There was an officer in charge, a man I knew from the Dublin Brigade. He said: 'Go and sleep. Others are coming in the morning too. You can get your orders then.'

'How are things here?'

'Bad enough. I think we'll all be up in Sackville Street tomorrow.'

'Should we go there direct, tomorrow?'

'You might as well.'

Their talk whirled around my head, half understood. The fight was by no means over, I was still in it up to my neck, and Dunne was my keeper.

I went with him along Kildare Street, then by back lanes to Baggot Street, where he let himself with a key into a long garden. It was still broad daylight, of course. Someone was cutting grass and I heard children playing, calling to each other in another garden. We entered a stone-floored kitchen, where a middle-aged woman in a white apron gave me warm milk and soda-bread.

Dunne said: 'Bridie is one of ours. We're quite safe here.'

We went upstairs, and he showed me into a bedroom at the back of the house. I fell onto the bed, and slept like a dead man for fourteen hours.

It all began again next day. I was awakened by Dunne shaking my shoulder, saying: 'Come on – we'd better get into town with the people going to work.'

'What time is it?'

'Seven o'clock.'

I didn't protest. I dragged myself out of bed, as I used to do at school, and followed him down to the kitchen where the housekeeper was cooking a huge breakfast on the range. She looked me up and down, then said: 'You're a bit better this morning. Last night I wouldn't have given tuppence for either of ye. Where were ye?'

Dunne said: 'In the Four Courts. We were arrested, but we got away. If anyone comes looking for us, you never saw us.'

With her back to us as she attended to the bacon on the stove, she said: 'Of course. What do you take me for? It's a hard thing to say, but I wouldn't trust the master. He doesn't know you spent the night here. You'd better keep out of his way. He was going on last night about the fighting, how it's ruining the country. Chalk and cheese will never meet. He won't change now.'

'Did he talk about me?'

'He hasn't said your name for a month. That's the best way to have him. If they come looking for you, he can swear his oath he knows nothing.'

'Has anyone come looking?'

'Not so far. Where are you going now?'

'Across the river.'

'I heard it's bad over there.'

After we had eaten, we went out by the back way and set out for Sackville Street, joining the crowds of workers as Dunne had suggested. Everything was quiet and peaceful at this hour of the morning and people seemed to be going about their affairs as they would on any normal day.

We got to Sackville Street easily and found that the Republicans had taken possession of all the buildings on the east side. We walked into the lobby of one of the big hotels and found a small group of officers standing around, looking as if they didn't know what to do next. All around them men were milling about, carrying guns and sacks of

117

sand, busy as a colony of ants. Dunne went over to the officers at once and got into deep conversation with them.

I could have joined them, of course, but I was too uneasy about my own feelings. I thought the whole idea of fighting for the centre of the city was ridiculous.

Perhaps I was wrong to keep quiet. Though they were our leaders – big names to me until now – most of them looked as hopeless as I felt. What really prevented me from speaking out was that there was an air of suppressed hysteria about them. Not one of them had the style of a leader – in that company, Dunne looked like Napoleon.

I watched them for a moment, then went to find the hotel kitchen. It was along a short passageway that led from the back of the hall, and before I reached the open door I could hear shouts of laughter and loud, cheerful talk. Our girls had arrived, and there was Pamela in the midst of them. They had been released as soon as the Four Courts were abandoned. Most of my objections to our situation melted away, even when she asked me anxiously if Dunne was with me.

'Of course,' I said. 'He's in the hall with the others.'

Horgan, my old companion from the Four Courts, was there too, drinking tea at the kitchen table as if he had lived there all his life. He said: 'Have some tea, and we may as well go up together. Have you any orders?'

'No one seems to be giving orders,' I said, 'but I may as well stay with you. Where are we going?'

'I have a lovely spot on the top floor; two grand beds in it.'

I drank some tea, delaying the moment when I would have to leave the kitchen. Horgan handed me a rifle and a Thompson machine-gun, saying: 'I'm not too sure how to work it – trial and error, as usual. Finish up that tea and we'll be going.'

I did so, and he led me to a bedroom on the third floor, where he had set up a post at the window overlooking the street. The glass had already been broken out and there was a sort of barricade of sandbags. When I leaned out I saw that we had a view of the whole street. People were walking about as usual, apparently unaware of any danger. I could hear occasional shots, but there was no sign of Free State soldiers.

All day long there was only sporadic shooting. Most of it came from the far side of the river, perhaps as a warning to us not to try to extend our conquest. I doubt if any of us dreamt of trying.

The walls between the different premises had been broken through, so that one could walk the whole length of the street without going outside. The men were enjoying this, helping themselves to cigarettes and chocolates and cakes from the various shops, as well as hats and scarves and any clothes that happened to fit. No one tried to stop them. This minor looting was a sign of disrupted discipline, but it seemed to me to be a sign of despair too – no day of reckoning was expected. We were all quite certain that the whole range of buildings would soon be blown to pieces, just like the Four Courts. This time, it seemed to me likely that every one of us would go with it.

My forebodings were intensified when someone – one of the countrymen or perhaps one of the priests who had come with us – started up the Rosary. The murmuring, droning sound carried none of the peaceful atmosphere that it brings to every farmhouse kitchen in Ireland at the end of the day. Instead it reminded me of country wakes and funerals in the Black-and-Tan days, when we had buried our dead with our version of military honours, often watched in bewilderment by our enemies.

We slept for a while in the two grand beds but were wakened over and over again by machine-gun fire from the street. Horgan got up after a while and started sniping from the window, but I had had enough of night fighting, and I lay in bed until what seemed to me the proper time in the morning.

When we went down to the kitchen, we found that several of our friends had been badly wounded and several were dead, picked off by snipers or blown up at their posts by the eighteen-pounder that was positioned at the corner of Henry Street. Darkness and depression had descended on everyone. There was no more joking, no more teasing the girls, only sadness that they would have to die with us. I was so weary now that the prospect of death didn't worry me much. At least it would mean a long sleep.

The day dragged on somehow. I stayed at my window, shooting at the post occupied by the Free Staters in a house across the street, never sure what my target was nor whether I was having any success. Again, a crowd of Dublin citizens had gathered to watch the battle, apparently unconcerned at the sight of the wounded and dead.

In the late afternoon I went to find Dunne, who was in charge of the snipers on the second floor. I had never seen him so animated. He seemed to be positively enjoying himself, running from one position to another, joining each group in turn to send volley after volley down into the street. An excited boy from the Dublin Brigade was with him, leaning farther and farther out of the window as if he were daring the enemy to get him.

Dunne pulled him in when he saw me and said: 'How are you doing? Where have you been?'

'Up on the third floor.'

'Can you go down to the hall and find out what's happening?'

'Of course.'

He turned eagerly back to his sniping, like a fisherman reluctant to leave the river when the fish are jumping. I went downstairs and found the senior officers, including de Valera, Brugha, and Traynor, O.C. Dublin Brigade, huddled together at a table in the hall.

Traynor was the only one who seemed to have a sense of what was happening. Brugha was like a man on the point of mental collapse, his mouth twisted, his hands gripping the edge of the table as if he were holding onto it for support.

De Valera looked bewildered, as if he had no idea what to do next.

While I hesitated, unwilling to join officers so much senior to myself, Traynor turned to me and said: 'Get the women out of the building as fast as you can. We're finished here. The top of the street is on fire. Tell them to leave by the front and walk down the middle of the street. While that's going on, get the men out by the back doors. One man can stay at each post until the others have got away. What are you waiting for? Any questions?'

'No, sir.'

They gave me an odd look at that. Since the intensive fighting began, we were all on first-name terms. As I turned away I heard another man say: 'He's all right. British army training, that's all.'

I ran upstairs at the double to ask Dunne to help me with the evacuation. He said: 'I'll stay, of course. I'll look after the men. You go down and give the order to the women.'

He didn't ask if I wanted to stay too. I don't think it occurred to him that I would leave. No one had used the word 'surrender', but that was inevitable now. Anyone remaining in the buildings would be in the hands of the enemy. The choice was mine to make. I made it in favour of freedom. My action was entirely selfish. All I wanted now was to get away from the whole lot of them and be alone with Pamela.

8

Now I come to the most difficult part of my story. It's no use trying to put it off any longer. Recrossing his bony knees, Dunne was watching me with a malicious expression. Perhaps it had something to do with his mention of Peter Hynes. He had said that my old friend had defended me, but there was some tone in his voice that I couldn't quite understand. Perhaps it was just his usual way of speaking about the Western peasants, as he called them sometimes. He had always disliked them, and thought I was a fool to believe in them, or to pity them. Once he said: 'They'd buy and sell you, those pure-souled Irish patriots. All they want is to get your land and the roof from over your head and enjoy it themselves. They have to be told what to think. You'll see, as time goes on.'

Now he had been proved right. Yet he risked his life over and over again in the cause of Irish freedom, as he called it. The worst mistake I had made was in thinking him a simple man.

When the surrender was decided on, Dunne knew that I was under no obligation to stay in that inferno in Sackville Street. He knew the women wouldn't be arrested – the age of chivalry was still extant – so I was quite free to save myself if I could. Dunne elected to stay. That was his affair. It wouldn't have surprised me if he had done what Brugha did, come out with two guns blazing so that he was mowed down by a machine-gunner up the street. Brugha must have known what would happen. He had even refused to go with an ambulance man who had gone in to fetch him out of the burning building. No one could blame the gunner, since a flag of truce had been shown and the garrison should not have fired another shot. In fact, as I soon found out, Dunne came out quietly with the other officers and was taken prisoner.

Running like a rat through the back streets of Dublin, I didn't waste much time thinking about him. This part of the city was strange to me, and I wanted to get back to more familiar territory at the south side of the river as soon as possible. I had to cross Sackville Street to reach Ormond Quay, where there were several bridges. This meant circling around behind the Rotunda Hospital and letting my sense of direction lead me to the river.

A melancholy, sooty rain was drifting down, turning the pavements black, making the crowds going home from work bury their chins in their collars and pull down their caps to cover their ears. This suited me – I did the same, and attracted no attention. My dishevelled appearance was probably a help. I kept my hand on my gun in case I were stopped. It would have been more intelligent to have thrown it away.

Where to go next was the problem. I could have gone back to my lodgings, where I would have been safe enough, or to the ghastly room in Terenure where I could burn some of the more dangerous documents in case of a raid, and wait for news.

The miserable city rain decided it. All at once I had a vision, if you could call it that, of the fields around Castle D'Arcy on a July day, with summer rain drifting, spinning, floating in a cloud, resting like a cobweb on my tweed jacket. Afterwards there would be sunshine, and the earth would breathe through the thin soil, covered with short, sparse grass, sown with harebells, or alive with furze and bell-heather. Instead of the clatter of traffic the air would be full of sounds so soft that one had to strain to identify them – a distant dog, sheep bleating, the corncrake rattling through the meadows, beetles ticking their way along, then landing with a thump, and always the wind, carrying drops of clean, sweet rain.

So I found myself walking up from Rathfarnham to Ferney. The rain stopped as I went and the sky was clearing quickly. I had no idea what I would find there, though I think I assumed the house would be empty. I knew it would not be hard to break in. There I would be free for a while to live in silence, and to sleep.

The avenue was muddy from the rain. I walked on the lumpy ground beside it, threading my way in and out among the trees, tripping over roots and unexpected hollows. These little misfortunes sent me into a passion of anger and bitterness, followed by a spasm of utter confusion. Once when I fell, I experienced an unreasoning panic, and was on the edge of tears. I pulled myself upright, knowing that I must somehow suspend all thought – forget the things that had happened, the things I had done since I was here last, the things I had seen: dead bodies of comrades stiffening on the floor, wounded men crying with pain, blood sliding under the feet, heads and limbs broken by bullets and flying masonry. Drift with the world – wait for my mind to heal itself – sleep – I knew the cures. I was too tired to think, to lay blame on myself or anyone else. My soul was filled with disgust and hatred, without any clear object.

The long evening was darkening at last. As I came closer to the house the windows took on a bluish glow from the dying light, filtering through the clouds. The clearing that we had done had given it a less desolate look. There had been no time for the grass around the steps to grow rank again, though dandelions were beginning to push through the gravel.

I tried the front door and found it still locked, then went around by the side of the house to the stableyard. The wicket was swinging, boltless, soggy with the rain, a puddle of muddy water under it. I stepped cautiously over this and went to the back door. I shook it tentatively. It was bolted on the inside, a good sign. We had done this when we were leaving. I forced the little window of the wash-house quite easily and climbed inside, then replaced the twisted hasp as best I could and walked cautiously along the stone-floored passage to the kitchen.

It felt warm and dry in there, in spite of the rain. I looked into the stove and saw that the fire had burned down completely. I stood and listened, and could feel no presence but my own. I tried to remember when I had last eaten, but it was impossible – ten or twelve hours ago at least. I hadn't thought of food until now.

Fire – if I could get that started, I knew there were potatoes I could boil. I found dry sticks in a tea-chest where we had stored them, then half a dozen logs of wood that could be stuffed into the stove two or three at a time; a sheet of newspaper, a match, a blaze, the twigs flew alight and held long enough for the wood to begin to burn. I felt a ridiculous glow of satisfaction, as if I had done something extraordinary. I went to look for the potatoes and found a few, old and rubbery, but probably edible. I put them in a pot with water from the pump and set them on top of the stove. The mice had got at the butter – it had little tooth marks at one end – but I was willing to share with them.

When the fire was established and the water had begun to heat, I went upstairs to look at the room where I meant to sleep, the one I had used the last time. Some lunatic of former times had painted the walls a violent red. The bed was lame in one leg, as I remembered. The sheets and blankets I had used were still there.

Downstairs it was an age before the potatoes began to boil, then a lifetime before they were cooked. I kept falling asleep, my head on the rough table, almost slipping off the chair, starting awake just in time, getting up to prod the potatoes futilely with a fork from the drawer. At last they were done. I drained them and ate them voraciously from the pot lid, coating each one with butter and a pinch of salt, then cutting them in pieces and putting them into my mouth with my fingers as the country people did. I put an extra log into the stove and opened the front to give myself light.

I was reluctant to light the oil-lamp lest it might be seen from a distance.

When I had finished, I dragged myself upstairs and fell on the bed, only pausing long enough to push off my boots before falling into an impenetrable sleep. To sleep like that after such a nightmare as mine, one has to be young.

The sun flooding the room woke me. I lay on my back while terror struck again, booming through my head like the thunder of the guns, bringing visions of horrors that would stay with me for many a day. I had to get up, in order to exorcise them, then go downstairs and open the back door to breathe the quiet air. Pigeons cooed softly, long drawn-out, gentle tones that always ended with a final, single note like a full stop. There was no other sound. Not a branch stirred in the wind, not a leaf moved. The long grass was heavy with rain, shining, bent over with its own weight.

After a minute or two I went inside and got the fire going again and put on water to boil for tea. Mechanically I looked into the larder for milk though I knew that if there were any still there it would be thick and sour.

The realities of my position began to come home to me. I was not on the run, nor did I intend to be, until I knew whether or not it was necessary. I would need to know from whom I was hiding. Getting news and food would be a problem. Pamela had said that I should keep away from the neighbouring farmers. Now, the day after the battle, they would be even more suspicious of a lone young man in filthy clothes, with several days' growth of beard and badly in want of washing.

There was at least something I could do. I looked into the kitchen, but the water in the kettle had not even begun to sing. The bathroom had been functioning when I was here last. I went upstairs and ran water into the bath. It came gurgling out of the tap in short bursts, brown with rust, but slightly warm from the fire in the kitchen. There were clean towels in the linen-room. I threw off my clothes and had a thorough wash, blissful to the skin and reviving to my spirits as well.

After I had rubbed down I washed my shirt and underwear, wrapped my lower half in the towel and carried the clothes outside to hang in the yard. The sun on my shoulders was a delight. I missed the chirping of hens, which should have been one of the comfortable background noises. The sun glittered on the clothes. They would dry soon.

Back in the house I sat down in the kitchen to wait for the kettle to boil. It was so quiet that a mouse came out and looked at me with little eyes like jewels. He took a short run into the room, then turned and went back. I remembered as a child imagining the secret lives of the mice behind the walls, their civilisation, their economy, their preoccupations and amusements, not always parallel with ours. It had never occurred to me that they might declare war on each other.

Drinking my foul black tea, I realised that I would have to walk down to Rathfarnham and buy some food. The prospect terrified me, but I would have to face it. I had almost ten pounds, enough to last the rest of the summer. Each day would have to take care of itself. This war was over. I had no more responsibility for it. My companions were in prison or dead. I was free. What use would it be to risk arrest? Even our enemies would think that foolish. Though they had fought against us ferociously in the recent battles, I had seen that some of them were bitterly hurt when the time came to take the surrender. There was no logic in them, no more than in ourselves.

The worst pain for me was in the knowledge that Michael Collins was my enemy. I remember tears running down my face at the thought of him. I couldn't understand how it had happened. Surely he hadn't been responsible for the order to bombard the Four Courts. He had always been strong enough to resist that kind of pressure. His Army of the North proved it. Where was he when that stupid order was given, when the Republicans were suddenly made the scapegoats? We had been positively encouraged to believe

that the treaty was only a step towards complete independence. We were certain that this was Collins' view of it.
Unethical, you may say, but our war, like many another,
had not been fought on purely ethical lines.

A wave of depression flowed over me, almost choking me.
I got up and walked around the house, opening doors
violently, banging them shut again. I stamped upstairs and
hurled myself onto my bed, then leaped up and began the
whole peregrination again. Nowhere was peace. My head
throbbed with pain, my hands sweated with it, my mouth
had a sour taste. I remember letting out a wild roar to ease
the groaning of my heart, then realising that if this went on
I would soon be in the hands of the men with white coats,
locked up in the bug-house.

It sobered me. I knew men who had gone raving mad
after a night with the Black-and-Tans. It could happen that
way, or it could come through weakness. Either way, it was
a real possibility. My Jesuit training came to the rescue, as
usual. I could hear the voice of Father Wingard: 'Naïveté
is not a virtue, though some try to make it seem so. *Sancta
simplicitas* is an expression of contempt, not of admiration.
Never allow your emotions to dominate your mind.' He was
referring to sex, of course, as closely as a Jesuit ever can,
but it was useful advice for my present purposes.

A walk down to Rathfarnham was imperative, to calm
me and to fill the larder. I hunted for a key to the front door
but found none – Pamela probably had it. I would have to
go and come by the little window, unless I left the back
door on the latch. In the end I decided to do this, since in
any case a determined person could come in and out at will.

I examined my trousers carefully for bloodstains. There
were none. I hadn't had so much as a scratch, but there
had been plenty of blood about. I put on my half dried shirt
and left the house, walking briskly down the hill. I paused
at a turn of the road to look down on the city, the estuary
of the river with a few ships tied up to the quays, the
wreckage of the Custom House and the Four Courts clearly

visible, a cloud of smoke still hanging in the air over Sackville Street. It was too far to hear shots, if there were any. Perhaps all the posts had surrendered. Pamela was down there, somewhere. She would have found a post that needed her. Or she would have tried to follow Dunne to his prison, wherever that was. I couldn't bear to think of her now.

I went to the same little huckster's shop on the outskirts of the village. Mrs. O'Grady came shuffling out from the back room. She looked me up and down, then said: 'I thought you were gone for good. Where's your wife?'

'She's not back yet. We've been away.'

'Did you see any of the fighting? Terrible doings, I heard, down in the city. Nothing at all around here. Did you ever hear of Robert Emmet?'

'Yes.'

'He used to live out this way, him and his friends, waiting to start the rising.' She sang a few notes in a thin, trembling voice: '"Bold Robert Emmet, the darling of Erin." Do you know that song?'

'I've heard it. Listen – was anyone asking about us?'

'No, and if they did they wouldn't hear anything from me. I suppose you're staying above in the big house?'

'Yes, for a while at least.'

'You'll want something to eat.'

'Bread, butter, oatmeal, milk if you have it, sausages – anything at all. And a razor.'

She made me up a parcel, humming the melancholy tune of 'Bold Robert Emmet' to herself. As she handed it to me she said: 'There's no one will go near that house. You might be better to come down for your groceries after dark all the same, in case anyone is on the lookout.'

Finding a Republican here was a piece of luck, though I had no idea whether a search would be made for our scattered army. On the way back with my parcel I tried to imagine the men as they would be: ragged, hunted, filthy, dispirited, embittered, like every defeated army. If I were with them, it would be my business to help the countrymen hide out in Dublin, then break through and get home to their villages as fast as they could, and rejoin their own units. I would have had no heart for that, nor courage either.

The walk back up the hill was a diversion, lifting my spirits a little, but once I was inside the house the silence oppressed me again. I found myself listening for tiny sounds, starting when a board creaked or a draught blew cold through the open door.

I put my parcels in the larder, then went out and collected branches for the fire and stacked them in the kitchen. For a mad moment it occurred to me that I could barricade the doors, but I realised almost at once that it would be worse to be shut in than to fear an intruder.

Building a fire in the stove kept me busy for a while. I set some sausages to fry on top and went to sit at the table, my mind a grey mass of total sadness. Slowly I laid my arms on the table and put my head down on them, and wept as I had never done in all my life.

Her hands stroking the back of my neck came hardly as a surprise, just as one is never surprised in a dream. I knew it could only be Pamela, and I accepted her presence there as quite natural.

I lifted my head to look at her and said: 'I thought you wouldn't come. I thought I'd never see you again.'

She said: 'I had to come here. There was nowhere else.'

'Everything is over, then.'

'Everything. They've taken him away. I tried to find out where, but no one would tell me. I think they didn't know themselves.'

Dunne, of course, always her first concern. I wanted only to comfort her. I took her in my arms, stroking her gently, feeling her shudder again and again. At last she whispered: 'Something terrible is going to happen now. I don't know what it is, but it frightens me more than anything ever did before. I saw the faces of those men, the way they looked at the prisoners. They were mad; some strange new madness, nothing to do with Ireland at all, only with winning. I couldn't bear to look at them – and to see them taking him away –'

'How many were there?'

'About twenty. They put them on a military lorry.'

'They are all Irishmen,' I said, but I no longer believed that this was a safeguard. The officer who had taken our surrender outside the Four Courts proved it. A terrible change had taken place, as I knew very well.

I asked: 'Where have you been, since you left Sackville Street?'

'Several of us went to some other posts, but no one needed us. The men were all leaving. They wanted news, but we couldn't tell them much. So I went back to Sackville Street, to find out what was happening there. That's how I saw the men coming out.'

'You went back into that battlefield? That was a crazy thing to do.'

'It's all crazy. I can't understand it – men that fought together, going over to the enemy, turning on their old comrades, how can they do it?'

'I don't know.'

The sausages were ready and I made her sit down and eat with me. She was ravenously hungry, as I had been when I came, and she finished her share of the food in no time. Afterwards she looked less distracted, almost like her old self.

I asked: 'Where did you sleep last night?'

'In Paul's room in Terenure. But I was afraid to stay there in case it's raided.'

'Does anyone know about it?'

'Lots of people do. Paul says some of the men who worked with him have gone over to the Free Staters. I went through the papers and took away the lists and files that you used to work on.'

And that I hadn't fetched myself. She didn't seem to blame me for not having done it.

'Where are they now?'

'Here, in a suitcase in the hall. I thought we should take them out to the dump and put them in there, for safety.'

'I suppose so.'

The dump had been on my mind ever since I came, but I had resolved to keep away from it. I began to see that there was no hope of opting out, especially now that Pamela was here. Already by taking away those papers, she had put both of us back into the war.

I said: 'Whether we like it or not, we'll have to lie low for a while. We'll be useless if we get arrested.'

'I knew you'd know what to do. When I came in just now and saw you with your head on your arms, I thought at first that you had lost your nerve. I thought you were thinking of running away. I should have known you would never do that. Paul always said you have more courage than any of us.'

And in her delight she jumped up and came running around to hug and kiss me, throwing her arms around my neck and clinging to me so that I had to hold on to the edge of the table for support.

What could I do? Explain to her that I had changed sides too? I hadn't, in fact. I was just finished with the whole thing. I was ready to settle for any solution that would bring peace and sanity back to ordinary life. I made very sure that she didn't doubt me – that would have ruined everything. I wanted her in a place of safety and she had given me the chance. If I had rejected her, she would simply have gone to someone else.

All right, you may say: stop making excuses. In fact, I didn't need any excuse. I stood up and took her in my arms and held her close to me, feeling her warmth revitalise me with every moment. When I released her, she gave me a long look full of understanding and pity. I couldn't return that gaze. I clung to her again, burying my face on her shoulder, clutching her wildly to me, until at last she said: 'Michael, let's make a fire in the drawing-room and sit down quietly for a while.' Her voice shook, but she managed better than I did to control it. 'If I had known how much you care about me, I wouldn't have come back.'

'If you hadn't come back I would have died,' I said with certainty.

She said very softly, almost as if she were talking to herself: 'You know Paul is my whole life.'

'Does he know it?'

'How can I tell? Why do you say such an ugly thing? He must know – he must feel it.'

'He doesn't feel much,' I said angrily.

I had only succeeded in making her angry too. She said: 'I'll go away. I won't stay here if you talk like that.'

'What do you expect me to do?' But it was dangerous to continue. 'No, I won't mention him again. Please don't go. I couldn't bear it if you were to leave me alone now.'

Carrying the wood for the fire calmed us. We pulled the huge shaggy sofa close to the hearth and sat watching the branches and logs begin to crackle and blaze. After a while she said: 'Do you think we can stay here?'

'Yes, for the present. It would be safer than trying to leave Dublin. We can get news when we go down to the shop. Mrs. O'Grady is on our side.'

'I can go into the city and find out what they've done with Paul.'

'I'll do that myself. I've been to his house. The house-keeper will know.'

I would have promised her anything, so long as she would stay with me. Besotted, obsessed – call it anything you like. There is nothing in the world like first love: the ecstasy, the pure, holy, bodily blessedness that flows through one's being as easily as one's own blood. Now that she was with me, all the pain, the frantic pain seemed worth it. Even jealousy of Dunne seemed unnecessary.

I went very carefully that first evening, afraid of disturbing her sympathy for me. I knew it was my strongest weapon. Instinct led me, I suppose, and a feeling of superiority to my rival which gave me the idea that once I possessed Pamela she would recognise that superiority and be won over to me forever.

We made love at last in the warmed room, sleeping in each other's arms far into the next day. I was the first to wake. I slid off the sofa and stood looking down at her, my darling, my salvation, her red-gold hair spread on the cushions, her transparent eyelids closed calmly in sleep.

I went out quietly and started the kitchen fire. When I came back she was sitting on the sofa. I could see she had been crying, but she spoke calmly enough: 'What can we do now, Michael? This is a disaster. It should never have happened.'

I sat beside her and took her in my arms, so that she couldn't see my face. I said: 'It's not a disaster. Don't look too far ahead. How can we? We don't know what's before us, any of us.' I couldn't bring myself to mention Dunne, but I knew she was thinking of him. 'We must take each day as it comes and wait for news.'

She said sadly: 'I never knew I could do so much injury to other people.'

'You haven't injured anyone. How can you talk like that? You've made me so happy, it's like a miracle. Everything in the world has changed.'

She took my hand affectionately, saying: 'Well, that's something, at least.'

Then she seemed to throw off her mood of guilt and to assume my own attitude. All that day I was afraid she would never again let me make love to her, but I think she pitied me too much to refuse me.

So we began our new life, the one I had dreamed of for so long, but it was nothing like what I had imagined. No one came to the house, though we kept a watch for the men who had set up the dump. For all we knew, they were dead – or perhaps they had been arrested and were in one of the camps. Mrs. O'Grady at the shop told us about those: a huge one at the Curragh where the old British military camp had always been; one nearby in the barracks at Newbridge; two in Cork – one in the female gaol and the other in the old gaol beside the university – others scattered throughout the country.

Why all these prisoners? Who was going to feed them, or guard them? How long were they going to be kept locked up? That side of the war made no sense at all.

Talking to Pamela, I had to be very careful what I said. I didn't care what happened next, nor what became of those men. I had other things to do. I swear my mind was totally occupied with the new game of love. There was no room for anything else.

Not so Pamela. She never lost herself as I did. Sometimes I would see her looking at me in amazement, not disapproving, but with an expression that said she had never imagined anything like this in all her life. Instead of alarming me or making me uneasy, I was pleased as Punch with her reaction. I was like an expert acrobat, or a man who has discovered how to fly.

Of course, I thought about marriage, but I didn't think I should mention it then. I was certain it would follow naturally. This present life of ours was so satisfying, it was unthinkable that it might be cut off. In domestic things we worked as a perfect team, often suggesting the same task at the same moment, so that we would laugh and look at each other, enjoying a new aspect of our understanding. We scraped walls in the house, ready for painting that we planned to do some day. We mended creaking boards and hinges and window-hasps and doorknobs and bolts. We cleared away more weeds and bushes around the front and sides of the house, so that it took on a lived-in look. We trimmed the old climbing roses at either side of the front door and the bushes in the rose-beds that bordered the croquet-lawn. The days were long and sunny – days spent in and around a house are very long indeed, as I knew from Castle D'Arcy.

Once she asked me about my own home: who was there now; whether or not I had been in touch with my parents to tell them that I was safe and well. I said: 'They're better not knowing too much.'

'I can't believe that.'

'What about yours, then? Have you sent word to your aunt?'

'Of course, before I came up here. She would be wild with anxiety. I wrote her a letter when I was in Terenure.'

'So she knows we're here?'

'She doesn't know about you, of course.'

But I felt that our paradise had been desecrated. I asked: 'Will she come to look for you?'

'I think not. I told her in the letter that I'll write again. She'll wait for that.'

It was some comfort. The thought that anyone knew about our retreat brought all my fears to the surface again. Instantly she saw this, and I was overjoyed at the speed of her reaction. So long as I had her pity, she would continue to love me.

I liked it when it rained. The house creaked to a different tune. Though it was summer, on wet evenings we brought logs and branches into the drawing-room and made huge fires which might have burned the house down. We kept the old sofa in front of the hearth and sat together watching the blaze. Behind us the glass of the long windows was splashed with rain and an occasional drop sputtered down onto the burning wood. The bare room seemed cold, and we huddled like cats for warmth. We could hear the heavy trees moaning in the wind. The birds were all silent, though this was the hour for their evening song. It was like being in a ship at sea, isolated, invulnerable.

On one such evening, when I glanced at Pamela, she seemed equally at peace, as if she had at last managed to shut out the whole world. But a moment later she said sleepily: 'How easy it is for us here, away from everything. I wonder what the men are doing.'

I held her closer, saying lightly: 'God knows. Playing chess and cards, probably.'

'Is that how they pass the time?'

'And learning Irish. There's always someone who knows it well enough to teach. They've got to invent things to do. I've heard them talk about it often enough.'

Her mind was on Dunne, of course. There was no point in pretending I didn't know. I said: 'He's safer in there than he would be outside.'

'I don't believe it. I don't trust the Staters. They're desperate. They know they can't keep order by force, so they'll try to do it by terror.'

I remembered what she had said when she came back to Ferney: that she had been horrified at the look on the faces of the Staters as they took their captives away. I had seen the same thing myself. Still I thought we might be mistaken, that our judgment was distorted by the things we had been through.

Before the year was out we knew that we were right, but throughout that summer I continued to hope that we at least were finished with it all.

9

From the beginning I knew that we couldn't keep up this slow, peaceful life forever. When we had been nearly three weeks alone in Ferney, one morning I walked down to Rathfarnham and took the tram into Dublin. Now that I was on the verge of the real world again, I was surprised to find myself almost ashamed of my victory over Dunne. It was not as if he valued Pamela – I couldn't understand why I should suffer feelings of guilt.

Pamela had given up expressing regrets, since she saw how they upset me. She planned to spend the day in the garden, she said, where the weeds were running riot in the warm, damp summer weather. The cabbage plants that Mrs. O'Grady had given us were infested with soft green caterpillars. Murderous little black flies covered the bean-stalks. It seemed as if our labours would not be very productive, but Pamela was willing to put in the work just the same. As I left the house she called after me to bring back some fruit, if I could find any.

The tram had its usual quota of women going shopping. I listened for news, but no one mentioned the war, nor the ruin we had made of Sackville Street. I travelled all the way into the city, consumed with the need to make sure it had really happened.

Both sides of Sackville Street were wrecked: buildings burned down, roofs gaping to the four winds. Most of the shops were gone, but there was plenty of business going on in the side streets. I was afraid to start a conversation with anyone, lest I might arouse suspicion. I had no idea how the citizens of Dublin felt towards us, after what we had brought on them.

I walked about for a while and then crossed the bridge to College Green, where I went into Bewley's in Westmoreland Street and ordered a cup of coffee. While I was waiting for it, I looked around cautiously. Bewley's was a favourite resort of Republicans, but I saw no one I knew. When the middle-aged waitress brought the coffee, I used my Galway accent and said innocently: 'I've just been up in Sackville Street. 'Tis an awful mess.'

She looked at me sharply, then said: 'I've often seen you in here before. What are you up to?'

'Just hoping to meet a few of my friends,' I said.

'Well, you won't find them here, if they have any sense. Don't try that game again. People would think you're some kind of a spy. How is it you're not in gaol with the rest of them?'

'I got away in time.'

'Lucky. Take my advice and keep out of here for a while. The Staters aren't all asleep.'

'I thought the soldiers would be swarming everywhere, stopping people and asking questions and prodding with guns, like the Black-and-Tans. I haven't seen any of that.'

'No. But how do we know when they might begin?'

It looked as if what Pamela had said was true, that everything was finished.

I went to Dunne's house in Baggot Street and rang the doorbell. The housekeeper opened the door, and when she saw me she said at once: 'Come inside. Are you on the run?'

'I suppose I am. Paul was arrested – perhaps you know where he is?'

'In the Curragh Camp. His father got a message nearly two weeks ago. We can send him parcels of food and clothes.'

She led me into the kitchen and made a pot of tea, talking all the time and asking questions. I told her how I had escaped at the last moment and that I had a place to stay, where I would be safe for a while.

She said: 'You could stay here, but I think you're safer out of it. They might come raiding, on account of Paul. They're as bad as the Tans, if you ask me. They learned that lesson, all right.'

I told her of the risk I had taken in going into Bewley's and she repeated what the waitress had said, that I was lucky not to have been spotted.

She had heard stories of outrages by the soldiers, raw recruits most of them, young men out of jobs who joined the army and were loosed almost without training on the population. Their instructions seemed to be simply to put down the Republicans once and for all. Some of the army officers were already in a bad mood, as I had seen. Now these seemed to have become fanatics, bearers of the truth. I knew the seed was the same that had made them into dedicated nationalists in the first place, but that only made it all the more dangerous.

Before setting out for Ferney I bought a bag of oranges, and a small box of chocolates for Pamela, with some idea that these would be a diversion from my bad news of Dunne. I saw it as excellent news, since he would be out of the way for a long time to come. I practised a few consoling remarks – Dunne was safe so long as he was in gaol; he appeared to be in good health; there would be letters, perhaps even visits would be allowed later. The best thing all round was for us to remain out of sight until the situation cleared.

I left the tram at Rathfarnham and walked up the hill in the darkening evening, feeling the real world drop away behind me. I could almost believe, as the country people did, that one could overstep the bounds of our world and move into faery at this time of the day, without being aware of the change. Ferney was certainly not of this world. In the few weeks I had lived there, I had become so attached to it that I felt more at home than I had ever done at Castle D'Arcy. The sagging boards in the hall that I had fixed with nails, the dripping tap in the kitchen, the draughty windows and doors and the impossible garden, all had combined to make an endearing, exasperating *raison d'être*, a lifeline and an entertainment all in one.

As I came close to the house I felt a rush of longing for Pamela. She was its perfect match, her hair still untidy in spite of all my brushing, her humours unpredictable, her energy inexhaustible. There was no knowing whether she would have remembered to cook a meal. I might find her in the musty little room at the back of the house where there was a small bookcase with a strange collection of damp volumes, mostly about the care of horses and dogs, but with several books which, as she said, had great eating in them. *War and Peace* was there, and a few Jane Austen novels, and Proust, and some obscure Balzac, a three-decker novel by Trollope, some bound copies of an American children's magazine called *Saint Nicholas*, a thumbed complete Shakespeare. With these one could winter at Ferney in great comfort. When Pamela went into the book-room she lost track of time and had to be fetched out by force for the next chore. There was a fireplace, and I had a plan to spend a lot of our evenings there when the weather turned cold.

No light showed from the windows – perhaps it was too early. There was still a good deal of daylight, but a soft glow from the kitchen would have been reassuring. Suddenly frightened, clutching my bags of groceries and fruit, I hurried around by the side of the house to the back door. Since we had come here, I had never been away from her for so long. I should have taken her with me, to keep an eye on her. Supposing she had used this opportunity to leave me? She had never said she loved me. In fact, in the midst of our wildest love-making she sometimes murmured his name.

Reassured at finding the back door on the latch, I walked quietly into the house. Just as I reached the kitchen door, a terrible realisation hit me without warning. The door was open. I saw his boots first. A last dim shaft of light fell across the floor, filled with dancing dust. Just beyond it, seated comfortably in the chair that had become mine by tradition, was Paul Dunne.

It was a moment or two before Pamela spotted me, so I had time to collect my wits. There was no need to cover my surprise – it was the most natural thing in the world. She said triumphantly: 'Of course, you're bowled over. He escaped yesterday. He sneaked onto a train and got off near Dublin, and then he walked for miles and miles.'

I put my silly parcels down slowly and asked in the deadest voice I could manage: 'How did you do it?'

'A tunnel,' he said nonchalantly. 'We began to work on it the moment we arrived. A lot of us got out before anyone noticed what was going on. I waited until the end, to make sure the rest got away safely.'

'Naturally,' she said, in the same tone. 'He was the C.O.'

I had seen him do that 'after you' act before, when we were herded into the distillery.

I said: 'I had only just heard that you were in the Curragh. I've been down to the city, to your house.'

'They won't look for him here,' Pamela said. 'He'll be quite safe.'

So began the craziest part of my existence with Pamela. As easily as a young cuckoo ousting the rightful heir to the nest, Dunne became the C.O. of Ferney. He never questioned our devotion to him and to his cause, which was of course to fight to the last Irishman for the restoration of the Republic as declared in 1916. Out came the lists of loyal men throughout the country, the ones that Pamela had taken from Terenure. The little book-room became Dunne's office, and I – who else? – his secretary. He took our service for granted. I never heard him thank Pamela for removing those essential papers, but perhaps he did it in my absence.

I made sure not to leave them alone together much, but in fact his interest in her seemed to be confined to her accomplishments as a cook and general messenger. When he began to spruce himself back into his former elegance, she even offered to polish his boots. He refused kindly, then stood for what seemed like an hour at a time in the kitchen, one foot after the other on the seat of a chair, swishing the brushes back and forth until the leather gleamed like glass. He let her iron his shirts, however. I had to protest when I saw this for the first time. I said: 'Where did he get those shirts? I've got only one.'

'He must have a change of shirts,' she said with a desperate note.

'When I want a change,' I said, 'I pick a fine day and wash mine, and then hang it by the fire for the night.'

'I know. I'll try and get you some too.'

'Where?'

'Mrs. O'Grady got them. You're being childish.'

'Childish!'

I left the kitchen biting my tongue. She had got him a dark-green tie too, which he tied like a valet. Later I saw her pressing his old jacket and trousers, something she had never offered to do for me. I suppose she knew I wouldn't have let her.

She began to look ahead, to plan meals for us, in a way that she had never done when we were alone. She trudged down to Rathfarnham almost every day and brought back food, then spent hours watching over stews and roasts to tempt his appetite. I had to make sure of my share before he swiped the lot, but she always kept up the myth that he would never bother to eat unless she was there to coax him. I've seen people take their pleasure in the same way, watching small children and pets eating.

I insisted that we fix up a bed for him in the dining-room, which we never used. I didn't want him upstairs. The dining-room had French windows that opened onto the garden, and I pointed out that he would have an escape route if a party of soldiers came out from Dublin to arrest him. I didn't think there was much hope of this – it was true that Ferney was not known as a hiding-place for men or weapons, and the days passed in complete safety for all of us.

On her trips to the shop in Rathfarnham, for a while Pamela was our only messenger to the outer world. Every

143

day or two she posted off the letters I wrote at Dunne's dictation, to various Republicans in Dublin and around the country. He used military language, summoning what he called key men to meetings of three or four, to decide on policy for the future and for the counter-attack. I began to wonder if something had happened without my knowledge – was Eamon de Valera dead? Where were Liam Lynch, Oscar Traynor, Ernie O'Malley, Séamus Robinson and all the others that I had assumed were still our leaders? How could I find out from Dunne, without asking him straight, if he had been elected to greater power since I had seen him last? I knew, of course, that the planning continued in the gaols and camps throughout the country, and there could well have been a reshuffle among the powers.

I waited, and men did begin to come. Most of them were from the Dublin area, and most of them were full of complaints that they had been left out of things when the new plans for reorganisation were made. From these, Dunne began to compose a faithful following, sending them off two by two, like the disciples, to do great things. I thought that this was possible for the countrymen, but I couldn't believe that anyone would accept the leadership of the Dublin City men that I saw.

At last I could hold my patience no longer. I said to Dunne: 'Those are not leaders. They'll never be taken seriously. The Dublin brigades are accustomed to men like O'Malley and O'Connor – people with education and discipline. That's why these men have been left out.They're real rank-and-file types. They don't give orders. They take them.'

Dunne said easily: 'What a snob you are still, D'Arcy. Everything has changed in the last few years. We'll need new leaders. They can come from the people. What about James Connolly?'

So as usual he maddened me by what seemed to me deliberate misunderstanding. I was too angry to explain that I was not talking about class but about a quality of determination and certainty – the usual things one finds in a leader – above all the special clarity of vision that is unmistakable and compels respect. Dunne obviously believed that he himself had all that, but he certainly had none of the humility that one finds in truly great leaders. Connolly was an unfair example of a working man who became a leader. He had educated himself in the things he needed. None of the men I saw at Ferney were like him in this. I saw that it was no use talking. I had no faith in Dunne, nor in what he was doing now – playing soldiers was what it looked like to me.

For Pamela, it was deadly serious. One squeak of protest out of me, I thought, and I would be suspected of treachery, or spying, or loss of courage, and I would risk banishment from her presence for good. It was marvellous to watch the hero's welcome she gave to each and all of the men, from Dublin gurriers to tongue-tied country boys who looked as if they felt they had come to the wrong house. Her fluting English voice left them quite at sea, until they came to know her better.

She would say, in the only way she knew: 'Do come in. Won't you have some tea? What a dreadful day. All this rain is ruining the raspberries.'

But when they had been fifteen minutes in her company they always felt at ease, and some even began to tease her about her accent and the way she spoke. Then she would say ruefully: 'I know. But I can't do a thing about it.'

The summer dragged on, full of boredom for us because we had to keep out of sight. As an escaped prisoner, Dunne considered himself particularly vulnerable, but after a while we heard that the government was not too anxious to rearrest anyone who had got away. There was a shortage of places to keep prisoners and those that they had were a continual embarrassment. General MacEoin, who was very successful in the Sligo area, always sent his prisoners home when his battles were over.

Most of our news came from the little shop in

Rathfarnham, where Mrs. O'Grady kept us a copy of her daily paper and as much gossip as she could hear. One morning in late August, Pamela came running in with her parcels, calling out: 'Michael Collins is dead.'

'When? How?'

I couldn't have concealed my dismay, but in any case no one was paying attention to me. Dunne was sitting sideways at the table he used as a desk. He straightened up and stuck out his jaw, and almost seemed to expand as the news sank in. He didn't speak until he could control hs voice perfectly. Then he said: 'How did it happen?'

'An ambush, in West Cork, late last evening.'

'Are you quite sure?'

'Yes, yes. It's in the paper. They're taking the body to Dublin by sea. Look at it yourself – she gave me the paper to take away.'

Dunne's self-important air was increasing by the minute. He read through the report, then said solemnly: 'He was quite a good soldier in his day. Now I hope the Staters will see that the Republic can't be so easily finished.'

The next day we got more news. Dunne was particularly scathing about the fact that as the ship carrying Collins' body passed a British gunboat off Queenstown, the sailors presented arms and a British trumpeter played the Last Post. He said: 'You see how they know their friends.'

'No!' I shouted. 'They always do that for a dead enemy that they respect.'

He gave me a strange look, then said: 'Of course you would know that, D'Arcy.'

I fled out of the house, leaving him to mull over the details of the funeral. That day I think I might have deserted Pamela and made a run for safety and sanity, but I didn't. Instead I came crawling back, and resumed where I had left off. It was some comfort that Dunne spoke very little about Collins after that first morning, but he never again lost his busy, important expression.

The house was swarming with strange young men at all

hours of the day and night. Pamela and I were never alone together. The hair-brushing was finished. Then I noticed that she seemed to be sending me signals with her eyes. I understood that she wanted some private conversation with me.

Though I was increasingly bitter about my position, I never thought of refusing. I invented an excuse to get away and waited for her at the gates one afternoon. No more work had been done to clear the grounds. Dunne had decided that it was better to keep the derelict look. The brambles still ran wild and the avenue was muddy and overgrown as ever. I stayed out of sight behind a tree until she came toiling up the hill with her basket of groceries. She looked flushed and weary after her walk, and the basket hung heavily from her hand. I took it from her at once, cursing Dunne for using her like this, and made her sit down to rest on a fallen tree just inside the gates. I put the basket down and took her in my arms. She made no protest, just leaned against me quietly as she used to do.

After a long pause she said: 'You must help me. No one else can do anything.'

Such an appeal was certain to warm my heart. I held her more closely, asking gently: 'What is it?'

She said excitedly, suddenly moving away from me: 'We must conspire together, and get Paul to leave here. Mrs. O'Grady told me today that someone has noticed how much food I buy. She thinks there might be a raid.'

Good riddance, I thought, while I tried to look very concerned. Above all I didn't want to start her crying. I said, dead-pan: 'You're quite right. He must go away. We must tell him he's in danger – he knows how valuable he is.'

'That mightn't be enough reason for him.'

'What about the dump? He could sleep down there.'

'Too near. I want him as far away as possible.'

There was a more personal note to this, and I began to question her. Then, in floods of tears, she informed me that

147

she was pregnant. In a blind fury I said: 'Dunne, of course.'

'No, no. He wouldn't dream – it's yours – there never was anyone but you – I never – Paul would be shocked – he would say I let down the whole cause –'

I looked her over closely. She seemed to me more beautiful than ever, her skin clearer, her hair more shining red, her eyes more brilliant and lively. I said: 'How do you know?'

'Easily – lots of things – *morning sickness* – can you imagine it?'

I said: 'You could be wrong.'

'I'm not wrong. What are you saying? Won't you help me? You're the only one in the world that can do anything for me now. Why are you holding back?'

To stop her from wailing I said: 'Well, I'm glad. Now we can be married. That's what I've always wanted.'

'No – that would be the worst of all.' She seemed quite unaware of how she was hurting me. 'Paul believes in me. He trusts me completely.'

Her whole mind was on Dunne. It never seemed to occur to her that I would have any interest in our child. I gave up trying to reason with her. She was beyond that, for the moment at least. I said slowly, soothingly: 'Now, don't panic. Of course we'll think of something. I could fake a message that would get him to go down the country to meet some of the men who have been here.'

'He'd come back. He'd find out.'

'Supposing he were arrested?'

She understood me immediately. She went perfectly still. I held my breath in terror while she thought it out. She was so long silent that I ventured to continue: 'There's no habeas-corpus now. It would be ages before anyone would manage to get him out. It might be as much as a year. His father won't help him, I'm certain.'

Still she said nothing, but I could imagine the struggle that was going on in her mind. Now when I look back on it, I can see the funny side, but just then it was all deadly serious. I pointed out that he would be safer in gaol than out of it, and that he could get on with his plotting in there as well as he was doing now. There was an heroic cachet in being a martyr for the cause, and when he got out eventually, he would have gained greatly in his reputation.

At last she said: 'Yes, it would build up his name, and he could do more good. Can you arrange it?'

'I think so.'

'I knew you would have a plan. You're so clever. Paul always says that you're cleverer than anyone else, except himself.'

Her eyes, gazing up into mine, were glowing with admiration. I helped her to her feet and we set out for the house, I carrying the basket. Of course I had no plan, but how could I tell her that? The thought did cross my mind that I might be putting my own neck in a noose, but it was too early to consider details. I felt fiercely protective towards her and our child, though I only half recognised the power of that emotion.

Before we went into the house I asked: 'Is it true that some stranger noticed you're buying too much food?'

'Not at all. I just made that up so that you would help me.'

Of all things I longed now to have the house to ourselves again, but there seemed to be no hope of that. A constant pair of visitors were Paddy Horgan, my old mate from the Four Courts and the hotel, and a young man named Kevin Meldon from the West. Most nights they shared a room along the passage from mine, and were Dunne's trusted messengers. I knew they sometimes went into the city by day, but Dunne never allowed me to go with them. In my irritation it seemed to me that he kept me close beside him so as to supervise my movements. I made one half-hearted attempt to save myself. One day I said to Dunne: 'I don't think you'll be able to hide out here much longer. People will begin to notice.'

'Has something happened?'

'No, but it's only a question of time.'

'I've often been in danger before. I'm not in the least afraid.'

'You're too important. What if you're arrested?'

'You would be in charge. You'd do at least as well – better, probably.'

'I haven't your experience.'

'Nonsense. You know as much as I do. You could carry on everything. And I won't be arrested. No one knows we're here. The boys are very careful. I'm surprised that you're so nervous.'

This was dangerous. If I didn't watch out, I would be the one to be sent away. I had to drop that line altogether.

Weeks passed, and we were into November. Still I did nothing. The weather turned cold. Everywhere in the grounds there was a squelch of wet leaves underfoot. The air smelled of decay. In the dark, gloomy evenings it was easier to move around without attracting attention. At last Dunne began to go down to the city now and then.

Encouraged by the death of Collins, the Republican chief of staff, Liam Lynch, had moved his headquarters to Dublin and there were frequent meetings. Dunne always went alone. Each time I hoped he would be arrested and my problem would be solved. Each time he came home safe and sound and received a hero's welcome from Pamela. Whatever was going on in her mind had nothing to do with me, though she couldn't conceal her agitated glances in my direction. Dunne assumed that all the excitement was for him, allowing himself to be seated by the fire and given the best of suppers while he told us the news.

That news got worse as the weeks went on. In Kerry the Free State Army was under the command of General Daly, our old adversary of the Four Courts. Stories began to filter through of men and women tortured and murdered by methods that would have been appropriate to the Black-and-Tans. Even now I can't bring myself to describe them. All I can say is that when an army of whatever nation-ality is given a free hand, its members seem to lose their reason. Hatred accumulated to monstrous size on both sides.

It was astonishing to see the Free Staters using methods which had failed remarkably so very recently. The Republicans responded in kind, with equal lack of judgment. There were reprisals and counter-reprisals. An Army Emergency Powers law was enacted, prescribing the death penalty for carrying arms. I remember how clearly I foresaw the disasters that would follow this, when Dunne told us about it.

He had a copy of the letter that Lynch wrote to the Provisional Government of the Free State, as it was to be called until the treaty was ratified. Lynch said that the new law amounted to justifying the legal murder of soldiers, and he promised unspecified drastic measures in retaliation. Three days later Dunne told us what those measures were to be. I couldn't believe my ears. My habit of silence was never more useful. Instructions had gone out to the C.O.s of all battalions of the Republican forces that people who belonged to certain categories were to be shot at sight, and their houses and offices destroyed. These included all members of the parliament who had voted for the Army Emergency Powers resolution, unfriendly journalists, High Court judges, anyone who had accepted nomination for the Senate and indeed anyone who was loudly in favour of the Free State. I could foresee nothing but mass murder.

As no one else spoke, I asked after a moment: 'Is the judgment to be left to the commanding officer or must he refer back to the Council?'

'No. He can go ahead on his own.'

'Won't that lead to terrible mistakes? Some of these people are civilians. Will there be no trial of any kind?'

'No.'

He was watching me with that flat, animal look that I had never succeeded in understanding. Meldon and Horgan had been playing a half-hearted game of cards when Dunne came in. It was a dark, windy night and the rain was beating against the kitchen window and running noisily off the roof where the gutter was leaking. These sounds seemed to fill the room when he finished. Now Horgan gathered up the cards saying: 'When do we begin?'

'It has begun already. There was an ambush this evening – I can't give details, except to say it was successful.'

So began the final disaster which divided the two sides beyond repair. The four young men who had set up the ambush were captured and executed by firing squad within a few days. Erskine Childers was executed on the charge of carrying a tiny revolver which had been a present from Michael Collins. On the seventh of December, the day that the sixty Senators of the government were named, a deputy named Seán Hales was shot dead in the street. In retaliation four of our leaders from the Four Courts garrison, including Rory O'Connor and Liam Mellowes, who had been in gaol since the surrender, were executed.

The ruthlessness of this reaction appalled the Republicans. Until now they must have thought that some spirit of comradeship remained alive, in Dublin at least. There was a rumour that the men had been denied the ministrations of a priest, perhaps lest he might try to dissuade the government from their purpose, but I was rather sceptical about this since it was never confirmed. Still I thought it was a crazy enough idea to be true.

Pamela was frantic with fear for Dunne's safety, and with reason. Even I couldn't be cynical about him any longer. The plan that had been vaguely forming in my mind included his being arrested while armed, so that there would be no question of his being allowed to go free. If I were to achieve this now, it would amount to murder. Much as I hated him, I was not prepared to go to such lengths.

My main difficulty so far was that for all his posturing, Dunne was never an important member of the Republican executive, though he had always been a reliable officer and a good fighter. Now, however, with so many of our leaders dead, he moved into a different category. Messages began to come from Lynch, the chief of staff, mostly about country organisation. Wearing his busy look, Dunne went almost every day to Dublin. From the reports he gave to me of what happened at the meetings, I saw that I would have to act quickly.

The opportunity came quite soon. On the morning of the nineteenth of December, a date I can never forget, Dunne sent me into the city to meet an officer named Ryan from Tipperary. I was very glad to go. Pamela had taken to cornering me in different parts of the house when she imagined no one was listening, and asking me when I was going to do something. The baggy clothes that she always wore concealed her condition, but that couldn't last forever. Dunne was noticing a change in her. Once he said to me, in that patronising tone that made me want to kick him: 'Look at Pamela – she's the best soldier of all. She thrives on excitement.'

She was indeed shining with health, as pregnant women often do, and the frantic look in her eyes could be mistaken for excitement, to use Dunne's word. Sometimes she seemed to me to fawn on him like a frightened dog, and this above all tore my heart with pity for her. I made some vague reply, though I might then have asked him to send her away for safety. It hadn't been much use when I tried that before. I let the opportunity go.

10

Dunne had arranged that I was to meet Ryan in a small, sleazy café in Rathmines. I had seen him once before and I recognised him immediately, sitting uneasily at one of the iron tables near the door. The tables were decorated with scruffy bunches of holly in glasses, in honour of Christmas, and a paper garland had been slung against the wall behind the counter.

Ryan was short and dark, the kind of man one doesn't notice in the country, but here he looked out of place. I knew he was an active member of the Tipperary Brigade, which was mounting an aggressive action under the command of the best guerilla fighter of all, the Corkman Tom Barry. On the day after the executions of O'Connor and the others, they had attacked and captured Carrick-on-Suir. And a few days later they were in possession of Callan, Mullinavat and Thomastown. More important than possession of the little towns was the fact that the captured arms made it possible for them to plan an attack on Dublin.

Ryan gave me first-hand news of these operations and details of the plans for the next few weeks. Quite truthfully, I said: 'I can hand on all of this to the chief of staff, but I can't give you any instructions. You'll have to see someone higher up.'

He looked uneasily around the café. It was filling up with tired women, their parcels of Christmas shopping piled around their feet, cups of tea and buns on the tables to sustain them until they got home. They were not in the least interested in us, but he said: 'I don't like this. Can't we go somewhere else?'

Almost without thinking I said: 'Yes. There's the house in Terenure. I have the key.'

'I know that place,' he said. 'I thought no one was using it now. There was some talk that it's not safe.'

'I heard nothing.'

That satisfied him. As we left the café I asked: 'Are you carrying a gun?'

'Of course. A fine soldier I'd be without one.'

'You'd better ditch it somewhere. It's dangerous in Dublin.'

'Dangerous!' He gave a funny little happy chuckle. 'It's a bit late for me to think of that. I'd feel naked without a gun.'

I said: 'I can order you to dump it. I'm your superior officer.'

'So you are. Well, Dublin is different, I suppose. I'll get rid of it.'

'How?'

'Bury it in the back garden after dark, I suppose.'

His manner became less friendly after that, though he continued to give me the information I asked for. We sat for a couple of hours in the room in Terenure. It hadn't changed since I saw it last, and Dunne's spirit pervaded it like a miasma, raising the pitch of my hatred of him.

Ryan's news alarmed me. If the Republicans' march on Dublin resulted in the loss of the city to them, we would be back where we started. The rumours were wild – the strongest one was that the British Prime Minister, Lloyd George, was monitoring events from London and urging the Free Staters on. I didn't know whether or not to believe this, but if it was true, and the British sent help to the Staters, the result could only be a massacre. In the meantime, our reputation in the eyes of the world was being destroyed. I could never be on the side of the Free Staters. I simply wanted to stop the whole thing as soon as possible, by whatever means came to hand.

All right, you may say, these are only excuses. What kind of porridge was boiling in your head? Even now I don't know. There were so many vague pains in there that it's no wonder I acted as I did. But I had had time to reflect. This was a long-term plan. I had agreed with Pamela to get rid of Dunne so that I could have her for myself.

That was only part of it. Ever since I came up from the West long ago, I had suspected, or rather feared, that I would abandon the Republicans sooner or later. My soldier's nerve was gone, I no longer believed that we might displace the Free Staters. Then why had I fought as if I were as dedicated a Republican as Ryan and Dunne and O'Connor and O'Malley and the rest of them, who never seemed to have these problems at all? To them it was quite simple: the war of independence was not over yet. They would fight to the finish. Their point of view affected me strongly while I was with them, but it had quite worn off in the last few months.

I persuaded Ryan that he could safely stay the night in Terenure and that he should see a higher ranking officer next day. Then I went back to Ferney to tell Dunne what I had heard.

It was after dark when I got there, and I saw that there was a light in the little book-room. I slipped in quietly by the back door, past the kitchen where I could hear the voices of Horgan and Pamela. Dunne was sitting at the table, going over his lists of names as usual. I had a moment of compunction, but by now I felt that there was no turning back. The fever in my head gave a glow of excitement to my manner and must have added conviction to what I was saying: 'Ryan's news is extraordinary. It looks as if the tide might be turning. He says that Barry could be in possession of Dublin in a week.'

'That hardly seems likely,' Dunne said wearily. 'If things were as good as that I would surely know about it before now.'

'They have more men in the field than we thought. They

have captured arms. Everything has changed. You'd better go and talk to him yourself.'

'Where is he? You should have brought him here.'

'He's in Terenure. I was afraid someone would notice him on the tram.'

'He should be safe enough there. Let him have a night's sleep. I'll go down first thing in the morning.'

There was still time to get out of it. As we sat around the kitchen table eating our supper, neither Dunne nor I spoke of where I had been. Pamela watched closely all evening, as if she were trying to divine my thoughts. She kept glancing from Dunne to me and back again, so that I was afraid he would notice it. Meldon and Horgan were missing. Gone on a job, Dunne said casually when I asked about them.

Dunne would never allow any drinking in the house, so there was not even Dutch courage to comfort me through that long night. I went over the whole business a thousand times and could see no other solution. There was one, of course, that Pamela should go away, but I was convinced that if she left me now, I would never see her again. Besides I had to make sure of her safety, and the safety of our child. The thought of this creature of ours made me miserable and blissfully happy by turns. I have never forgotten the force of that emotion, never again experienced.

The morning was better. I found Dunne in the kitchen soon after eight o'clock, ready to go, strapping on a holster with his Webley 45 under his jacket. There was no sign of Pamela.

I was afraid that he would want me to go with him, but he said: 'When Meldon and Horgan come back make sure they go to bed for a while.'

'Where have they been?'

'They went after Mulcahy.'

The casual tone sickened me. I asked: 'When can we expect to hear?'

'They'll tell what happened when they come. They may bring the others here too.'

'How many?'

'Four, as usual, including Meldon and Horgan, of course.'

And Ferney would be full of guns, fresh from the assassination. If I needed any stiffening in my resolve, this news would have done it. I said firmly: 'You'd better leave your gun at home. If they succeed there will be searches.'

'I suppose you're right.'

He took it off and handed it to me, saying: 'Just put it in my room, would you?'

'Certainly.'

My relief must have been obvious. He looked at me sharply, probably mistaking my concern for devotion to himself, then said: 'Thank you for mentioning it. No sense in taking silly risks.'

Once he was out of the way, it would not be hard to clear the house of Meldon and Horgan and anyone else who might come. Only then would we have peace.

After Dunne had left, I waited for half an hour before following him. Pamela had not yet come down. I wanted no questions about my movements this morning. I knew that she would be wild with anxiety, but for this one last day she would have to endure it. By evening I hoped to have good news for her.

Telephones were rare enough in those days. The only one that was accessible to me was in Dunne's own house. I hated the idea of using it, but in my desperation I saw that there was no alternative.

I approached Dunne's house from the back, as I had done that first day when we were fleeing from the burning city. I slipped into the kitchen, and there was the housekeeper, just as she was on that other occasion. This time she was peeling potatoes at the sink by the back door. For the life of me I couldn't remember her name. She looked up, startled, her knife held high in her hand. I said: 'It's all right. I just need to telephone.'

She relaxed at once and said, 'You gave me a fright. You look as if you'd seen a ghost.'

She dried her hands carefully on a towel, then led me up the kitchen stairs and along the narrow hall. She paused at the first door and said: 'It's in there. The master is out. He never comes back before lunch-time.'

She turned and went back to her kitchen. Of course, she had assumed I was on Republican business. Still I had to be careful. I had memorised the number I wanted and I gave it to the operator in the accent I had planned to use – the Dublin city accent is easy to imitate. In a moment a strong voice barked into my ear: 'Yes?'

I started as if he had bitten me, but recovered after a second and said softly: 'This is your agent.'

Before I could go on he said: 'Who? Speak up.'

'No. Listen.'

I went into my carefully planned speech. He listened, all right, then said again: 'Who are you?'

Shaking with self-disgust I hung up the receiver, then had to go and sit in one of the heavy leather chairs. For the first time I observed my surroundings. The room was darkly furnished, with panelled walls and a long window that looked over the garden. There was a heavy desk, with the telephone, and some bookshelves full of aged books. A big game-table in one corner struck the only skittish note. I could almost pity Dunne, growing up alone in such a house.

My thinking had only taken me as far as this room. Now I longed to lose all consciousness of what I had done, but I knew already that this was impossible, that it will haunt me until the day I die. The shock brought on a kind of drowsiness, so that for a while I couldn't bring myself to move.

At last I realised that if I stayed any longer the house-keeper would come to fetch me. In a daze I heaved myself out of the chair and went to the door. There I paused and made an effort to control myself, but it was no use. When I reached the kitchen she looked at me with horror, then said: 'What in God's name has happened?' I shook my head, unable to speak. 'Is it news of the boys?'

'Boys?'

'Last night, the shooting.' Realising it was hopeless trying to talk sense to me she went on: 'Sit down there and eat something. I'll make tea. You're not fit to go out.'

She pushed me into a chair at the table. I laid my head down on my arms while she went about making tea, talking to me as she worked. I knew she was trying to calm me down, but what she was telling me only added to my horror. The boys had not succeeded in killing the Minister for Defence, but she was not sure whether or not they had been arrested. There was a rumour that at least one of them had got away and was in hiding somewhere in the city. It occurred to me now that the man to whom I had spoken on the telephone may have thought the important people he would find in Terenure included this fugitive.

Of course I shouldn't have telephoned until after I had heard news of the assassination attempt. Hindsight – or perhaps subconscious suppression of the knowledge that the Free Staters would be out for blood this morning. I remember moaning to myself quietly, like a sick child, while I tried to bear the pain of what I had done.

The housekeeper placed her hand on my shoulder and said gently: 'It will be no disgrace if you go home to your father. You've done your bit. Many a one has done less.'

I remembered hearing that before, or perhaps even saying it to someone myself. For me there was no escape. In a few minutes, when I had drunk the tea and eaten the slices of cake that she laid beside me, I would have to go out into the same world that I had left and try to make some sense of it. I was grateful to her for her attempt to comfort me, but most of all because she didn't ask me for news of Dunne. I suppose she thought it would only upset me further.

After I left her I wandered around the city for several hours. I went into Bewley's café in Grafton Street, but once inside I changed my mind and went out into the street again. I couldn't rest anywhere. Still it was too early to go home. I knew I must stay in the city until I had some news.

And it would have to be first-hand news to be any use to Pamela.

Gradually the pain eased, and I began to console myself with little frantic details. Neither Dunne nor Ryan was armed. The Staters would be disappointed at not catching bigger fish, but there was a good chance that they would put them away in prison all the same. Ryan had told me himself that he was not an important man, though he had been entrusted with important messages. Even if someone recognised him, he was not in much danger. Dunne's was not a big name.

It was one of those clear, still, frosty afternoons that make the Irish winter a pleasure. The trees in the Green were bare and the ducks were huddled on the edges of the pond, but still people were walking about taking the air. I spent half an hour there, after I had left the café, and then walked towards Harcourt Street, to a house where I knew I would find some of the Republican Army executive. I thought I had recovered from the worst of the shock, but when I opened the door and looked in, all conversation stopped.

Three men were there: Commandant Fahy, from East Galway; a Donegal man named MacGinley and another that I had never seen before. They were all older than me, probably in their thirties.

MacGinley said after a moment: 'You've heard the news, then?'

'The news?'

'Of Dunne and Ryan. Obviously you have.'

'Yes,' I said dully.

MacGinley explained to the others: 'D'Arcy has been living up in Rathfarnham with Dunne. Sit down, D'Arcy. You look fit to drop.'

I sat at the table, feeling as if I were in a cage of lions. They looked at me kindly. The third man said: 'Dunne is safe enough. It was a pity that Ryan had a gun.'

I said: 'He wasn't supposed to –' I stopped, terrified.

MacGinley said: 'The countrymen never understand that. He must have realised it, in the end, or he wouldn't have put up such a fight.'

In the end. Poor Ryan. I hadn't wanted that, God, I hadn't wanted that.

Fahy said: 'What happened is better. They wouldn't have opened fire if he hadn't pulled his gun, but they would have found it on him later.'

And he would have been executed after days of terror and anger. I grabbed at this bitter comfort. Dunne was safely on his way to gaol. This was the most important thing. The plan had worked. Now she would be happy.

If only the knowledge of what I had done were a secret between me and God – but Pamela knew all about it. She was equally guilty, since it was she who had insisted on getting Dunne out of the way.

The men were going on with their business, unaware that there was an informer in their midst. Quietly they discussed a plan to lay another ambush for Mulcahy, by now the Republicans' most hated man. If they could get rid of him, they said, the whole picture would change.

Then the stranger said: 'Horgan is a great loss. He knew the city like the palm of his hand. Meldon was from your part of the world, D'Arcy, wasn't he?'

Both in the past, both dead. I said: 'Yes.' I stood up. 'I'd better bring the news back to Ferney.'

With Horgan and Meldon dead there was no one but Pamela to receive it.

Commandant Fahy said: 'We don't know where Dunne is, but we'll find out soon enough. You can come again in a day or two. Go home and get some sleep.'

They didn't ask how I had heard the news, nor why I was in Dublin that day, nor who was living at Ferney now. The organisation was so loose that it wouldn't have occurred to them to question me about such things.

She was waiting for me in the kitchen when I arrived, sitting slackly in a straight chair in front of the stove. In the dim light her face looked old and sick and frightened. She made no move to get up when I came in, just glanced at me and said: 'No one has come home.'

'It worked,' I said abruptly. 'He was arrested.'

'Go on. Why do you stop?'

'The man who was with him was killed. I told him to get rid of his gun but he didn't.' She closed her eyes, and immediately I regretted my brutality. Still I had to continue: 'Horgan and Meldon are dead too. They were killed in the ambush, probably the two others as well. I didn't ask about them.'

'Thank God he's safe.'

She began to come back to life. I knew she had taken in what I had told her, but it was as if she had never known the two young men who were dead. They were part of the war, toy soldiers, expendable. I remember thinking that her weeks with us in the Four Courts and in the hotel had done this to her.

She started to prepare supper and I sat in the big chair and watched her. She went about it more efficiently than she used to do. She had learned a great deal in the last few months. Now I could see the new curves of her body. In a few weeks her condition would be obvious to everyone. We were just in time. Even Dunne couldn't have failed to notice the change in her.

While she worked, she scarcely looked at me. We were alone in the house at last – I had my wish. For this I had committed an unspeakable crime. I was just as crazy as she was, for all my notions of superiority.

The pain of waiting for her to look at me was unbearable. She hadn't thanked me, nor shown any sign of understanding what I had sacrificed for her sake.

At last I said: 'I'll take care of you now, Pamela.'

'Yes.'

I thought that would be all. There was nothing more I could say. She prodded her potatoes to see if they were cooked, then drained them in the scullery and brought the pot back to set it on the stove. I watched her, leaning back in my chair, making no attempt to help.

Suddenly she was kneeling on the floor at my feet, her head on my lap, shaking in agony. I put up one hand and stroked her hair gently. Over and over she said, in a dreadful half-whisper: 'What will become of us? What will become of us?'

I murmured what comfort I could, but it was several minutes before she was quiet again. Then she said: 'I haven't lost my nerve. I'm all right now.'

We got through the next two days silently. I chopped wood for the fires, stacking it in the shed by the back door with fanatical neatness. At night we slept in each other's arms, in Pamela's room.

On the morning of the third day I went into the city to pick up news. I found Fahy alone in the Harcourt Street office, walking nervously around, taking things up from the desk and putting them down again without looking at them. He said he was waiting for the others to come in, and that Dunne was in Harepark Camp in the Curragh, with hundreds of Republicans. There had been a big sweep on the day of the raid in Terenure.

'And Ryan?' I asked.

'His body was sent home to Tipperary. MacGinley went to the funeral. He should be back today. Ryan's parents are old. His father had a stroke when he heard the news. Someone had to go. We thought it had better not be you.'

But if they had sent for me, I would have had no choice.

Fahy went on, a little more calmly: 'We heard they're looking for you, probably because you were always seen with Dunne. You'd better keep out of the way unless you want to be in the Camp with him.'

'God forbid.'

This time he managed a smile.

'I thought you might feel like that. A little of Dunne goes a long way.'

I began to like Fahy more. I asked: 'What will you do?'

'Go back to Galway, I think. There's not much I can do here. I'll soon find out if I still have a following in the West. Mellows was their man, not me. Did you hear that President Cosgrave has a red Court suit with a red velvet cloak, and white silk stockings to wear when he goes to London?'

He pronounced the word 'president' contemptuously. For him there was only one president, de Valera, the President of the Republic. I certainly couldn't imagine either of those men in Court dress. I said: 'I don't believe it!'

'Oh yes, it's true. I wonder if Collins would have worn duds like that, if he had lived.'

'You think it's all over.'

'So many are dead.' I waited. He threw me a peculiar, nervous glance and went on after a moment: 'I don't think there will be much to do in Dublin from now on.'

'What about Ryan's message, the march on Dublin, Tom Barry's plans?'

'You know about that?'

'Yes, Ryan told me himself. It was I who took him to Terenure and arranged for Dunne to meet him there.'

'Dunne had no doubts about going to that house?'

'No.'

'We can expect a lot of raids from now on.' He was fiddling with the ink-bottle again, looking down at his hands, embarrassed. 'Where is the English girl, Pamela?'

'At Ferney. She's been there since the summer.'

'Can you look after her?'

Suddenly I was in a panic. 'Yes. You don't think anyone would touch her?'

'Only if they thought she's not reliable.'

'Have you heard anyone suggest such a thing?'

'No, but people said it was funny the Staters raided the room in Terenure just then. It hadn't been used for a long time. I said it must have been coincidence.' So there had been a discussion. 'I said the Staters have lists as long as your arm of places like that. It could be someone who once worked with Dunne. This is not like fighting the English.'

'Do you think I should get Pamela away from Ferney?'

'She's as safe there as anywhere.'

It was a warning. Pamela – I couldn't believe it. How sharp they were, except for Dunne. I said: 'I'll keep a close eye on her. She's been with us from the start.'

'That's no guarantee of anything.'

'She's wildly Republican.'

'I pointed that out. But some people are probably too nervous for their own good.'

These devious countrymen could say more in a series of hints than I could in ten minutes of explanation. Pamela and myself were like children compared with them. Perhaps that was why he had suggested that I look after her, whatever that meant. It could just possibly mean that he knew we were two of a kind in more ways than one, neither of us to be trusted, both of us capable of actions that Fahy couldn't even contemplate, like betraying a comrade. That was Fahy's language.

After a moment I said: 'I'd better go back to Ferney. I'll think about what you said.'

'Don't take it too seriously.'

Why couldn't he say it straight, whatever it was? But I was glad he didn't. I wouldn't have been able to answer. My acting days were over. It seemed to me that anyone could see through me from now on. It was just as well I had a reason to stay out of sight, away from the action, if there was any action left. I said, knowing he would refuse my offer: 'Don't you think I should report for duty in the West? If everything is finished here, as you said –'

'No. It's not certain that anything will happen there either. I'll send for you if I need you.'

'I'll wait until I hear from you, then.'

But I could see that he was hinting again, that they had become uneasy with me and my kind. From now on I might find I was unwelcome in their company. This was good news, and still I felt a momentary sense of disappointment. I was the one who should reject them. If I showed my feelings, he misinterpreted them. He said: 'I won't forget you. Be careful leaving here.'

'What about you?'

'I'll wait a bit longer.'

'There may be a raid.'

'I'll have to risk that. I've got to see MacGinley. The Northerns are going to have a bad time of it if we have to give up now.'

I left him still moving restlessly around the room. I came out onto the street and walked up to catch the tram, expecting at every step that one of the quiet people behind me on the footpath would lunge forward and grab me by the collar. The temptation to look back over my shoulder was almost irresistible, but if anyone were really following me it would be like running up a flag. It was worse in the tram. It seemed to me that one man in particular was eyeing me closely, every time I looked up, but when we reached the stop at Rathfarnham he got out and walked away.

In spite of the sunshine, the frost had not melted from the grass at either side of the road. I heard a robin give his desolate little cheep in the woods, cold little feet, poor pickings. The chill bit through my overcoat. I should have bought some food in the village. I would have to come down again later.

As I ploughed my way up the ridiculous avenue it occurred to me that with Dunne out of the house we could clear it. The desolate look of the place might attract attention, if peace came. I had never agreed with Dunne that it was better to neglect it, that this would keep people out. Besides, it would give me something to do. Since I would have to live off Pamela's bounty now, at least I could make myself useful.

She was in the drawing-room, waiting for me. She had built a fire and had brought in some branches of holly and ivy to decorate the mantelshelf and trail around the window ledges, making the big shabby room look inviting and comfortable. She was sitting in a corner of the sofa, looking tired to death. I said: 'You should have waited for me to help you.'

'I thought you might be late. Christmas Eve is tomorrow. I had to do something. Did you get some news?'

'Yes. He's in Harepark Camp. Nothing will happen to him there.'

'Are you sure?'

'Yes, unless he tries to escape.'

'He did that before.'

'They'll be guarded more securely this time. I think they have some important people in that camp.'

'Obviously.'

'The camps are safer than the gaols,' I said quickly, not to go into the question of Dunne's value to the nation. I went to sit beside her and put my arm around her shoulder. In that position she couldn't see my face. 'Pamela, we should be married. You have no one else now. Don't you see that?'

'Yes, I see it, but it's not a good reason. I couldn't marry you just for my own convenience.'

'What about the child?'

'That's the woman-trap, always. We don't live in that age. Everything has changed.'

'When it comes to our problem, nothing has changed.' I felt her draw away from me and I said frantically: 'Pamela, I have some rights too. You must know that. I wasn't being casual with you. I loved you from the first day I saw you, in the room in Terenure.'

'I found that out too late. And I didn't know then that it mattered so much.'

'But now that you know, won't you trust yourself to me?'

'That's not the point. Listen to me: the worst thing I could do to you now would be to accept your offer. It's tempting. It would solve a lot of things. But Paul would always be there. We could never forget about him. I can't – I won't do that to you. Why don't you see that as clearly as I do?'

'I see it, all right.' In despair I asked: 'Would you never consider me at all?'

'You mean if Paul were dead?' That was what I had meant, but I wouldn't have put it so straight. I made no answer. After a moment she said: 'Who knows what I would do then? I know what I can't do now. Don't try to understand everything.'

So I allowed myself to be talked down, put aside, as if I were some inconveniently demanding outsider. She hadn't spoken to me so directly for a long time, and that at least was a gain.

11

Though I had gone to such desperate lengths for her, there was no satisfaction in my success. My peace of mind was gone. I saw no hope anywhere. I tried to get Pamela to discuss what must be done next. She said: 'Why should we do anything? Can't we just rest a while?'

'You can't order the whole world to stand still.'

'At least we can draw breath over Christmas.'

'I suppose so. But afterwards we'll have to be more sensible.'

I agreed to wait, and the next few days felt almost like a holiday. On Christmas morning I walked down to Mass and mingled nervously with the local people in the church, automatically noting that there were several doors through which one could escape if necessary. That was ridiculous – it was the most reverent, peaceful group of people that one could possibly imagine, heads all bent in prayer, minds all concentrated on the birth of Jesus, the crib with its animals and figures of Joseph and Mary and the shepherds, arranged lovingly on clean straw, in one of the side chapels.

As they left the church, most of the congregation went to kneel for a minute or two in front of the crib and pay their respects to the holy family. The children were full of wonder and excitement, the parents charmed and childlike too, forgetting their own troubles in the presence of such simple pleasure. I hadn't been to Mass for a long time, having found the bullying tone of the sermons intolerable, but this priest seemed to have a different attitude from the official one and he confined himself to wishing us all the joys of Christmas and praying that peace would come to our country soon.

Pamela had wanted to come with me but I wouldn't allow it. I knew that her Protestant sensibilities would not be shocked at the pieties of Catholics – in fact she loved them, and saw them as an essential part of the Irish character. But Commandant Fahy had frightened me. I couldn't tell her my reason for making her stay at home, but I felt it would be madness to expose her to the possibility of being attacked as a spy. When I realised that nothing of the kind would have happened, I was sorry I hadn't taken her.

We celebrated the day with a chicken which Pamela had bought from the neighbouring farmer, when she went to get the milk on Christmas Eve. We dredged up memories of how a plum pudding was put together, and I got materials and advice from Mrs. O'Grady. We tacked some ivy and red-berried holly to the kitchen walls and stoked the fire, and smells of Christmas began to fill the room. Our Brussels sprouts had yielded some bitten clusters, and we cleaned them and left them ready, with a few potatoes, to put on when the chicken would be almost done.

These domestic occupations soothed my nerves, especially since we went through them so naturally together. Pamela always had an extraordinary capacity for attending totally to the business in hand, whatever it was. Everything else seemed to drop away while she concentrated on the moment. That afternoon, anyone peeping through the kitchen window would have thought we were a contented married couple. She laid the table carefully and had even found some smilax in the broken-down greenhouse, to trail among the dishes.

'It's not Christmas without smilax,' she said. 'Aunt Molly always has it – I wish she were here.'

At that time of the year darkness falls in Ireland soon after four. The kitchen was filled with soft lamplight, and with light from the two red candles I had placed on the dresser. I can still see her standing by the table, her eyes widened with satisfaction as she gazed downwards, her hair glowing like a halo in the shimmering light.

171

Later, when we had finished the meal and were putting the things away, I said: 'Would you like to go to Mount Sanders for a while?'

'Do you think I should? Will the prisoners be released soon?'

'I don't think so. I just thought you might be safer there.'

I didn't want Dunne's image to join the company, so I dropped the subject then. I brought it up later when we were sitting drowsily in front of the drawing-room fire after dinner. I said: 'Your aunt could come here, if you like.'

'You think we'll need someone?'

The 'we' delighted me. I said: 'Yes. And we'll have to find you a doctor.'

'I suppose so. I haven't thought about it.'

'Will your aunt be shocked?'

'I don't think I want her to come. But in any case she wouldn't be. My mother would say something about camp-followers, but then she says that kind of thing about everyone.'

'Tell me about your mother.'

'I don't think of her very often. What do you want to know?'

Her indifferent tone surprised me. It was true that she had never mentioned her mother, but I had somehow assumed that they were on good enough terms. I said: 'Does she live alone? Do you have brothers and sisters? You never talk about these things and I've never had a chance to ask you.'

This was not strictly true. There had been time, but I had been too timid to question her. She had talked freely enough about her aunt and her father but never about the rest of her family. She said: 'Yes, she lives alone, or rather with a housekeeper who has always been there. I'm the only child. I was sent away to school when I was five, so I don't have strong family feeling. I envy you that.'

'Envy me?'

'Yes. Your father and mother mean a lot to you. Paul

172

told me about them, and how you used to play with the local boys when you were small. He admired you for that.'

'I wouldn't have dreamed of doing anything else.'

'In Ireland it's possible. My mother didn't like it when I went to Ireland, but then she disapproved of everything I did at that point. She thinks all the Irish are invincibly vulgar, a sort of national failing that they can never shake off.'

'What did she want you to do?'

'Marry a general who would arrive on a white horse, I think. She adores the army. Aunt Molly hates it. It's a good thing Aunt Molly doesn't live in England – she says all the generals in the war were fools. You can't say things like that in England.'

'Not yet, I suppose.'

'She always had a mind of her own.'

'Tell me about Mount Sanders.'

'It's bigger than this, and, of course, in much better repair. Big, elegant rooms. It was built about 1750, so it has the kind of roof that gives trouble. She gets it painted often, and she keeps the gardens properly, and the greenhouses. Yes, I would like to go there. I wish I could do that.'

But it had occurred to me that a visit from Pamela might put Mount Sanders and its owner in danger. I said: 'We have plenty of time. Let's begin by clearing the grounds here. We've made a good start and we know exactly what needs to be done.'

I thought she might object in homage to Dunne but she said: 'Yes, we can start cutting back the shrubs even while the ground is wet.'

I had promised to call a halt to planning until after Christmas, but though she hadn't objected to my talking about clearing the grounds, I was unwilling to prolong the discussion now. Any reminder of Dunne might lead to a guilt-ridden, acrimonious argument. And I knew we didn't have plenty of time. If he arrived back from the Camp sooner than we expected, she would have to face him with some version of the truth. Better to wait and let her come to recognise all facets of her situation gradually. I would help her to deal with them one by one as they emerged.

It never occurred to either of us that she might have an abortion, nor even give away the child for adoption. Those were not the mores of the time. My secret plan was that in spite of her refusal we would be married later, when she would have finally realised the hopelessness of her position. I was prepared to bide my time. The young are generally accused of impatience and impulsive behaviour. I disagree. I have never seen a mature adult plot and plan as a young person does, to get what he wants. One reason may be that the young don't see the difficulties, nor the possibilities of failure, and this gives them the strength of ten.

I needed strength. Part of my tactic was not to seem to press her in any way, to let her make her own discoveries and come to her own conclusions. At the same time I was to become the support she needed, who would always be there through thick and thin to take care of all her needs. So I brushed her hair every night and then went to sleep in her bed with no promise of future happiness.

A few days after Christmas I went down to Rathfarnham with my shopping-bag to fetch some groceries. I always approached the shop cautiously, since any public place was potentially dangerous. By now many people must have noticed me, but so far no one had shown any interest. Dublin people are not very curious, and besides they probably thought the times too dangerous for talking to strangers. Still I usually picked the quiet period at about noon, when the women had gone home to cook dinner.

The shop was empty when I went in, but a moment later Mrs. O'Grady came out of the inner room, having seen me, I suppose, through the lace curtain of the glass door between. Two wooden trays of fresh bread were laid on the counter, filling the air with their sugary smell. Another, smaller tray had Bath buns and a round, thick kind with jam inside. Suddenly ravenous, I picked up one of these and began to eat it, while I told her what I needed. As she poured tea into a paper bag from her little shovel she said: 'I was thinking about you over the Christmas. How did the pudding turn out?'

'Very well. You gave me good advice.'

'Nothing like your first Christmas. No one to bother you. Next Christmas you'll have your baby. When is it due?'

For a moment I was dumbfounded, then I said: 'Some time in May, I think. How did you know?'

'She had that look on her face, the last time I saw her. You should know the date. What did the doctor say?'

'She hasn't been to him yet.'

'I can send Dr. Cummins up to you. He comes in often for a packet of cigarettes. He's one of our own.'

'The avenue is such a mess, he'll have a hard time getting in. We can hardly manage it ourselves.' I hesitated, then said: 'I want to clear away some of the growth. What do you think?'

She glanced towards the door to make sure no one was there.

'You could start up by the house. Leave the part by the gate a bit wild. You needn't make it easy for them.'

'You think there could be a raid?'

She said angrily: 'Isn't it all around us? We don't know what they'll be up to next. They're every bit as bad as the Tans, going around on lorries, raiding in the middle of the night, or whenever it suits them. Now they're saying they'll shoot the prisoners in the gaols around the country, whenever there's trouble outside, the same as they did in Dublin a couple of weeks ago.'

I stuttered in horror: 'But they can't – prisoners of war – it's impossible – surely they couldn't go on with that –'

'Nothing is impossible for those fellows. Didn't they do it before? They have the country by the throat. They're gone mad, if you ask me. If the English did the like of that we'd be howling all over the world about them. There's a few of them in there that think they can give orders to God himself.'

'It's murder. That's not war.'

But it could be argued that the Republicans had started it, by attacking members of the government. I didn't believe that would excuse this new policy. There could be no comparison between the helpless countrymen who were held in gaols everywhere, most of them rank-and-file soldiers, and the men who formed the Provisional Government.

'You're dead right,' she said. 'Can't you take your wife away from here altogether? Where's her mother?'

'In London.'

'That's where she ought to be.'

'She doesn't want to go.'

'What about your own people?'

'They're not on our side. We must stay here, I'm afraid.'

What she had told me had sickened me utterly. I couldn't take it in properly yet – could the men I knew in the Provisional Government really commit murder so cold-bloodedly, in the name of war? In the name of winning? There might be some justification for executing men caught carrying guns, but shooting hostages in prison could be called nothing but murder. I began to realise that once I had described those executions as murder, there was no escape for me. As I saw it, in getting Dunne arrested I had committed a minor, almost forgivable crime, by comparison with the crime of deserting now.

As I packed the groceries into my bag I said: 'Yes, she must see the doctor. Do please ask him to come, any morning.'

'I'll do that. I could send you a man to help with the garden and the house, if you want.'

'I'll think about it.'

Anyone she would send would be a Republican sympath-iser. She seemed about to say more but then she was silent, as if she felt she had intruded on me.

Still in a daze, I said: 'And I'll take some buns to my wife. She seems to be always hungry.'

'It's natural,' she said, more cheerfully. 'Give her plenty of good food. That's the best doctor of all.'

She cashed Pamela's cheque and gave me the change, then said: 'Come down any time you need help. I'm always here. God help us, we live in terrible times.'

I told Pamela nothing of this conversation, and she had no idea of the wild turmoil in my mind. How could she? It had never occurred to her that I had contemplated deserting the cause. To her that was as unthinkable as if the sun failed to rise.

Dr. Cummins came the very next morning, before Pamela was up. I saw him through the window of our bedroom, when I came in with her tray of breakfast, and guessed who he was from his heavy overcoat and boots and his generally prosperous appearance. All the same the sight of a stranger approaching made my stomach twitch nastily. I said: 'It's the doctor. I'll let him in. Make a start on your breakfast.'

She sat up slowly and wrapped the quilt around her shoulders, and I laid the tray on her knees. From downstairs I heard heavy hammering on the door panels, the sound that used to announce a Black-and-Tan raid. The bell-wire was broken. I should have fixed it long ago but Dunne would never let me. He hated bells, he said, but he didn't explain why.

It was a typical January day, gusts of wind blowing rain relentlessly before them, no shelter anywhere. I went down and let the doctor in. He was crouched against the door, trying to avoid the drops that fell through the leaks in the porch roof. He was a middle-aged man with receding grey hair and an expression of permanent irritation directed against no one in particular, as if he were always trying and failing to catch up with his responsibilities.

It was not much warmer in the house than outside. I led him into the drawing-room saying: 'Sorry there's no fire. I didn't expect you so early.'

'The sooner the better. How is she?'

He made no move to take off his overcoat. I said: 'Very well. She was in no great hurry to see you, but I thought she should.'

'Quite right. You're both mixed up in the racket, I've heard.'

'The racket' was one of the many euphemisms for our war. I said: 'Yes. I don't want her to go into the city, if it can be avoided.'

He looked around the room with disgust. 'Is that why you're living in this dump? I remember the people who were here before you. They never did a thing to the place, sat in the greenhouse when they felt the cold, always sniffling and wondering why they were crippled with arthritis.'

'We're going to clean it up. We have a repairing lease. They don't want to sell it, in case they might come back.'

'They'll never come back. They couldn't afford to, even if they wanted. It will be an enormous job, even to fix the roof. Can't you get her out of here?'

'She's safer here than she would be in most places.'

'I'm afraid the war is over. We're beaten to the ropes. Any minute now there will have to be total surrender. I should feel quite free to take her away, if I were you.'

'There are reasons why we can't leave,' I said, and added when he looked sceptical: 'This is the coldest room in the house, when there's no fire.'

'Well, let's have a look at her.'

I took him upstairs and left them together. While I waited for him, I stoked the kitchen fire and put on some water to boil, so that I was able to offer him a cup of tea when he came down. He said: 'I'll be glad of it. I've got to go up the mountains now – just pray it won't snow. Your wife is very well. I don't expect she'll have any trouble. The baby has a good strong heart-beat. I've heard of her – she went as a nurse to the Four Courts, I think.'

'Yes.'

'She's come out of it all right. Just as well she wasn't pregnant then. What brought her to Ireland?'

178

'Sympathy for us. She has an aunt down the country.'
'You English too?'
'No, just my accent. I come from Galway.'
'I'd never have known it.'
'I was at school in England.'
He left then, promising to come back in a few weeks' time.

We began our programme of clearing that same day, defying the weather, getting as much done as we could before darkness fell. We started with the wild hedge of flowering shrubs, bare of leaves now, that bordered the far side of what had once been the croquet-lawn. A robin worked alongside us, picking up morsels now and then when we turned the earth. Pamela said: 'That bird is almost as good as a dog. I wish we could have a dog or a cat. I can ask at the farm.'

As with everything we did together, we had a sense of natural communion, constantly anticipating each other's needs. I did the heavy sawing and chopping and she hauled away the branches and made a pile of them, to be burned later. Sometimes, when the growth was hopelessly lop-sided, I pulled out a whole shrub by the roots and took slips of it to put into stock for planting when we would have space. Gradually I felt a glow of physical well-being as I got into the rhythm of the work, so that the time passed quickly.

The darkness and cold drove us indoors eventually, and we drowsed before the fire while we waited for the stew to cook. It was the most elementary kind of satisfaction, primeval, as old as man, requiring no thought and no conclusions. Neither of us had ever worked like this before and we had not anticipated the sheer mindless bliss of being exhausted from natural labour, waiting to be rewarded with dinner and sleep. We appreciated it all the more because it had nothing to do with the fatigue of battle, which we had both endured so recently. I could imagine no greater pleasure than to prolong this way of life for ever.

There was not much hope of that. The first interruption

came a couple of nights later, after supper. We were still in the kitchen, lingering over tea and buns, when we heard a series of rapid taps on the back door. We both leaped to our feet. I took one of the candles and went along the passage to the door. I stopped to listen for a moment, then asked: 'Who is it?'

'I.R.A. on duty. Let me in, for God's sake. Let me in.'

This couldn't be a trick of the Staters. They usually burst into a house without ceremony. I slid back the bolt and opened the door a crack, then wider as the candle lit up a little, lop-sided figure. He was wearing what had almost become the uniform of the Republican Army, a worn British army surplus trench coat and a tweed cap.

Tim O'Brien – I remembered him as one of Dunne's Dublin Brigade, as I had called them to myself, one of those who had come to him to make sure they would be involved in the war to the end. He was a fierce little die-hard, implacable in his hatred of England. This had been increased by an encounter with the Black-and-Tans, which had left him permanently crippled in one leg but apparently no less active.

I thought of him many years later when I was in a State forest near San Francisco and stood for half an hour to watch two tiny lizards fighting for possession of the top of a warm rock. It was astonishing to see how such small bodies could contain such massive anger. They changed the colour of their throats repeatedly, from blue to red, to terrify each other, facing up like fighting bulls, then darting in and out, back and forth, lashing at each other with fists and tails, until one retreated, vanquished, and left the other to sun himself in triumph.

O'Brien shouldered his way past me, then turned and snapped the door shut and replaced the bolt. He looked up at me with a grin, saying: 'No wonder you're nervous. This is a queer way to come visiting. I have a message for you.' I guessed who had sent it before he went on.'Commandant Dunne, from the Curragh.'

'He hasn't escaped?'

'There won't be many escaping from the Staters. They know all the tricks.'

'Were you followed here?'

'No. It's just that I'm as nervous as yourself.'

He walked quickly along the passage and straight into the kitchen. Pamela was standing by the table, watching the door. She relaxed at once when she saw who it was and said: 'Good evening, Tim.'

'He has a message from the Curragh.'

I saw her eyes light up as they never did for me. She said: 'Well?'

'There's nothing written. A soldier in the Curragh that's a butty of mine, he came up to Dublin for the day and told it to me. He'll be coming again whenever he can.'

'A soldier! Can he be trusted?'

'He's a cousin of my own, as a matter of fact. Got a wife and chisellers – he had to take a job somewhere.'

'Well, what's the message?'

'That you're to carry on, Captain, as he would if he was here. You know the ropes, he said, and we were all to take our orders from you. He's sent a message to headquarters too, saying the same thing. You'll hear from them in a few days. Commandant Dunne says I'm to stay here on guard and in case you need a messenger or dispatch carrier or whatever you like to call me. He thinks the prisoners will be kept in the Camp for a long time, maybe a few years, but he'll get word in and out as often as he can.'

A few years. And I was to be his deputy as long as he remained a prisoner. I could almost have laughed, but O'Brien and Pamela would have been horrified. She was in a state of ecstasy, looking at O'Brien as if he were an archangel with good news for the world. He kept glancing quickly from one of us to the other. She asked: 'How are the prisoners? How is their morale, their courage?'

'The cousin says they're all right. You know the way it is in gaol.'

I tried to imagine Dunne spending his time on chess and football but my mind couldn't rise to it. I said: 'Did he ask for anything?'

'A few books. He said you'd know which ones to send.'

'What about his father?'

'I suppose he's able to write letters to him, but he wouldn't be likely to give away the address of this place. I'm on the run myself and I'm mighty glad to have a safe house to go to.'

'Why are you on the run?'

'Bomb factory in the back yard. The Staters found it last week. I haven't been home since. The cousin had a job to find me.'

We put him to sleep in the downstairs room that Dunne had used, so that he could act as watch-dog. This also meant that I could continue to sleep in Pamela's room without having to make any explanations. In fact he never questioned me, but I saw him glance at her curiously sometimes, obviously aware that she was pregnant. It probably never occurred to him that we were not married to each other. As I said, times were different then and the moral tone of our comrades was unbelievably high. And it was obvious too that he was fully sympathetic to us.

I warned him not to tell Pamela about the threat to the lives of the prisoners. She had taken to going to bed rather early, so it was easy to keep our military discussions until she had left us.

That first evening he informed me that a new dump was to be built, perhaps more than one, and I was to be ready to receive consignments of arms at any time.

'Captured arms?' I asked, thinking of the march on Dublin.

'No. But we may get an order to dump our guns if we have to surrender. Some of us are going to make sure to dump them anyway. It's hard enough to get a gun when you need it. The Staters want the guns handed over to them, but that would be madness, until we know which way the cat is going to jump.'

Other men would come from Dublin to build the dump, he said, and he would be able to supervise them, since he had a great deal of experience in this work.

While we waited for the men to come, O'Brien adopted the role of general handyman. Each morning we divided the tasks between us, continuing our plan of clearing the grounds close to the house. At the same time we tackled the building itself. We found a stack of slates lying against the wall of the greenhouse, bought presumably with the idea of repairing the roof some day. They were overgrown with moss and weeds, as if they had been lying there for years, but they were in perfect condition. O'Brien went crawling on the roof and spotted the worst parts, and quickly replaced the missing slates with new ones. Almost at once we felt the house become warmer. We built fires in all the rooms, to dry them out, and planned a campaign of painting. O'Brien said he had worked as a painter and builder, and he was glad not to be idle. He even talked of rebuilding the greenhouse.

Within a week of O'Brien's arrival, a team of three men came to dig the new dump. They chose a place in the wood, where the trees grew sparsely and had obviously once been expertly thinned. We scarcely saw them. O'Brien took full charge of them and kept them well away from the house. I went to inspect the work from time to time, and to make sure that their tools were hidden when they left in the evening, but we managed to keep Pamela out of the secret of what they were doing. It was slow, heavy work but towards the end of January they had finished one underground room and were planning the second.

During this time I lived from day to day, savouring every hour of the breathing space and watching our work on the house and garden progress. This was what Pamela had recommended. I began to appreciate her wisdom, though I could never exorcise the devil that was on my back, as she seemed able to do.

One morning I had taken a saw and had gone to cut branches off a fallen tree, and to make sure that the new dump had not been damaged by the recent rain. The ground was just dry enough to make it possible to work in the wood. It was one of those still, winter days when sounds travel a long way and there is a scent of growth in the air. The stream that ran downhill through the wood was full, roaring noisily over the stones. It should have masked every other sound, but I heard a twig crack a little way off, then another. I felt that someone was watching me. I straightened up, letting the saw fall by my side, and looked around.

A man's head appeared from behind a tree, then the rest of him. Trench coat, tweed cap. Of course he was one of ours. I walked towards him. Then I recognised him – Tom MacGowan, a Donegal man. He had a delightful, soft Northern accent.

'Commandant D'Arcy, dispatch from the Chief of Staff.'

So I had been promoted.

Still holding the saw, I put out my free hand for it, a half sheet of writing paper with a typed message, signed by Liam Lynch. I was to report for duty at the office as soon as possible. I said: 'Very well. Do you want to stay and have something to eat?'

'No thanks. I'll be off. When can you come?'

'In an hour or so.'

'I'll tell them. I've just had a look at the dump. A nice job.'

He slithered off down the hillside, digging in the heels of his boots to prevent himself from falling.

A sudden pain in my wrist made me realise that I was still tightly clutching the handle of the saw. I let it fall to the ground and went to sit on the tree-trunk. General Lynch – what could he want with me? I wasn't important. Without Dunne I was nobody. I hadn't worked with anyone else for

184

a long time, except when I was a judge on the Western circuit. It must be that with so many in prison or in camps, even men like me were needed.

One thing was absolutely clear: this was the moment of truth. I found that I had already made up my mind. My months of vacillating were over. As long as it had seemed that the ordinary rules of decency were being kept, the rules of war if you like, I had imagined I was capable of dispassionate judgment. Now I realised that while I still loved Pamela with complete devotion, I loved justice better than life itself. I had come full circle. I could not accept the notion that victory should be pursued at any price, regardless of morality – I had probably never believed it. My original, burning reasons for joining this army were the same as those that would keep me in it now. I felt no more doubts, only a kind of happiness, as one feels in the face of inevitable death.

I went back to the house and found Pamela working a hoe on the gravel sweep in front of the door. I stood to watch her. She swung it like a man, no delicate prodding but a long, sweeping movement that used the energy of her whole body. She stopped when she saw me, and pushed the hair back from her forehead, saying: 'This is wonderful exercise, as good as swimming.' Then, suddenly: 'What's happened?'

'A man came through just now to say the Chief of Staff wants to see me. I must go at once.'

'Who was it? I saw no one.'

'Tom MacGowan, from the Second Northern Divison. He came by the back way, up the hill. I was working in the wood.'

'Then you knew him already?'

'Yes. There's no doubt. The despatch is signed. Look.'

I showed her the paper with General Lynch's name. She came with me to the house, trailing the hoe, which she left propped against the side of the front steps. While I was changing into clean clothes I said: 'O'Brien will stay here.

Others will come. I'll send a message if I can. I don't know what to expect. I may even be back this evening. If I'm not able to come, will you be afraid?'

'Yes, but what can we do?'

I found O'Brien and instructed him to take charge of the house and the building. Pamela walked with me to the gate that led onto the avenue, and I held her in my arms for a moment. Then she turned back to get on with her hoeing.

12

I had to cross the city to get to Tower House, in Santry, the home of the Fitzgerald family, where the Republican headquarters had been established. Dunne had given me exact directions once, saying they might be useful some day. From the outside it looked like an ordinary, well-kept big house, but he had told me that like many other houses around the city it had a secret room where men and guns and all evidence of its real use could be safely hidden at a moment's notice.

By the time I reached the house I was extremely nervous. My recent elevated mood had evaporated. The pain of my guilt for Dunne's arrest and for the death of Ryan hurt like a raw wound. Passing through Sackville Street in the tram I found that it was full of ghosts.

Lynch took my anxiety as natural. He was thin, ascetic-looking, seven or eight years older than me, wearing spectacles that gave him a blind look when the light caught the thick glass. It was hard to believe that this man was the fiercest fighter of all. He had been a draper's assistant, landed into his present position by force of circumstances rather than by any special military genius. He was a countryman, but not like Peter Hynes or John Kelly or any of the other strong-bodied men that I had known in the West. Lynch had an aura of innocence about him that made him seem rather helpless and childlike, like some academics. But his exploits in guerrilla warfare during the Black-and-Tan war were second only in daring to those of Tom Barry. I had heard of these in detail from John Kelly, when we were together on Rabbit Island. Kelly said that Lynch's political sense was better than Barry's, which was why he found himself in his present position.

I had met him on one or two occasions, but had never had any conversation with him. When he came into the drawing-room where Mrs. Fitzgerald had left me to wait, he looked like a tired old man. He said: 'Commandant Dunne sent a message to say you could take over from him. I've heard that you know everything he was doing.'

'I think so.'

'And he said you get on well with the countrymen.'

'Dunne is a real city man.'

For the first time he smiled and looked a little less anxious.

'Yes. Most of us are bewildered in the city. You can go down the country, then?'

It was a question rather than an order. I said: 'Of course. When?'

Instead of answering, he began to walk back and forth, talking in a low monotone as if he were rehearsing a speech. 'You know the Staters won't settle for anything but unconditional surrender. When we were all comrades together they refused that offer themselves, from the British, but they seem to have forgotten it now. They won't even agree to negotiate. Our position is that we won't be forced into the British Empire. We have stated it over and over again. I want you to visit the country brigades and give them our message clearly.' He turned away and rubbed his forehead, as if he were suffering from headache. 'I'm sure you know these things as well as I do. You may not know that the country brigades, especially the Cork ones, have been sending messages since Christmas, asking for a meeting of the executive. They want to end the war. After the executions that would look like weakness, or fear. It will be your business to explain that to them. We fought this kind of terror before and we must do it again now. You must impress on them that there can be no meeting of the executive for the present, but there's to be no slacking off.'

'What are the alternatives, if they won't agree?'

'They must agree, at least until the point when the Staters will be forced to negotiate. There must be no split in the Republican ranks. They must not surrender their arms.'

'What about dumping them?'

'Rather than give them up, yes. That's been discussed, but I don't want to order it unless there's no alternative. Tom MacGowan will go with you. You'll have lists of officers you must see.'

'When do you want us to go?'

'As soon as possible. I'm going to the South myself at the end of the month. Try to visit as many of the brigades as you can before I do. The list is almost ready. You can go over it before you leave and make sure you have the names correctly. If you're captured, of course the list must be destroyed.'

He took me to an upstairs bedroom which was set up as an office. Three very young men, hardly more than boys, were working at typewriters, placed on the wash-stand, the dressing-table, the bedside table. They stopped typing when we came in, then stood up. I had never seen any of them before. They all looked cheerful and eager, in strong contrast with Lynch's gloom.

Lynch said: 'This is Commandant D'Arcy. When can you give him the lists?'

One of them said: 'Tonight, if you like.'

'Tomorrow morning will do. You had better show them to him as you go along.'

Suddenly I felt very old and sad. Instead of heartening me, the sight of these simple young men forced on me a sense that the end was indeed coming. A true blue Republican would have been glad to find that the ranks were filling up with younger men, but that was not how it struck me. As I had suspected, the fact that I was suddenly given such heavy responsibility meant that there was no one else to take it on.

The rest of the day confirmed this. Lynch summoned me from the office to sit in on a conference. Several Dublin generals of the G.H.Q staff were there, as well as two officers of the Dublin Brigade. The leaders I had known were in gaol, but I knew these by sight. They remembered me from the Four Courts and the Sackville Street battle, though they hadn't seen me since.

One of them said: 'I thought you were in the Curragh with Dunne?'

'I've never been in gaol,' I said.

'Lucky man. That's where we'll all be, soon. Where have you been, then? I haven't seen you around.'

'I was with Dunne, all right, out in Ferney.'

'You weren't with him when he was arrested?'

'No. That was in Terenure.'

'Of course. It was a bad business. We don't know who put them onto that house. Someone did. I've heard of Ferney. A good place for dumps.'

'Yes. We've been working on them.'

Just then Commandant Fahy and Commandant MacGinley came in. I had last seen them in Harcourt Street. I thought Fahy looked a little put out at finding me there.

We sat around the shining mahogany table in the dining-room. Lynch opened the proceedings in a curiously formal, stiff way, saying: 'As you know, I've called you to this meeting to discuss our next moves. Michael D'Arcy will go to various brigades in the country over the next few weeks, to stiffen their morale and instruct them to keep up the fight. They keep sending demands for a meeting of the executive, but I'm certain the time hasn't come yet. I'd like your views.'

After a pause, one of the Dublin officers said: 'The simple truth, Liam, is that we're hopelessly outnumbered. The Staters have a trained army of thirty-eight thousand men. We have – maybe – eight thousand that we could put in the field.'

Lynch made no reply, nor did he show by any change of expression what he thought of this. He simply looked at the next man, who said: 'Apart from military strength, we've lost ground with the people. The Church has condemned us out of hand – well, they always do that with nationalist movements in Ireland, but it always has the effect they want. You'd think the people would see the way the bishops plumped for the Free State even before it was off the ground. One good thing will come out of it eventually – this will finish the power of Maynooth. But the ordinary people are tired of the war and we can't be too sure of their support. They're still a bit frightened of the bishops and some are glad of an excuse to turn against us. They're even beginning to inform on us to the Staters for private reasons. That's the thing that I find most significant.'

He paused and shrugged his shoulders, as if to say that any of them could continue his speech as well as he could. Lynch looked at the next man. He was one of the G.H.Q. officers, a stocky sharp-eyed man with a slight northern accent. I had never seen him before, but he was obviously well thought of by the others. He said quietly: 'Once again I want to press the need for a meeting of the executive. President de Valera should be present. As you know, I've laboured long and hard, first to prevent this miserable war and then to bring it to an end by any means possible. I believe the time has come for us to abandon all hope of achieving the Republic by force. From now onwards we must look to political means. It's time we took our places in the Dáil –'

Fahy interrupted: 'And take the oath? I could never do it. My tongue would fall out. And accept partition? You could never do that yourself.'

One or two of the others murmured agreement.

Lynch said: 'When we go into the Dáil, there can be no oath. This is one of our chief principles – there's no need to repeat it. Please go on.'

But the officer who had spoken said: 'That's all I have to say. The only possible road for us now is the political one. If the Staters won't negotiate, we should simply disappear until our time comes again.'

'Surrender?'

'I said disappear. Go under ground. It can be done. We'd have to make statements, naturally. The first necessity is to have a meeting of the executive.'

'You recommend dumping our arms?'

'Of course. They can't be surrendered.'

'Commandant Fahy, what about the West? Michael?'

I said: 'I haven't been to the West for a long time. It's always different from Dublin.'

'In what way?'

'Poorer. People have less to lose. There are some good fighters there, but they feel out of touch with Dublin. Commandant Fahy knows more about them than I do.'

Fahy said: 'We could stand firm in the West for a while, but I should point out that the people are not all poor. Business people are tired of the war. They think we've got enough for the present. They're in favour of a political solution now. Some of them are on the edge of taking the law into their own hands. I don't think we can go on much longer. There have been heavy raids. Some of our best men are in prison. Liam Mellows is a great loss, but even if he were to come back now, I wouldn't be certain that they'd follow him.'

Lynch looked around the table as if to make sure that no one else had anything to say. Then he said quietly: 'Thank you. Now I know how you all feel, I'll give you my own thoughts. You know some of them already. You agree with me that the oath is intolerable. It's intended to humiliate, and that would be its effect. It would certify us as slaves. Some people argue that it's only a routine part of entry into the Empire. The Labour Party has adopted that line. But an oath can never be routine for us. Mr. de Valera's oath to the first Dáil is what makes it impossible for him to enter this one. None of us here present could enter the Dáil under present conditions. But the Staters can. Do they believe in it? Or do they take it lightly? Can one take an oath lightly? Can one call on God to witness, and then disregard Him?

They are not irreligious people – they don't intend to do that. And by taking the oath they agree to abandon our comrades in the North to their fate. It's one thing to say that we can do no more for them now, that we have no hope of winning a war which was undertaken partly for them. It's quite another thing to swear in the sight of God that we will never again attempt to lift a finger for them, to free them from tyranny and safeguard their lives and the lives of their families. The Staters can swear to that. Or else they are trying to deceive both God and man.

'These issues are cut and dried. We must ask ourselves the question, whether by surrendering now we would not be morally guilty of collaborating in their crimes. Crimes they are. There is a second question, which may help us to solve the first one. Can we in conscience hand over the people of this country to men who have no qualms of conscience, not only about the things I've described but about the morality of executing prisoners of war in reprisal for acts of war that have taken place elsewhere? As we know, these prisoners have been executed for political reasons, to create terror among the people and to get rid of intelligent critics who wouldn't tolerate the slave-minded attitude of the Staters. Even if one takes the line that we are rebels, criminals, it would still be grossly immoral to visit our guilt on helpless prisoners.

'This savage policy is the one that has formed my mind in its present mould. If we were to surrender, could we trust them not to continue with this policy? Might they not simply exterminate all the prisoners, on the principle that it would be well to get rid of the Republicans once and for all? They're like killer dogs. Mulcahy has said that he's proud of the stand they've taken. We have no evidence that they would stop now. When men have hardened their hearts like this, killing is easy. So, as chief of staff, I must in conscience order the war to continue.'

One of the Dublin officers said quickly: 'Collins wouldn't have allowed what they're doing now.'

Lynch said: 'Who knows?'

No one else spoke, but as they left the meeting it was clear that they had all accepted their orders. A few weeks ago, I would not have understood Lynch. Now I found that I shared the other officers' final gloomy, dogged, hopeless determination to stand together behind him.

I spent the night in Santry, in a nearby house where MacGowan was billeted. There was no possibility of sending a message to Ferney. MacGowan talked for a while as we both lay in the darkness, too nervous to sleep. His wife was in Donegal, he said, living with her parents in a remote valley near Dunlewy. They had married two years ago and he had an infant son that he had never seen.

'She says he's black-haired like the rest of us,' he said. 'Long hands and feet, going to be a tall man. I'd like to see him.'

'When can you go?' I asked, glad of the darkness.

'I don't know. I haven't been home for four months. The way things are, there's no telling when I'll get off. Nora doesn't say a word in her letters, but I know she'd like me to see the baby. Why wouldn't she? You're from the West – what part?'

'Near Oughterard.'

'A big house, I heard.'

'Yes.'

'Big or small, you'd want to go home sometimes. We got no orders to go to the West. Commandant Fahy can do all the talking there. Liam didn't say he was going there either – I wonder why was that.'

'There will be meetings in the South. That's the only reason he's leaving Dublin.'

'Yes.' I heard the bed-spring creak as he turned over. 'Are you married, Michael?'

'Not yet.'

'I'm glad I am, before anything –' He left the sentence unfinished, then said: 'But you'll get married some fine day when all this is over. How old are you?'

'Twenty-three since last October.'

'Sure, you're only a child. You have plenty of time. I was thirty-two at Christmas. Time for me to settle down.' He gave a satisfied sigh, then said: 'This is a good bed. We'll be lucky if we have as soft a sleep tomorrow night.'

Before leaving next morning, we called at Tower House for the list of Brigade Commandants that we were to meet. There was only one copy, which Lynch gave to me to put in an inside pocket. He looked even more distracted this morning. He handed MacGowan a second packet, saying: 'These are some copies of General Order No. 9. Give them to everyone – make sure they all have them.'

I remembered General Order No. 9, which stated in part: 'Our troops are strictly forbidden to carry out reprisals on the enemy for the recent cruel and cold-blooded murders, and no such acts can under any circumstances be tolerated.'

The order had been made as long ago as October, after revenge was taken by the Republicans on innocent people in West Cork and Kerry, in reprisal for an outrage by the Free State Army. Dunne told me at the time that the Republicans did respect the order, but it would be too much to expect that they would continue to do so in the future.

Lynch was saying: 'You've heard the news?'

We hadn't, and he told us: 'Eleven more prisoners shot – five in Athlone, two in Limerick, four in Tralee – that's twenty-four already this month. You're going into the middle of it. They won't stop now.'

I said: 'No change in our orders? If I may say so, it looks to me as if the brigades will want to step things up now. They'll say it's not much use shooting at the enemy's feet.'

Lynch looked distressed. 'No. The rules of civilised war must be kept, at least by us. You must impress on them that there is to be no retaliation.'

This was the man who had ordered the shooting of Senators, judges, prominent people of any kind who supported the treaty. I had wished a plague on both their houses then. There was a world of difference between that policy and his present one, and I remember wondering how he would explain it. I knew it would be useless to ask him.

MacGowan had a bicycle for each of us, and he led the way across the city by a roundabout route. It was a typical January day: cold sleety rain falling, borne on gusts of wind so that there was no escape from it. Within half an hour we were soaked to the skin. MacGowan forged ahead with total disregard for the weather. I kept him in sight, through the smelly streets near the cattle market, then down towards the river and across the bridge beyond the main railway station for the South. Rain ran down inside my collar, tickling my back like a flea. My trench coat felt loaded with water. My feet squelched with every push on the pedals.

It was worse when we left the city and were in quiet lanes with hedges, too bare at this time of year to give us shelter. The wind howled through them, sending the puddles splashing up our legs, sometimes almost knocking us off our bicycles.

The bicycles were very old, and MacGowan's gave way after we had covered no more than the first forty miles. We were pushing laboriously up a hill when the front fork cracked and jerked him off into the road. As he picked himself up he said: 'There's a queer way to die for Ireland – am I killed?'

'No, but the bicycle is,' I said.

Mine had a slightly buckled front wheel which had happened in the morning when I went over a stone, but I had managed somehow to carry on.

'Shanks mare,' MacGowan said. 'This is the end of both of them. I doubt if anyone around will be able to mend these veterans. It's the hand of God.'

We hauled them to the farmhouse where he had planned for us to stay the night. The farmer said he would try to repair the bicycles but we hadn't time to wait. Instead we took a ride in a pony-trap next morning, by muddy lanes and byroads, to Leighlinbridge. The incessant rain was a protection, since there were few people out. We stayed that night in a cottage where there was only one old man. He was expecting us, but was disappointed to find that neither of us was General Lynch. MacGowan said: 'Keep the beds ready – he'll be along this way with a few Dublin generals in a couple of weeks.'

Members of the local company came in when they heard we were there, and they all had the same question – when would Lynch come and tell them what to do? They had no more than ten rounds of ammunition each, though they were hoping for supplies from the South in a few days' time. The Staters had lorries and machine-guns and rifles and were roaring around the country attacking anyone and everyone.

'They're like the Tans, only worse,' one man said. 'They know who they're looking for and they're out for murder. If we had a few of those guns they're getting over from England, we'd have a different story.'

Rain, cold, hunger, misery are the things I remember about that journey. We seemed to live under water, like fish, fording streams in flood, crawling over mountainsides that ran with water, walking along endless muddy, rutted roads, even swimming across a narrow stretch of the river Suir, rather than cover eight miles on foot to the nearest bridge. MacGowan was always in charge of planning our route. He seemed to know every track and waterway in the whole countryside, and to have friends that he could call on everywhere. He was usually cheerful, even when he cursed the weather, but he sometimes went silent for miles at a time, as if he were saving his energy.

When I was a judge on the Western circuit I had experienced the same kind of hardship, but this time there was a difference. Everyone seemed to have lost hope. We were often warned that the neighbouring farmers and shopkeepers were our greatest danger, and would send for the Staters if they knew we were present in the area. This had been a hazard in the Black-and-Tan times but on a much smaller scale. The priests were noticeably absent, though we were told that some were clandestinely friendly. Instead of music and dancing to end the evening, now there was always bitter, angry argument and talk of revenge for the execution of the prisoners. We quoted General Order No. 9 and handed out copies of the document, which had the effect of reducing the threats to a mutter. It was quite clear that no one any longer believed in a Republican success, and still the faithful few were determined to follow orders.

Everywhere we went, we met the same questions: 'When is General Lynch coming? When is the executive going to meet? Where is President de Valera? Can't we dump our guns, such as they are, and rest for a while?'

What they were really saying was: 'Has everyone forgotten us? Who is our leader now? Will we still be fighting this war when we're old men? Why don't we get a chance to say what we want?'

But their loyalty to Lynch was complete, and their determination to follow him forever.

Because of my youthful appearance, the farmers' wives always took special care of me, giving me extra food and a warm place by the fire, as if I were a child. If I hadn't had the rank of commandant they would have called me 'boy' in every sentence. I must have looked like a countryman, with my hair grown long and wild and my worn jacket and trousers, a shirt without a collar and frayed shoes. MacGowan was just as bad. The women washed our clothes for us if we stayed more than one day, and some gave us socks and shirts to take away.

On the evening of the fifth day we started to climb by way of a sheep track over the mountain into County Waterford. Our guide was a black-browed young man named Phelan, a Waterford man whose brother was in Clonmel prison. We were given these details by the man in whose house we met Phelan, but he himself scarcely spoke to us. Not even MacGowan's cheery remarks could get a smile out of him. He seemed possessed by a devil of silence, plodding along through the mud a few yards in front of us,

198

turning every now and then to make sure we were still with him.

After a couple of hours of this I said quietly to MacGowan: 'What do you know about him? Do you know where he's taking us? I don't like the look of him.'

'Neither do I,' MacGowan said, 'but I was told he's all right. We're going to his uncle's house on Mount Melleray. If I knew the way, I'd tell him to go home and we'd find it ourselves.'

We rested in a hut on the mountainside, lying on dry branches of heather, the air heavy with the smell of sheep droppings. For once the rain had stopped and it was a clear moonlit night. Through the open doorway of the hut we could see away off down the valley to the winding, glistening river. Isolated points of yellow light showed where there were houses. A cold north wind wailed miserably around the hut and brushed up the grasses and heather. All around us there was the sound of falling water. The moonlight drifted in on us, giving the peculiar comfort that only light can do. Softly MacGowan began to sing:

Both night and day I'm dreaming of the hills of
    Donegal,
The heather on the hillside and the sunlight over all.
And westward I'll be going across the ocean blue
To seek again the happiness that long ago I knew.

Behind us, Phelan spoke up. 'You have music?'

'My mother loves that song,' MacGowan said, 'though it always makes her cry. Her sister sang it the night before she went to America.'

'Can you finish it?'

'Indeed I can.'

He went on with several more verses, each with a melancholy chorus, still in that intimate, almost whispering tone, though there was no one within miles to hear us. At the end Phelan said to me: 'What about you, Commandant?'

He had spoken so little that it was only now I noticed he had difficulty in speaking at all. It was not that he had a speech defect of any sort, but that bringing out the words seemed to cause him pain, as if each one had to be lifted separately and laid down again, like a stone. Suddenly I knew the reason – he was speaking a language that was foreign to him. I said: 'I have some songs in Irish.'

MacGowan said: 'That's a queer one – I never knew you had a note of music in you. Strike up an old song there for us, in any language you fancy.'

'Which language would you like?' I asked Phelan.

'Irish, of course,' he said, suddenly liberated, using the lovely soft Waterford Irish that I had never heard before. 'What song have you?'

'I have "The Blackthorn Tree". Do you have that one?'

'I've never heard it,' he said. 'On with you, boy.'

It's a love song with a long wandering line, a great favourite in Connemara where there are many blackthorn trees. When I was young I had a light tenor voice which was greatly valued for singing in church. That was only at school, of course, but I had picked up some songs from our neighbours in Connemara, when I was a small boy, and for some reason they have always remained fresh in my memory.

While I sang the first verse, Phelan was twitching with excitement and pleasure. Then he said: 'That's a fine song, and you sang it finely. You must write down the words for me, and sing it over and over until I know it. Have you got all of it?'

'I have five verses. There are more, but I don't know them. What songs have you?'

'I have "The Connerys". Give us the rest of yours first.'

I did, and afterwards he sang the song of the Connery brothers who were transported to New South Wales from Waterford for a political offence, at least a hundred years before. The last verse consisted of a ferocious curse wished on the oppressors, unless the young men were allowed to come home and see their aged mother before she died.

At the end of it, when we complimented him, he said: 'That's a sad song, but we have some cheerful ones too. I have a fine one about a Bandon trawlerman. When we get to my uncle's house, we'll make a night of it.'

When we had rested, we continued on our way, and now the conversation was in Irish. Phelan no longer kept at a distance. Singing and hunting hares were his two passions, and he chatted amiably about days out with the dogs and about the words of songs, apparently tireless as we trudged higher and higher.

'I thought the two of you were from Dublin,' he said. 'Why didn't you tell me you're from the country? But that's a lame kind of Irish you have, without wishing to insult you,' he said to MacGowan, whose northern dialect he had never heard before. 'It's like another language.'

'Never mind,' said MacGowan. 'I'll give you lessons.'

It must have been four in the morning before we reached the summit and turned down the mountainside at last. We went cautiously now, slipping and sliding on the gravelly surface, until we came without warning to a low, slated cottage built against the slope and sheltered by a wind-break of pines. Our track ended at the back of the house and Phelan said: 'I'll go in first, and make sure it's safe for you.'

We waited, shivering, close to the house wall in a vain effort to shelter from the evil wind, our wet clothes agonisingly cold. Within a minute he was back and leading us inside. His uncle had waited up for us, but the rest of the family was long gone to bed.

Every moment of that journey and of its end is etched on my mind and will lie there forever: the straw-filled mattress in the loft overlooking the kitchen where we slept; the flea-ridden feather quilt that covered us; the drip of the rain through the leaky slate roof; the false feeling of safety that let us sleep long into the morning of the next day.

Murmurings below in the kitchen awoke me first. The family was up and about, trying to move quietly so as not to disturb us. I leaned over and saw a woman and a girl gently rattling milk-cans, or cans of feed for hens, padding quietly to and from the open door. I looked down at Mac-Gowan, sleeping still, the black curls spread over his forehead giving him a boyish look that was belied by the firm lines at either side of his mouth.

I crawled from under the quilt and climbed down the ladder into the kitchen, my finger on my lips to indicate that MacGowan was still asleep. I went outside to look for the privy, then walked a short way up the mountainside to see in daylight the route that we had taken last night.

It was bitterly cold, but the rain had stopped. I was glad to fill my lungs with clear air after the fug of the loft. I could hardly make out the track that we had used, it was so worn by the rain. There was a sort of shoulder to the mountain, which was probably why the house was built in that exact place. The force of the wind was broken by it, but when I rounded the shoulder it struck me like a blow, sending me hurrying to the shelter of an overhanging rock. I crouched close against it and gazed downhill, where a curving road wound along beside a stream.

That rock saved my life. Leaning against it, I heard the lorries roaring up the hill. There were three of them, nose to tail. By the time they came into view they were already almost at the house. There was nothing whatever to be done. I was fully a quarter of a mile away, much too far to raise the alarm. Flattened against the rock, I heard the old nightmare repeated: rifle butts pounding on the door; men shouting; one shot; then half a dozen more; then silence for a few minutes before the soldiers came out half carrying their prisoner. One or two turned to look up the mountainside. I froze against my rock, waiting for the bullets. None came. They turned away and followed the rest, climbed into the lorries and roared off down the road.

13

Once I had decided to seek out Dunne, I had known I was in for a flood of poisonous memories. There was no one to blame but myself. Memory is a peculiar business; it can't be entirely stifled, no more than conscience can, and it has an odd way of jabbing at you when you're quite unprepared for it. It's like awakening from sleep to find a thief, or a devil, in your room. Sometimes it can be exorcised by talking it out, but in all the years I was away from Ireland I never met anyone to whom I could talk about MacGowan and his death, and the appalling sense of guilt that I felt because I was not with him at the end. Perhaps it would be possible with Dunne. At this stage, surely there was nothing to lose.

I had known MacGowan only for a short time, but I had come to admire him most of all for his determination and uncomplicated honesty, so different from my own wavering, uncertain cast of mind. A steadfast man, free of hatred, no matter who was the enemy, he never doubted that right would triumph eventually. And I had come to love him, as you love a person who has shone a light into the darkness of your mind. His death was as bitter to me as Peter Hynes's would have been, or John Kelly's.

Dunne leaned in to put some wood on the fire. It sputtered and crackled as he adjusted it. Now was my chance. I was tired of facing his bright stare. I said: 'Did you know Tom MacGowan?'

Dunne went on prodding the fire, saying: 'Of course. He used to come often to G.H.Q. with messages from the North. You were with him when he was killed.'

'Yes. Not in the house – I had gone out for a breath of air on the mountain.'

'I know. I heard all about it. You had arrived only the night before. Why did he shoot, do you suppose? He hadn't a chance.'

'Perhaps that was why. He had his gun under the bedclothes. It may have been instinctive.'

'You had taken yours with you?'

'Yes. Instinct again.'

'That was lucky. If they had found a second gun they might have gone to look for a second man.'

'Lucky?'

'You had a list of names in your pocket that they would have been delighted to find.'

'Yes.'

'And it's always lucky to be alive, don't you think?'

'Not always. Curiosity is the only thing that keeps one alive when one is older. Death seems outrageous to young people.'

'In normal circumstances, not in ours as we were then. I never worried about it at the time.'

This was true. He had never seemed in the least afraid, as I was.

'And later?' I asked. 'When you were in prison while the Free Staters were in power after the civil war was over? Weren't you afraid then, that you would be taken out some morning and shot?'

Only de Valera's entry into the Dáil in 1927, and his subsequent formation of a government in 1932, had put a stop to the Free Staters' policy of executing prisoners. I knew Dunne had been released and rearrested several times during the 1920s, along with hundreds of Republicans who continued to show that, though they were defeated in war, they had not abandoned their position. The guns had been dumped, and a small army could be raised at any time, enough to make any government nervous. At the time that the Free Staters were ousted, they had a long list of men

marked down for execution, some of whom became prominent in various sectors of Irish life afterwards. No doubt
Dunne's name was somewhere on that list.

He said: 'One gets hardened, like a professional jockey,
or an aircraft pilot. The married men were in the worst
position. They were afraid, but not for themselves.' He sat
back, still holding the tongs, admiring his fire which was
now blazing up in a symmetrical pile. Before I could make
any comment, he went on: 'As you probably know, poor
Tom MacGowan didn't die until the evening. I wonder if
you heard he said it was worth it – finding out that the
house was no longer useful. Liam Lynch wouldn't be taken
there.'

'I hadn't heard it. I only saw the men taking him
away.'

'But Liam was killed in open ground a few weeks later
anyway. It amounted to the same thing.'

'MacGowan had a wife, and a child he had never seen.
What became of them?'

'I don't know. I was more than a year in Harepark Camp
after the civil war ended. We used to get news through
various sources, but we never knew whether or not to trust
it. There was a friendly soldier. A cousin of that man
O'Brien.'

'I remember him.'

Dunne said calmly: 'Of course you do. He went to Ferney
with a message once. Well, I went on hunger strike with
most of the others, in the end. You had gone away by the
time I came out.'

'Yes.'

'You'll hear strange stories, but in fact, it was the hunger
strike that broke the Staters down. It was one thing to shoot
a few of us now and then, and quite another to have a few
thousand dying of starvation in a prison camp. Some people
have tried to make that strike seem ridiculous, but it was
nothing of the sort. I've never seen such a mixture of despair
and courage. That's what kept the men going.'

The warm room and the medication I had taken just before coming out were making me drowsy. This was probably one reason why the atmosphere of suspicion seemed to have softened – I may even have thought that old enemies could become friends if they live long enough. Dunne was saying: 'They caught Phelan the same day, and his uncle who owned the farm. At least they left the women alone.'

'Yes. I saw them go away, else I suppose I would have had to go down and fight. It seemed useless. And I had the papers, as you said. Was that what they had against me – that I didn't show myself and get killed too?'

'Partly, I suppose. They were talking about you already, how you were never arrested though you were often connected with people who were. There was a man from Galway – Commandant Fahy.'

'I remember him.'

'When the rumours started, he was the first to take them seriously, so far as I know. Since he came from your part of the country, people thought he had special knowledge. Unfortunately I wasn't able to get in touch with them until it was too late – I would have tried my damnedest to save Castle D'Arcy.'

But Fahy had only warned me that Pamela might be suspected of spying.

Of course I had gone down the mountain to the Phelans' house as soon as the coast was clear and tried my best to comfort the women. Mrs. Phelan and her daughter were sobbing in each other's arms when I went in, rocking back and forth as if each was supporting the other. They sprang apart when they saw me, then the girl said: 'Thank God you're safe. You heard what happened?'

'Yes. I saw them from the mountain.'

'They were tipped off. What else would bring them up here? We never see a stranger on that road from year's end to year's end.'

'Where is Mr. Phelan?'

'Gone down to my uncle's house.'

I remembered all that now, and the long, drawn-out aftermath when I tried to find the people on my list, without MacGowan's help, and to explain why I was alone. Back and forth across country I went, climbing mountains, floundering in streams, taking guides wherever I could get them, until I fetched up in John Kelly's house about four miles north of Cork city. It was there, in early April, that I learned of Liam Lynch's death. It was the first news they gave me, but I was so weary that I was barely able to understand what they were saying.

Kelly lived with his family in a two-storey farmhouse which looked comfortable enough, except that it was crammed with people. Both of his parents were there, four unmarried sisters and two brothers that I saw, and they mentioned one or two more who were away at a fair on the day that I arrived. All of the brothers were in the Movement and they lived in daily danger of raids and arrests. Still they made space for me, on a mattress on the floor of the big room where the men slept. It was like being in barracks. I fell asleep that day at four o'clock, and didn't wake up until the following evening.

After I had eaten something, John took me for a walk up the hillside, so that we could have a quiet talk. Spring had come, and the lush Cork green was beginning to show through the dry winter ferns. From the top of the hill we could see for miles along the river, with a segment of the broad, circular harbour at the end. John said: 'Isn't it beautiful? Did you ever see anything like it in all your travels? And down there we'll have to see battleships at anchor for the rest of our lives, to remind us that we lost everything in spite of it all. I can never understand how Collins could let himself be pushed down like that.'

'They say he meant it as a starting point.'

'Do you believe that?'

'I don't know what I believe now.'

Like myself, Kelly had escaped by a series of miracles. He had been in a dozen fights, but he was always the one that got away. That first day he said: 'It's a mystery why I was never caught. Look at all the good men that have gone since this began. Now Liam Lynch. Lord God, Michael, this will be the end of the whole campaign.'

'What about Barry? What about Dan Breen?'

'They'll give up now, if they're still alive. Most of the commandants have been saying for a while back that we'll have to give up. Anyway, Barry and Breen were never in Liam's class – too impulsive. Liam could plan like a general. He had a big heart. He hated fighting, but he drove himself to it for love of Ireland. I think he'd rather have been captured and killed by the British than to see brother fighting brother, as they're doing now. Did you know him well?'

'Hardly at all,' I said, 'until the day before I left Dublin.'

'What will you do now?'

'Wait and see what happens. That's all we can do. I'll probably go back to Dublin as soon as I can.'

'I know what will happen. By the end of the month we'll have a cease-fire. It's overdue. That was the one flaw in Liam – he didn't know how to retreat in good order.'

I didn't share in this hero-worship, but I wouldn't have said so for the world. I had thought Lynch was too simple a man for the tasks that had been forced on him. Wars are not won by saints.

I asked: 'What about you? What will you do? There will be sweeps for a while.'

'I'll take my chance here. The guns are all dumped. We'll get our orders soon enough.'

He included me automatically, but I had different plans. I would get back to Ferney by hook or by crook, and wait there with Pamela until peace came, as it must do now.

Dunne, still prodding the fire, still with his back to me, said: 'One of the things that was said against you at the time of the court-martial was that you didn't rejoin your brigade in Connemara.'

'That was nonsense. I was on the staff at G.H.Q. by then. I actually offered to go, but Fahy himself said I shouldn't.'

Dunne said sharply: 'I didn't know that.'

'I was just as pleased – all I wanted was to go back to Dublin, to take care of Pamela.'

At last her name had been said. Dunne sighed, as one might in remembering a very old sadness.

'Ah, yes, Pamela. She was so devoted, and she had the courage of ten men. The day I was arrested in Terenure, the day poor Ryan was killed, I nearly went out of my mind with worry about her. If I hadn't known you were there, I think I would have fought my way out with my bare hands.' He turned suddenly to look at me. 'These are the things I remember about that war now, not the gunfights and the politics.'

I was struck dumb at this, as you may imagine. After a pause he said: 'I've always blamed myself about Pamela. She was strong, but not as strong as I thought. She had a kind of hero-worship for me, as you saw, and I should have been glad of it instead of mistrusting myself. I can see my reasons now, but at that time it was all fogged over with emotions that I could scarcely understand. Why were you in the Movement?'

The sudden question startled me and I answered cautiously.

'As John Kelly would say, for love of Ireland.' My voice sounded in my own ears like a sick mouse, but Dunne seemed not to notice. I sat up straighter and forced myself to speak more strongly. 'I couldn't bear the poverty of the people around my father's house. Its name was an insult to them – Castle D'Arcy! I loved England too, but England didn't love me. Most people I knew there had the greatest contempt for the Irish, as if we were a nation of servants. Pamela said that was her mother's attitude. I felt I was a stateless person, as they say nowadays. If I had to settle for one country, then it would be Ireland. I thought it all out very carefully.'

'You make it sound easy. Cut and dried. Right and wrong. It can't be easy to give up a big house and an estate on principle.'

I remembered the house in Baggot Street, the evidence of wealth and comfort. I said: 'You did the same, surely.'

'I never regretted it; no more than you did. There was no question of doing anything else. When I was young, I would have changed places with anyone in the whole world to get out of the future I saw before me.'

'What was that?'

Dunne said with extraordinary bitterness: 'Tailoring, high-class gentlemen's tailoring, officers' uniforms, evening-dress, my father with a tape around his neck and a mouth full of pins, the gentlemen being treated like royalty, myself – patronised so that my blood boiled. "Got a school prize again, boy. Your father just told me – here's a shilling for you. Keep up the work." And my father would glare at me and say: "Thank the gentleman, Paul." I thanked them, all right, and put away the shilling. They meant well, I can see now, but I hated them.'

The natty clothes, the fear of disrespect, the unease with country people, the wish for acceptance, or power, or at least something that would restore his humanity – friendship perhaps – a whole pattern of reasons fell into place. Dunne was saying: 'There's no one as class-conscious as those who serve the upper classes. My father had a different manner for everyone, though he served them all. A rich shopkeeper got different treatment from a baronet, a baronet different from a lord. Oh yes, he had a couple of lords. He employed seven tailors and a cutter in a back room, and he talked to them as he thought the lords would talk to their servants. It's another world, gone completely, or almost gone. We didn't know that. I'll never forget the excitement when we heard of the Russian Revolution.'

'We?'

'I was in the I.R.B. You were only a boy, of course.'

'I was seventeen. I was away at school. We heard nothing, until the holidays.'

'Bliss was it in that dawn to be alive – in my mind's eye I saw my father's customers lined up with the Tsar and shot. Can you believe that?'

'If you say so.'

'God help them, they were only working out their lives the same as we were, in that state of life to which it had pleased God to call them. If I had been a Catholic, I think it would have been different.'

'You were not a Catholic?'

I was truly astonished. It had never even occurred to me that Dunne was not one of the great mass of Irish people, who can never be understood except by their own, who seem so devious to outsiders, who have a private wire to the next world at all times and can see through walls and doors to whatever it is they want to find.

Dunne was looking pleased. He said: 'So even you didn't know? You didn't take one look at me and say: "That's a poor Protestant"?'

'Of course not. You were one of us. You even went to Mass.'

'No one knew, not even the priests who came to the Republican courts, nor the men who came out from Dublin to Ferney when the civil war began. But I thought you might. A poor Protestant is a servant forever. A poor Catholic is the king's brother.'

'Are you a Catholic now?'

'No. There's no need. Ireland is quite different now. Don't look so dazed. You were the interloper, not me.' Here was the maliciousness again, his true feeling for me. 'Some of them complained about you when you went on the circuit – a gentleman wouldn't understand them, almost like an Englishman; couldn't we send a real Irishman?'

Surely if this were true I would have felt it with John Kelly and with Peter Hynes and my other neighbours. I said, before I could stop myself: 'They called you a Dublin jackeen.'

He hadn't forgotten, and it still hurt. But I was sorry I had responded in kind to his gibe. Some holds were better barred. He said: 'They're like that in the country to this day. You'll see, when you go there. Dublin is the distant enemy. The Pale still exists. They don't like taking their orders from the city.'

I didn't believe this – in fact I might have said that it was still the jackeen in him that made him say it. City people never understand the fun that goes on in the country but country people are usually well able to enjoy themselves in the city. I answered with a generalisation: 'The capital is never popular. It's the same everywhere.'

A log fell from the fire onto the hearth, scattering tiny sparks. Dunne leaned forward and picked it up expertly with the tongs, and laid it back, then said: 'So you went back to Ferney in April, as soon as the cease-fire was ordered?'

'Yes.'

John Kelly's mother had cleaned my trousers and washed my shirt, then given me her husband's good overcoat and a pair of his Sunday boots so that I could travel to Dublin on the train without attracting attention. The Republicans had blown up the Mallow railway bridge, with the result that the railwaymen were hostile to the whole Movement. John warned me to trust no one. In fact, the train was raided by a party of soldiers somewhere near the Curragh, but they took no notice of me. Seedy gentility is always the best disguise.

It was a beautiful spring afternoon, the sky almost clear of clouds, the air light and cold. I took a series of trams to Rathfarnham, where I was tempted almost beyond endurance to stop at the shop and ask for news. Instead I hurried up the hill to Ferney. The gate still hung crooked. I saw that the avenue had been cleared and levelled to some extent, and the farther I went, the more evidence there was of O'Brien's work. Then I noticed that there were tyre-tracks in the soft earth – the doctor, of course. He had said he would come to see her.

I paused at the inner gate, perhaps foolishly hoping to find her where I had left her, hoeing the gravel. It was all neat and tidy now and there were daffodils in flower all around the bordering grass. A car was standing in front of the closed door. While I watched, the door opened suddenly and the doctor came out.

He stood on the top step, looking me up and down, then said: 'So you're back. Where have you been?'

'Down south. How is she?'

'All right, considering. She's been alone for the last few weeks, but she wouldn't leave. She said she's used to being alone.'

'Alone? What about Tim O'Brien – the gardener – ?'

'Gardener?' The doctor gave a short laugh like a bark. 'The Staters didn't believe that. He was arrested. The whole thing is over now. I hope you'll be able to stay at home and look after your wife. The child seems all right so far. It should be born in less than a month. Get her to rest, feed her well. I've made arrangements with the district nurse. She's been here to see her. Send for me if you get uneasy – or come yourself. Do you know anything about babies?'

'No.'

'If there's any bleeding, or if she begins to get regular pains, I'll come at once. I'll see her next week anyway.'

I found her in the kitchen, stoking the stove with wood. She had heard me come in, and she had turned eagerly, confidently, towards the door. Perhaps I imagined that she looked disappointed, but then she dropped the log she was holding and ran into my arms.

After a while I held her off to look at her. She was glowing with health, her hair shining in the sunlight that streamed though the window, her curving body seeming to move without awkwardness or strain. She said: 'Well, how do I look?'

'Beautiful.'

'You look scruffy. Where have you been? I've heard nothing at all since you went away. You know they came one night for O'Brien?'

'The doctor told me. I met him outside.'

'Poor O'Brien – I was hoping to hide him in the old dugout but there wasn't time. Anyway, they went there first, before coming to the house. One of the party knew about it – he had a hand in digging it, he said.'

'They didn't molest you in any way?'

'No. They were very polite, almost apologetic. Do you want a bath? I think the water is hot. O'Brien did wonderful things with the plumbing. It's good to have you back.'

She was hugging me again. She had lost none of her exuberance. I said: 'Have you heard any news of him?'

'How could I? But I think he's safe. From the way they were talking I thought that they were taking him to gaol. They didn't shoot – I stayed close to him all the time to make sure they wouldn't. They emptied the dump, of course, but they didn't know about the new dugouts. In any case, now that they know about the house, it's no more use as a hideout.'

'Have they been back?'

'No, as a matter of fact they haven't.' She seemed surprised, but I guessed the reason. Since she was so obviously pregnant they must have decided to let her alone, though they were not always so sensitive. 'Do you think it's safe for you to stay? I'd love that. It's creepy here at night, alone, though the evenings are getting brighter. I try to be in bed before dark.'

'Of course I'll stay. Did you really think I might leave you?'

'I should have known you wouldn't. You're always so good to me.'

While I bathed in heavenly hot water she cooked supper. Afterwards we sat in the drawing-room in front of the fire, as we used to do, her head on my shoulder, her shoes off and her feet drawn up comfortably.

She said: 'I've been making baby clothes – wait till you see. The nurse told me what to make. She brought me patterns. She's very nice and friendly. I can't believe anyone could be as small as that baby will be.'

She chattered on, twisting my heart this way and that as if it were a sponge that she was washing out, quite unaware of what she was doing to me. I was not much more than a boy but even a toughened man would have found it hard to endure. I held her closer and said as calmly as I could: 'Please let me take care of you forever. You must see that the time has come for it. Everyone assumes we're married – the doctor always speaks of you as my wife. Don't you love me enough to marry me?'

My arm was around her shoulder. She reached for my hand and held it tightly in hers, talking gently as if she were soothing a child: 'I love you, but not enough for that. Can't you understand? I told you before. We would both be miserable. I love everything about you. You're my dearest friend. But I couldn't possibly marry you just to make use of you.'

'I wouldn't mind. I'd spend my whole life with you and never care.'

'Yes you would, after a while. These are the things women know. You've done so much for me already, I know you would always be good to me, but I might not be good to you. It was one thing to throw myself on you when I was desperate, and get you to do something that went completely against your conscience – I know it did – but if I were to marry you now, in the same spirit, I'd never see God.'

'Do you believe in God?'

'Of course. He's our father.'

'Do you pray?'

'Yes, for Paul, and for you, and for the baby.'

At this I began to cry helplessly, stupidly, like a despairing child, and soon it was she who was comforting me. But she wouldn't give an inch in her decison. That night when I was alone in my old room, I cursed Dunne as I had never thought I could curse another human being. I wished him dead and damned and out of my way. Only then would I have a chance of moving into his place.

Life slipped back into the peaceful round that we had enjoyed long ago, before Dunne intruded on us. We were completely alone, except for the doctor who came every week, always with news of the outside world. In spite of the cease-fire, the Free Staters were still arresting any Republicans that they could lay their hands on. He advised me to stay out of sight, not to go into the city until things calmed down. I was quite content to do that, though as the days went on I felt more and more that we were living in a fools' paradise. I couldn't imagine anything beyond the birth of the baby, and neither could Pamela, though obviously she had more excuse for being so blind.

The clear weather continued and we were able to spend a great deal of our time in the walled garden. O'Brien had planted lettuce and potatoes and broccoli and radishes, which were all beginning to show signs of life. Around the house, buds appeared on rose-bushes that had been choked almost to death last year. Early in May, old gladioli sent up spears where the flower-beds had been weeded. We brought in bowls of narcissi and let the air blow through the open windows, so that the whole house smelt clean and fresh and full of their scent.

The doctor complimented us when he came one afternoon about the middle of the month. We gave him tea in the drawing-room and he said: 'I hardly knew this place could look so well. You've done wonders. You'll stay, of course.'

'I hope so,' I said. 'Otherwise all our work would be wasted.'

He said comfortably: 'It's a good house for children. Nothing like having enough space for them to play. Children love to be free. It's hard to imagine before your first child is born, but you'll be amazed at how soon these things will be important.'

I was watching Pamela. She got up at that moment and went to the long window that looked out on the side of the house, then turned suddenly, saying: 'I think something is happening to me, a sort of jerk. Do you think it could be the baby coming?'

'Why not?' The doctor heaved himself out of the depths of the sofa. 'Upstairs is the place for you. Lucky that I'm here on the spot.' He turned to me. 'I'll come down in a moment and tell you if I need the nurse.'

He was back in five minutes, literally rubbing his hands with satisfaction, saying: 'Can you drive my car?'

'No.'

'Then you'll have to run. Down the hill, first lane to the left, second cottage on the right. Tell her to come as soon as she can.'

'What if she's not there?'

'Her mother will be. You can leave a message. I'll stay here.'

He took over everything, so that after I had fetched the nurse I had no function whatever in the business except to keep the fire stoked and the kettle on the boil. I felt choked with excitement and fear, almost as if I were the mother of that child instead of only the father. It's a familiar sensation, I believe – I've often heard people joke about it, and wanted to run out of the room or box their ears. There was nothing humorous about it, that I could see.

Hours passed before I heard the doctor rattling the latch of the kitchen door. I ran to open it and he came in smiling, took my arm and said the magic words: 'You have a son. He's a little beauty, like his mother.'

'How is she?'

'Perfect. She's a fine woman, D'Arcy. A rare woman. You're a fortunate man.'

'When can I see them?'

'This minute. The nurse will let you in. Have you thought of a name for him?'

'No. We didn't talk about that at all.'

'Most people do. In fact, some have a whole string of them. I think your wife may have a name in mind. She said it several times when she was in labour.'

I knew what that name was. I said quickly: 'I'll ask her about it later.'

As I darted out of the room and along the corridor to the stairs I heard him call after me: 'Only five minutes!'

14

In spite of what the doctor had told me, I still had hopes that Pamela would relent when she saw our child. For a while this seemed possible. She watched me with an amused expression when I first held him in my arms, and on the following days while I sat looking down at him by the hour, at the side of his makeshift cradle. I had never seen a newborn baby before and the sheer wonder of him over-whelmed me. Though I had had advance signals, I hadn't even remotely imagined the force of the effect he would have on me.

What excited me most was that he looked so like my father, a reflection of myself, of course, but one that I rarely perceived. He had reddish hair and eyebrows, showing that this would be his colouring as he got older, but otherwise he was a D'Arcy through and through: the same long narrow head and high forehead, and especially something about the set of the mouth that was quite unmistakable. This was the miracle that filled me with the foolish pride of creation.

The nurse was very matter of fact about it all. She was a Wicklow girl, in her late twenties, very practical and competent and already with the authoritative manner that subjugates patients and their families everywhere. She let me stay only a few minutes that first day, while I held Pamela's hand and admired the baby, then sent me off downstairs to prepare dinner.

I think I sensed that the last vestiges of my happiness were contained in those two weeks when the nurse came on her bicycle for an hour or so morning and evening, and ordered us around. Taking care of the baby preoccupied us when we were left alone, so that we had scarcely any time for conversation. With so much natural excitement, I was able to ignore the fact that every hour was bringing it all to a close.

In those days, women stayed in bed for a week after childbirth and then began to get up cautiously for an hour or two every day until they felt strong enough to handle their households again. I said: 'Surely poor women can't do that.'

'Of course they can, unless their husbands are brutes,' the nurse said, fixing me with a look which might have included me in that category. 'Why shouldn't she have a good rest? It's her only chance, unless you're going to get a nursery nurse. She must not put her foot on the floor for seven days.'

So there was a hospital atmosphere: tiptoeing, lowered voices, no controversial subjects, frequent snacks to keep up her strength, lessons on nursing and bathing the baby, mostly conducted in my presence since, as the nurse said briskly, I had equal responsibility for his existence. And the washing – I could never have believed that so small a creature would need so many clothes. I became expert at this, under the nurse's direction, though she clearly thought it peculiar that I didn't hire a woman to come and do it for me.

The truth was that I was pleased to be the servant, since I imagined that it might bond Pamela to me. I simply wanted her to feel dependent on me for everything.

Pamela didn't change her personality enough for this to work in my favour, however. Before the week was out, one afternoon when I went into her room carrying a tray with tea, I found her standing at the window looking out over the gardens. She turned towards me, saying: 'I'd like to get out there and do some weeding. The place will soon be back to nature, at this rate.'

'But you're not supposed even to be out of bed.'

'That's all nonsense. I feel so well, I could walk to the gate and back and enjoy every moment of it. Now that she's gone home, I can come downstairs. You can take me for a walk along the avenue.'

It was no use arguing with her. She had her wish, giggling at the way she was deceiving the nurse, but she didn't get as far as the gate. Halfway there she said she had had enough and we went back, but after that she extended her clandestine walk every day, inspecting the vegetable garden and even the wood beyond. Though she was pale, I had never seen her so beautiful. A new freedom in her movements showed that she would increase in beauty from now on. I think I had never loved her so much as during that time.

The nurse left us at the end of two weeks, with instructions to send for her if we needed her. At the last moment she said: 'Surely now you'll get someone to help with the housework? You can't do it all yourselves. The house is too big.'

'We can't have anyone at present,' I said. 'We must lie low for a while.'

'Troubled times,' she said. 'The doctor told me. I could find you someone reliable.'

'No thank you. We'd prefer to wait.'

'Things will be better from now on. When are you going to baptise the baby? Have you thought of a name for him yet?'

She looked expectantly from one of us to the other. As Pamela was silent, I said: 'We haven't talked about it.'

The nurse obviously thought this was very odd, but she asked no more questions. When she had gone Pamela said: 'What name would you like? You have a right to choose that, at least.'

It was what I wanted and still I couldn't bring myself to give him a name. I knew she had meant to be kind, but that 'at least' had cut me through and through. It seemed always to be like this between us – not too little but too much understanding soured every one of my attempts at making her love me. I couldn't bring myself to utter a name while

221

I remembered what the doctor had said, though he hadn't mentioned that name either.

The apple-blossom had withered on the boughs of the old trees in the garden. O'Brien had pruned them under Pamela's direction and there would be some fruit. The weather remained sunny and dry though there was a cold edge on the wind. I had made a sort of carrying-cot for the baby and we took him with us when we went for our walks, holding one handle each. I found that O'Brien had opened the small gate that led from the garden into the wood, and we walked in there sometimes, always taking a look at the dugouts to see if anyone had been to visit them. The soldiers had wrecked the entrance to the old one and last year's dead leaves had begun to drift down into it. There were no new footmarks that we could see.

A third week passed, and we were into the early days of June: long sunny evenings, blackbirds and thrushes everywhere, woodpigeons calling all day among the heavy-leaved trees, our own robin, with his squeaky chirp, accompanying us everywhere as we weeded and cleared the garden.

Since I had been away, the farmer had taken to sending his small son down to Ferney with the milk. The boy had seen me often. Though I hadn't yet gone into the city, I had given up trying to hide myself from our neighbours. At the shop Mrs. O'Grady said that things were settling down a little. It seemed pointless to take excessive precautions. I thought I had developed a fatalistic attitude towards the possibility of being arrested, but in this I was quite wrong. I'll never forget the sickening shock that went through me when I looked out one morning and saw a Free State soldier slipping around by the side of the house.

I was in the drawing-room, working at the fireplace, brushing the ashes aside and stacking logs of wood for the evening. We always got it lighted for an hour or two before going to bed. I had glanced towards the side window while I straightened up from my stooping position. There was no mistaking the uniform: ill-fitting green, with a peaked cap.

The man looked furtive, perhaps a scout for a bigger raiding party. My suspicions were confirmed when he paused and looked back towards the front of the house.

My first thought was of flight, naturally, but where could I go? This house could be surrounded in no time. Its only advantage had been that no one knew about it, but since the last raid even that protection was gone.

Then I saw the man cross the grass and try to peer in through the window. I stood perfectly still, hoping that the sunlight outside would make the interior of the room invisible, but he saw me. To my amazement he pressed an agonised face almost against the glass and beckoned urgently, using his whole arm. This was no raiding party. Suddenly I remembered Tim O'Brien's cousin. I gestured quickly to indicate that he should go around to the back of the house and a moment later he was standing inside the back door, his cap in his hand, rubbing the sweat from his forehead.

He was twitching with fright. I led him into the kitchen and poured him a glass of water and made him sit down. After a moment he said: 'I'm afraid I gave you a start. I'm Jock O'Brien, Tim's cousin. I've been trying to get here for the last fortnight but there wasn't a hope. They took us out on the lorries today and I slipped off. If I'm caught I'll be in the clink.'

'Where is the rest of the party? What are they doing?'

'How the hell do I know? They don't tell us, only shove the gun in our hands and tell us when to let go.'

'Are they near us now?'

'No. They went on,' he said. 'We stopped to have a pumpship at the side of the road, and I just went down into the ditch. The lads might cover up for me, if they can, though I don't know how in hell I'm going to get back to barracks. I couldn't miss the chance when I saw we were near here.'

'Which barracks are you in?'

'Portobello. I could walk it after dark, maybe. Or I might

catch up with the lorries on their way back, if I'm lucky. I can say I was left behind by mistake.'

'Where is Tim? Still in the Curragh?'

'He's there, all right, but I don't see him any more. They took us to Dublin the week before last and I needn't tell you I haven't been back since. I have a message for you.'

'From whom?'

'I don't know. I just got it through some of the boys. I'm getting sick and tired of this. I can't keep on with it forever. Sure as God they'll catch me some day.'

'What is the message?'

'That the Englishwoman is to go to her aunt's house and bring the babby with her, if she has it.'

'When?'

'As soon as she can. That's all I heard.'

'Which camp did the message come from?'

'I don't know.'

And it was true. I questioned him over and over, but all he could say was that the message had come to him through some reliable means. I thought it might have been from Dunne, but he would not have known about the baby. Obviously someone knew she was in danger if she stayed at Ferney. I couldn't help feeling relieved – I had urged her many times to let me take her to her aunt's house. Now she would have to listen to me.

She came into the kitchen a few minutes later and I left it to Jock O'Brien to repeat the message. I could see that she was upset, but like myself she had to accept that the message was from a reliable source. Jock was quite incapable of acting. She simply had to believe him. She tried to get him to admit that he had seen Dunne, but he swore he wouldn't know him from a crow. At last she gave up and thanked him for bringing the message, which I had quite forgotten to do. Then she put him sitting at the table and gave him a pot of tea and some bread and butter and cold ham, which he wolfed as if he hadn't eaten for a week. When he had finished he said: 'That was grand, ma'am. You'd cry with the hunger in the army. Every penny we get goes on extra grub. Bread and tea – potatoes and cabbage and an inch of bacon – how can a man work on that?'

Pamela said: 'Why don't you get a different job?'

'Where would I get a job? There won't be any jobs for years, as far as I can see. You have to have someone to speak for you, and I haven't a sinner.'

'Can you send a message from us back to the Curragh?'

'No. It's a one-way traffic.'

He left us soon afterwards, though we offered to let him stay until the evening.

'I'll go a-hide by the gate,' he said, 'and I'll watch out for the lorries coming back. I'll stop the first one and play the innocent. I'll say they went off and left me, and I'll let on to be hopping mad. It's as good a trick as any other, as the cat said to the mouse. That tea done me good, ma'am.'

When he had gone, Pamela said tensely: 'Who sent that message?'

It was then that I told her of Commandant Fahy's hints that she might be in danger, and I said that I thought this message probably came from the same source. Obviously she must heed it, and she agreed that she must set out for Mount Sanders as soon as possible. The message had said she was to bring the baby with her, 'if she had it'. I couldn't imagine Fahy including that detail, but I said nothing about this to Pamela. She must have overlooked it, since she made no reference to it then or later.

I took it for granted that I would go with her to Mount Sanders but she wouldn't hear of it. Her aunt would get the wrong impression, she said, which meant that it would look as if we were married. She preferred to make her own explanations. She would not be far away. I could visit her after a while. She conceded that I might do that. I was forced to agree. I had a strong feeling that her aunt would support my cause, eventually. It might be a good thing to leave them alone together for a little while.

I went down to the village and sent off a telegram on her

instructions. Then I helped her to pack some clothes. She wanted to set off on the tram, carrying the baby and her luggage, but I pointed out that this would be impossible. At last she let me accompany her to the station and see them onto the train.

The next week passed like a year. My feet felt heavy as lead when I walked around the house and garden, doing all the things that had seemed so important while she was there and that seemed futile and stupid now. She had left me enough money to live on, since I still had no income, and I amused myself by keeping a record of what I spent so as to be able to repay her later.

The nights were the worst. A point would come when I couldn't work any longer. I would light the fire and sit there looking at it, waiting for the first yawn to indicate that I could go to bed. Then I would lie in the dark listening to the owls and the other night birds, sleeping at last and waking to the bright light at the window in the early morning.

I heard nothing from her, no letter, no message of any kind, but I was not surprised at this, since she might have thought it dangerous to write to me. No one came to the house except the boy with the milk, and he had clearly been told not to stop and chat. I would have been glad to have a conversation with him, with anyone at all – but he would say only a few words and then run off. It was better at the shop. Mrs. O'Grady kept me abreast of the news but she warned me that I should still keep out of sight. When she asked about Pamela, I said she had gone for a visit to her aunt in the country. Mrs. O'Grady said: 'That's no harm. She can do with a bit of a rest. I hear he's a fine little lad, the image of yourself.'

'Where did you hear that?'

'Nurse Donnelly, of course. Who else?'

Pamela had been gone for more than a week when I woke up one morning, still heavy with a dream about her, and decided then and there to follow her. Letting her go alone now seemed ridiculous. I should never have allowed it. I had been too easily persuaded. The message had not said that I was to stay at Ferney. I didn't even know who the message was from, nor whether I was under orders from anyone. As if my brain had been asleep and now came to sudden life, I locked up the house and set off for the railway station, without even packing an overnight bag. There was a train to Trim at noon, a journey of an hour or so, and from there I would have to hire a car for the rest of the way. It never occurred to me to announce my arrival.

The only vehicle I could get at Trim station was an outside car, but the driver said it was only three miles to Mount Sanders and he would do it in less than half an hour. We set off over smooth sandy roads, past gentle green pastureland. With the grinding noise of the metal-bound wheels and the heavy pounding of the horse's hooves, no conversation was possible. I was glad of this. I tried to spend the time preparing myself for our meeting, and working out some reasonable explanation of my relationship with Pamela, for the benefit of her aunt. Perhaps Pamela would have done some groundwork for me. But in fact, I was so excited at the prospect of seeing her and my son again, that I could barely think about anything else.

Pamela had described Mount Sanders so well that it was no surprise when I saw it. There was the long, winding avenue with the neat lodge at the gates, the Palladian house with broad, shining windows, the lawns and flower-beds all in perfect condition, a total contrast with Ferney. Trees kept their distance on a small hill, a beautiful circle of chestnuts and beeches, with here and there a single elm to shade the cattle from the sun.

A parlour-maid of whom my mother would have approved let me into the house and left me to wait in the drawing-room. A few minutes later Mrs. Sanders came in, again such a familiar presence that I felt I had known her all my life. Her eyes were her most remarkable feature, a reddish brown as her hair must have been once, with a

227

disconcerting sparkle of intelligence that seemed to take in everything about me all at once. She evidently knew as much about me as I did about her. She came towards me at once with her hands out to take mine, saying: 'I didn't expect you. Pamela didn't say you were coming.'

'She doesn't know. How could I stay away? I should never have let her come alone. We were confused.'

She turned away and brushed a trailing wisp of white hair back from her forehead. Every move showed her agitation. I was struck dumb by panic, waiting for her to speak. At last she said: 'They've gone, since yesterday.'

'Where?'

'To London, to her mother. Did she really not tell you? Did she not write to you?'

'I've had nothing. Did she say she would write?'

'I told her she must. She didn't promise. Oh, for God's sake let's sit down and talk. We can't stand about forever. Are you hungry?'

'I don't know.'

'My poor boy, that means you are. I'll send for something.'

The parlour-maid brought a tray and we sat at either side of the fire. I was ravenous, and while she talked I ate every single sandwich and piece of cake in front of me. Pamela had received a second message, which said that she must leave the country. The only place she could go was to her mother. She had told her aunt about the first message and the strange way it was delivered. This one seemed to come from the same source, through one of the gardeners whose brother was a prisoner in the Curragh. Mrs. Sanders said: 'Whoever sent those messages knows a great deal about her and about you. Who could that be?'

'Commandant Fahy, of the Connemara Brigade,' I said. 'I can think of no one else. Did she tell you that he said she was suspected of being a spy?'

'Yes, and I think it's nonsense. There was a man who came here more than once, during the Black-and-Tan times.

You know him well, Pamela says. Paul Dunne – she talked about him quite a lot. He was quite a high-ranking officer and he would have vouched for her.'

'But he's in one of the camps.'

'The messages come from that camp. They seem to keep in touch with what's happening outside. Someone must have thought she was in danger.'

I asked: 'Did she travel alone?'

'No. There was an English nanny here, whose job had come to an end, and she was on her way back to Yorkshire. I persuaded Pamela to employ her. She needs someone to take care of the baby. She said you were doing all that.'

'So I was. Did she leave a message for me?'

'She was supposed to write to you.'

Now Mrs. Sanders couldn't meet my eyes, and from such a forthright person this could only mean one thing. I said harshly, using a tone that would have been classed as rude if either of us had had time to think of such things: 'She didn't write. You know what she would have said. Tell me.'

'I don't know what she would have said. I only know what she said to me. I can see now that the baby is yours, but she said –' She paused for a moment and then went on in a rush, using a different, quite bitter tone, as if she hated the words she uttered: 'She said the father was someone she will never marry. She doesn't care enough for him, though she seems to have given him her favours without mentioning that.'

I was stung by this injustice to her. I said quickly: 'She always said she would never marry me, but I hoped she would change. I hoped the baby would change everything.'

'That was a foolish hope. I'm afraid you don't know very much about women. Do you have a sister?'

'No. I had a brother, but he was killed in the war.'

'The war in France?'

'Yes.'

'Well, she has taken your son to London and she says you are not to follow her. Had you thought of it?'

'Yes, I would go this very day. Why shouldn't I follow her?'

'I don't know. Give her time. She may write to me. Stay here with me for a little, and wait.'

'Do you know what you're asking?'

'Of course I do. I know Pamela very well. In a way I have some responsibility for forming her mind. She would never have come to Ireland if she hadn't learned something about it from me.'

'She has told me so, many times. She has a great admiration for you.'

'Not enough to take my advice, or do what I demand.'

'Did you demand?'

'Yes. But in affairs like this one can never demand beyond a certain point. One loses one's certainty, even at my age and with my experience. I told her where her duty lay, and that was with you, though I had never seen you. I know now that I was right.'

'How do you know?'

'By one look at you. She would do well with you, and you with her. You're two of a kind. If I had ever seen you, I would have been able to add that to my reasons.'

'She might not have seen it as an argument. Did she tell you that there's someone else she would marry?'

'No, but it's not hard to see that there is. Do you know who it is?'

Instead of answering, I asked: 'Did she name the baby?'

'Yes. She said his name is Paul. Hadn't you decided that together?'

'No.'

Obviously she didn't make the connection between this sickening statement and Dunne. Paul is a common enough name. And she didn't press the earlier question. I think she assumed I knew no more than she did.

I stayed at Mount Sanders simply because it was the nearest I could be to Pamela. I expected that she would write to her aunt, and I even hoped that she might come back, but the days passed without either happening. As I had no luggage, Mrs. Sanders drove me to Trim to buy some night-clothes and a shirt or two, but otherwise I never left the property. I drifted around the house and grounds, aware that she was full of pity for me. One morning at breakfast, after I had been there for a week or so, as she finished looking at her post, she said: 'Still nothing. You can really do no more.'

'I could go to London.'

'It would do no good. She made that quite clear.'

'What, then? I can't go back to Ferney.'

Beautiful Ferney, full of the ghosts of everything I loved – it would be madness to go back there without her. Mrs. Sanders didn't answer my question. I guessed that my presence irked her, though she would never have said it. There was only one place I could be sure of, unwilling as I was to make use of it. I said: 'I can go back to my father's house, like the prodigal son.'

'You don't want to do that?'

'No. But I think the time has come for it.'

'Pamela would know where to find you, if she comes to her senses.'

I left the next day. Mrs. Sanders drove me to Mullingar in time to catch the Galway train. I remember clearly how it was to follow that old route, so full of painful memories, so full of expectations that were never realised. The little station at Galway, approached over a rickety bridge, then the long wait in Eyre Square for a hired car to take me home, the long, slow progress through the little medieval town, the view of the river and its many bridges, all gave me a pain in my heart which reached its climax when I arrived at the gates of my father's house.

My driver was a stout, untidy, middle-aged man who told me that his name was Dave Brown and that he used to do a lot of driving for the officers in Renmore barracks in the good old times when the British army was there. He drove recklessly, with one elbow propped on the door of his car, so that he was perpetually canted sideways. This was exaggerated by his continual attempts to engage me in conversation, half turned to see the effect of his questions. Where did I come from? He knew Castle D'Arcy – was I one of the D'Arcys? Had I been away for a long time? What was the news from Dublin? Was the war over? In return he informed me that not only his own business, but the whole of Galway was ruined by the departure of the British army, that it would be a good thing if all the Republicans in the country were shot or deported to Australia as was the custom long ago, and that since the gentry had lost their money, there was scarcely a living for anyone. I had to answer some of his questions and I could see by his response that he knew nothing about my recent history.

When we reached Castle D'Arcy, the first thing that struck me was that the heavy gates, with their spiked bars, were standing open. They had always been kept shut. It had been sunny all day but now, as often happens in Ireland, suddenly the sky clouded over and a light wind stirred the trees. The driver swished between the two stone lions without a pause. I noticed that the grass at either side of the avenue hadn't been grazed down, nor the bushes trimmed back. With my experience at Ferney, I could see exactly what needed to be done here. If my father would allow me to help, I could spend my time very usefully. The realisation that I ought to be bringing home my son and my beautiful wife made me almost weep. At this moment I would be showing her my favourite places and telling her about the delights to come.

My mood of self-pity was halted abruptly when we turned the corner and took in the scene before us. The driver, who had been quite unperturbed by the hazards of our journey, swerved violently so that the car almost left the driveway. He righted it with an automatic reaction and said, in a half whisper: 'Jesus, Mary and Joseph!'

He pulled over to the left-hand side of the gravel sweep and switched off the engine. We sat in the car, I in the back seat and the driver in front, gazing in a state of shocked speechlessness, trying to make sense of what we saw.

Castle D'Arcy was on fire. The front door stood wide open, and so did the windows of the rooms at each side of it, creating a draught which was obviously finding its way up through the building to the very roof. On the first and second floors the flames looked out through the glass, and while we watched, one by one the panes split with a loud cracking noise. A gentle roaring sound, quite even and steady, filled the air like the humming of a giant swarm of bees. Slates began to slide off the roof as the timbers up there caught fire.

It took me a moment or two to realise all of this. Then I became aware of a small group of people standing on the grass lawn directly in front of the house. I flung the car door open. I would have given anything to slip into the woods and disappear but there could be no question of that. I crossed the gravel and walked firmly towards them. They watched me, their eyes temporarily drawn away from the burning house. There were four, my father and mother and two of the women servants, as I could tell by their uniforms, probably the cook and a kitchenmaid or housemaid.

They looked at me blankly as I approached. I must have been an odd sight, in the ill-fitting overcoat and baggy trousers that I had been given in Cork, and with my overlong hair. Then my mother said: 'It's Michael – thank God you're here.'

My father said nothing, just stared at me with an expression I couldn't understand.

I said, addressing the cook as the most likely to give a reasonable answer: 'What happened? How did it start?'

'It was Josie Cregan from Recess – I know him well. He was the leader.'

'Leader?'

'There were six of them. They came about an hour ago. They brought barrels of petrol. They ran up to the top of the house and poured it down the stairs. Then they got out matches and set it on fire.'

'Was Peter Hynes one of them?'

'God above! What are you saying? He wouldn't have anything to do with that scum. What are you saying?'

'I'm sorry,' I said. 'Of course none of my friends – did they give you warning?'

'Josie rang at the door and when Mary answered he said everyone was to get out of the house, they were going to burn it down. They said they had their instructions.'

'How did they come? In a car?'

'Yes. They seemed to be in a great hurry. When they had the fire going they all got in the car and drove away. That's a while ago – you didn't meet them on the Galway road?'

I remembered standing at the traditional place in the square in Galway, waiting for a cab, and noticing a country-man on a horse watching me closely, then galloping off. It was at least half an hour before Dave Brown pulled in to the kerb and I engaged him to drive me home. I said: 'There were no cars since we left Galway, only horse and donkey carts. Did they say why they were burning the house?'

'No. And we didn't wait to ask them, only did what they said. What else could we do?'

'You did right. Who else was in the house?'

The cook burst into loud sobs, holding her apron over her face. The other woman, obviously controlling her voice with a tremendous effort, said: 'Maggie – the parlourmaid from Recess – I'm afraid she's burned. She was asleep – it was her time off – I didn't think of her – they wouldn't let me go up to the top of the house when I remembered. They said – Josie said if I did, I'd go the same way. But he got the Master out – he got him out –'

I think I've never seen such pain and despair on any human face as I saw at that moment. I suppose my compassion was reflected on my own. My father said, every word charged with hatred and contempt: 'Now you see what you have brought on us.'

15

A sudden gust of wind shook the four walls of the cottage and sent a cascade of soot down onto Dunne's fire. He leaned back in disgust, saying: 'Push your chair away. That stuff drifts out into the room.'

I did so, waiting for another fall, but instead the fire began to burn brightly again.

Dunne said: 'Tending a fire is an old man's amusement. Of course you don't have fires in America.'

'That's a common idea,' I said. 'We have splendid wood fires.'

'Every comfort, I believe.' That peculiar bright stare was turned on me again. 'God's own country and the devil's own people, they say.'

'Where have you heard such nonsense? There would be no Ireland, but for the Irish in America.'

He said sardonically: 'I'm glad you support them so strongly. Did you associate yourself with the Irish in America, when you went there?'

'No. I had my parents to take care of. My father was very bitter about Ireland. He could never understand what happened to him. He blamed it all on me.'

'Wasn't there some justice in that?'

'He thought that Castle D'Arcy wouldn't have been burned if I hadn't been a member of the Irish Republican Army. But in the letters I had from the Land Commission, they said quite clearly that the motive was land hunger. It was a stupid waste – Peter Hynes had plans for my father to use his skill in horse breeding, sheep too. If the house hadn't been burned, he might have become a happy citizen of the new country.'

'I told you, I would have prevented it if I could.'

'I'm not blaming you. But there was a good deal of hysteria – sending Pamela away from Ferney, and then out of the country – that was a sign of paranoia. You heard the story that she was a spy?'

Nothing like taking the bull by the horns, I thought, and waited for his reaction. It was not what I expected.

'I felt very bad about Pamela,' Dunne said after a pause. 'She was so much one of us, she deserved the best we could possibly give her in return. But we had to put the general good of the country before any personal considerations.'

'A great many people were confused by that kind of thinking.'

'Some preferred not to think at all. Some deserted us, rather than take on the burdens that we did.'

'People like myself? I had no choice. I had done everything I could. Once I was suspect, there was no point in staying on.'

'Yes, it was a pity you were associated with Pamela's case.'

'It wouldn't have made much difference, in the end. The least I could do was to take care of my parents, after what they had suffered.'

'You were always good at considering other people's sufferings,' he said with heavy irony.

'Wasn't that why we were all in the Movement?'

'Some saw further ahead than others.'

'I've heard that you never gave up, all through World War Two.'

'Yes. I was one of the people who hoped Germany would liberate Ireland finally, at the end of the war.'

'Do you still believe it might have happened? Did you really think the Germans cared what became of Ireland?'

'Who knows what would have happened, if they had won the war? It might have suited them to have us as an ally. A pan-Celtic Republic was one of the suggestions. Pamela's son was one of the people we had working on that in Berlin.

We didn't really believe in the pan-Celtic Republic but it kept us in touch with the Bretons. They might have been useful to us some day. I thought it was worth a chance. I could never have gone off and left the problem to the next generation. One has to make hard decisions.'

He said this as if he were talking about a reasonable course of action, taken by another person. He seemed to have no idea of the strangeness of the position he had taken, in the light of history. And he was clearly unaware of any special interest of mine in Pamela's son. Still I held off, waiting for more information.

I said: 'I had to make hard decisions too. Yours must have been easier, while all the final actions in the civil war were going on. You were in the Curragh then.'

'You think that was a good place to be?'

'You seem to have managed to keep in touch. You spoke a moment ago as if you were consulted about Pamela's future.'

'There were a great many consultations. Where did you go, after the fire?'

He was fobbing me off. Perhaps he was becoming suspicious. I would come back to this later. I answered his question: 'I drove with my parents to Woodbrook. Nicholas de Lacy was there, with his family. They took us all in. Mrs. de Lacy's Aunt Jack was a tower of strength. She gave my mother her own room and took care of her as if she were her sister.'

'Ah, yes, de Lacy. He dropped out too, quite early. I thought he might have stayed with us until the end.'

'There is no end.'

'And we were not to know the future. Still, de Lacy meant well, even when he followed de Valera later. Some people are happier with the winning side.'

'That seems entirely natural to me. What's the use of prolonging a losing battle?'

'Who wins the last battle is all that matters. We haven't come to that yet.'

I said: 'De Lacy was essentially a moderate man. He had plenty of courage too. He sent his men out to catch the horses that had been turned loose from the stables before the fire was set. He forced the men who had taken them to hand them back. My father approved of him – I was glad of that, at the time. It took his attention off me.'

'Did your father ever become reconciled?'

'To me, yes. But he was never comfortable in America. You have to start from scratch in that country. You have to turn your back on Europe. He was too old and too suspicious of what he called the lack of tradition. And we were too poor, for a long time. My mother accepted it better, though I know she found it harder. She learned to depend on me. What about your father?'

Dunne gave a little barking laugh. 'He called me a traitor until the day he died. He said that I and my friends had ruined his business – that was true enough, though he could have built it up again if he had kept his head. When I refused to go into the business with him, he gave it up completely. I had no time for business – my whole life was filled with politics.'

So that was why he had fetched up in this miserable shack. Perhaps I glanced around the room – somehow he divined my thoughts. He said: 'My father began to gamble on the Stock Exchange. By the time he died there was barely enough to bury him and to buy this place for myself to live in. The house in Baggot Street had been sold and he was living in an old people's home.' He was enjoying my expression of shock, waving his hand around as if to show off the special qualities of the room. 'This suits me. I never had much comfort so I don't miss it.'

'But what do you live on?'

'You've been away too long. One need never starve in Ireland. I have the old-age pension, and all kinds of free benefits – electric light and fuel, free trains and buses too, if I want them. Everyone has these things. I could have an old-I.R.A. pension but I balk at that. All of the recent governments want the civil war forgotten. They're prepared to honour anyone who helped to set up the state. I'm not in want, and I'm still called on sometimes.'

'Called on?'

'I try to teach the lessons of history to the men who want to conquer Ulster by force.'

'Don't you want to do that?'

He didn't miss my ironic tone but he chose to ignore it. He said: 'I would if it were practicable.'

'You have a following? They come to see you?'

'They like mascots, though not as much as we did long ago. They know I've spent my whole life fighting for Ireland in one way or another. I sometimes get a chance to say something useful. They know I don't believe in making the civilian population suffer to gain political ends. I've taught them some history. I've pointed out the parallels – for instance that indiscriminate bombing is the equivalent of the Staters' policy of shooting prisoners in reprisal for actions outside. They tell me that things change, but I say that principles do not.'

This was the Dunne of the room in Terenure, one I recognised all too well. Even when I agreed with him, as I did now, and admired him for his life of self-sacrifice, his sententious moralising had the usual effect of arousing an almost palpable resistance in me, as if I were holding off a heavy weight that threatened to crush me to the ground. There were still some things I wanted to ask him. I said: 'Where did you go when you came out of the Curragh?'

'Back to Ferney. There was nowhere else. I could have gone home, I suppose, but there were still raids and I thought my father had had enough of that.'

'His house was raided too?'

'There was one raid while I was in the Curragh and they came again after I was released. They found nothing because there was nothing for them to find, but they caught me later. They played cat and mouse with some of us for a long time.'

'I heard you were arrested several times.'

'Yes. None of us were able to learn a profession or even take up a trade. Just when a man was getting properly started, he was hauled off to gaol again. It was just as bad after de Valera was elected. First he let us all out but he had us back in again within a couple of years.'

Because they continued to usurp the functions of the elected government. Dunne didn't give any reasons.

I asked: 'Was Ferney raided again?'

'Never after the first time, when Tim O'Brien was arrested. That was noticed, but I always insisted that Pamela was innocent. I was terrified that they would shoot her. Whatever she had done, there could be no excuse for that.'

Memories of the day when I had him arrested crowded into my mind: the pain, the anguish of mind when I telephoned from Dunne's own house. I had never felt clean again. I would never have done such a thing but for Pamela. I said: 'You mean – people thought she was being protected? That's nonsense. The one raid they made should have proved it.'

'She never understood herself what had changed everything. In all her letters to me she kept asking why anyone should have doubted her. I never told her.'

'She wrote to you?'

I could barely trust myself to ask the question. Mrs. Sanders had promised to forward my letters to Pamela in London, though she wouldn't give me her address. I wrote as soon as we were settled in Woodbrook. I described the fire, and my anxiety for my parents, and our anguish over the death of the maid, and I implored her to write to me: news of herself and of our son. As the days passed and she didn't reply, I comforted myself with the fact that she hadn't written to her aunt either. Without her address it would be useless to go to London, though I suppose I could have gone to Hampton Court and looked for her there. But it was impossible for me to leave my parents. I wrote again explaining this, saying that I would join her the moment she said that I could. Still no answer. And at that time she was writing to Dunne. He was watching me, again understanding more than I wanted, asking: 'Didn't she write to you? That was bad of her, after all you had done. Of course, she never liked to lose her independence. She may have felt under too much of an obligation to you.'

'Did she tell you what I had done for her?'

'Oh yes, once she was safely away. In her first letter she said that when I was arrested I didn't know about the baby, but that she wanted to break the news to me now. I fact, I did know. It was quite obvious. The men were even joking among themselves about it.'

'Joking?'

'Yes, about who the father was and all that. I felt responsible, having left her so open to temptation when I was away, sending those young men to stay in the house. It never occurred to me that she couldn't protect herself. I saw it afterwards, when it was too late. I was furiously angry with them, and with myself, but of course I couldn't say anything to her. I was determined that whatever happened, I would look after her. Then when I was arrested, as I told you, I was frantic with worry about her until I realised that you would step in and take care of her.'

I reached into my pocket for my little bottle of pills and my hand touched the gun. It felt warm from my body, and from the fire. I moved my chair back a little farther and Dunne said: 'Yes, now the room is warm, we needn't sit so close to it. You have to take pills?'

'Everyone does, at our age.'

'Not me, so far. I keep away from doctors. Haven't been to one for at least fifteen years. What's the matter with you, or may I ask?'

'One of those chronic things. These are the solution, it seems.'

'Can I get you a glass of water?'

'Please.'

241

'Whiskey, if you like.'

'No thank you, just water.'

Whiskey would be the end of my control, even a small amount, as I had discovered recently. I was never a drinking man and my toleration of alcohol was not high. In the hotel bar in Dublin, when I went in the evenings for a little company, I found that one drink made me tipsy, while it left the regular drinkers quite sober. They noticed it too, and some who were not as friendly as John MacDonagh took the opportunity of questioning me about my history. They thought I would be communicative, but I kept a tight grip on my tongue and told them only as much as I wished to tell: that I had emigrated in the '20s and gone into business. And my reasons for visiting Ireland? Curiosity, I said. One more visit before I die. This was accepted as a witticism. The Irish are always joking about death.

Dunne went into the little kitchen off the living-room and I heard him turn on a tap and fill a glass. He came back in a moment and handed it to me, looking down at me solicitously while I swallowed my pill and some water. He said then, as he took the glass: 'I'm afraid all this revival of old memories is wearing you out.'

'Not at all. It's what I came for.'

He carried the glass into the kitchen, talking as he rinsed it under the tap: 'I didn't give you much of a welcome but I'm glad you came. I often wondered about you. So many lives were torn apart at that time. In a way, the people who didn't leave Ireland had the best of it. Everyone was very poor but we were able to make our own destiny, for good or ill. You may have had long spells when you didn't think of Ireland at all, nor of Pamela and her problems.'

'Oh yes. I thought of her. I always had the latest news of her. Mrs. Sanders was very good about letting me know what was happening. She wrote several times a year, until she died. After that I heard nothing. No, it was not any easier, being away.'

I was talking too much. Let him talk – he was very willing.

'One thing must have been easier,' he said, 'not seeing your old enemies walking the streets all around you. You remember how we hated Mulcahy? He was a good Minister of Education later. A good Irishman too. We tried many times to have him killed, but somehow he always escaped.'

'I never believed in assassinating individuals. I thought we had had enough of that.'

'Killing political figures is different,' he said calmly. 'Your ideas weren't very realistic. I remember you came to Dublin once, all hot and bothered about an official that had been killed in the West. Do you remember that?'

'Very well.'

'You thought we should draw up two lines and fight a battle – *après vous, messieurs les Anglais*. It was charming in its way, and we needed some people like you to give tone to the thing.'

I felt a thrill of rage go through me. He was condemning himself. But the time was not yet.

I said: 'Was it the same thought that made you so sure I would take care of Pamela?'

'Now I've offended you. I'm sorry. Yes, it was. And I was right, about that at least, though I underestimated you in many other ways. I thought I knew you through and through. I realised much later that I should have consulted you more often. You had better judgment than I had in a great many things, in spite of your innocence. Pamela thought the world of you, but she was a little afraid of you too.'

'Afraid?'

'Of your disapproval. She said in her letters that she didn't want you to follow her to London. At first she was even afraid to write to her aunt lest you would get news of her, and follow her.'

'Did she say specifically why she was afraid of my disapproval?'

'No. But she said you were so high-minded, she could never live up to your standards. Considering what you had done for her, that was not fair. It was the same high-mindedness that had kept you at her service until the baby was born.'

'Did she mention the baby in her letters?'

'Only in the first one. She said her aunt had got her a nurse. It all seemed very practical and orderly.'

How he despised all that domesticity – it showed clearly in his tone.

Very quietly I asked: 'Did you write to her often?'

'Yes, in the beginning.'

'How often?'

He hadn't missed my agitation, but perhaps he put it down to my illness.

'Once a week or so, as often as she wrote to me. She seemed very upset and anxious at first. Then she calmed down, and I felt I was no longer so necessary to her. I had judged rightly in that, at least – she was better out of the country.'

'And you were busy.'

'Yes. The war was not over for us. We still had to go on organising, planning, but more secretly than ever.'

'In the camp?'

'Yes, and later in various houses, just as we always did. Ferney was very useful.'

'You still used Ferney?' I said in amazement.

'Yes, Pamela kept it on for several years. She said we were to use it in memory of old times, and she would gladly pay the rent. None of us could have afforded it, and the organisation had no money for that kind of thing, as you remember.'

'I remember.'

'Of course we would have nothing to do with her after she married. She herself knew that it was impossible.'

'Why?'

'The wife of a British army Colonel playing host to the I.R.A. – it would have been crazy. You heard about her marriage, of course?'

244

'Mrs. Sanders wrote to me about it.' That was when I gave up all hope. After a pause I asked cautiously: 'Did you instruct Pamela not to write to me?'

'Only in a general way. I said she shouldn't write to anyone she had known in the Movement. I thought a clean break was best, and I was thinking of her safety.'

'About the question of Ferney – surely what she did with her money was her own business?'

'Perhaps. But I wrote to her pointing out that we didn't need to be supported by traitors.' Here was the old venomous tone, the first time I had heard it in full cry. It brought me with a shock to a sudden realisation of the forces of implacable hatred that were still housed in that skinny body. Then he changed back to the easy tone he had been using until now. 'Dear old Ferney. The owners died and the house was sold. I think it has been pulled down.'

'Yes, it has. A new house has been built on the site. You can see where the garden was.'

'You went to see it? Wasn't that a painful thing to do?'

'Yes, but it was worth it.'

'You really have been making the rounds.'

'It was dear to me too. Once I had made the decision to come to Ireland, I had to see everything.' Then, still pursuing my plan, I said: 'So you kept in touch with the boy?'

'With Paul Hurst?' He said the name easily. 'Oh yes. When he was older and getting curious about Ireland, he came to see me.'

'With Pamela's approval?'

'Of course. She suggested it. Did you know he was named after me? That was touching. She was anxious for him to learn about Ireland. She wrote a strange little letter about it, after a long silence. Then she sent him to Ireland alone, for a visit. That was when I met him.' He was staring at me sharply, so that I had to drop my eyes. 'Do you think I should have rejected him? I would have thought it very cruel.'

'I don't see how you could have done that. Once he was interested.'

'He was interested, indeed. He wanted to know everything. At first I didn't quite see why, then I realised that
Pamela had talked to him a great deal.'

'When did he come?'

'Let me see: he was fifteen on his first visit – it must have
been in the middle 1930s. Yes, about 1937.'

'He was born in May, 1922.'

'Well, I was right. That was before our involvement with
Germany, before we had any ideas other than overthrowing
our own government and setting up the Republic again. If
we had had the country behind us, that would have been
possible. There were economic difficulties in the '30s – you
were not here for all that. The farmers were in a state of
ferment. We thought that if we offered something better,
they would follow us. We were wrong. They hadn't an ounce
of patriotism – all they wanted was higher prices for their
cattle. The towns were not much better. The days of sacrifice
for Ireland were over.'

'How long did he stay?'

'On that first visit? A couple of months – July and August.
I sent him off with some other young fellows, to stay
in summer Irish colleges and go to Irish dances and get
the feel of the country. I saw at once that he was the very
thing we needed. He was tall and thin, with an English
accent. Rather like you, in fact, but he fitted in better. He
tried very hard to learn Irish. He stayed out in Rosmuc for
a while, and then he and three of the Dublin boys went to
Donegal.'

'What use did you plan to make of him?' By keeping my
voice low I managed to remove the tension from it.

Dunne said: 'We were beginning to see new possibilities
in these idealistic young people. They knew next to nothing
about the civil war, even if their fathers had been in it. That
was kept very carefully out of the history books. They knew
all about Queen Elizabeth and Cromwell and the rising of
1798 and the great famine and the land war – not too much
about Parnell. They knew about Pearse. He was their saint.

When they were in Donegal they learned more about the partition of the country. They came back from that trip all eager to fight.'

'And Pamela? Did she come?'

'Never – surely Mrs. Sanders told you that? Paul went home, to go back to his school, but he was in Ireland again the next summer and this time he stayed.'

'When did you send him to Germany?'

'Just before the war began: the first of September, 1939. I knew Germany would close up once war was declared and we had been promised hospitality and work for anyone we sent over. He was in the radio station in Berlin for a while. They trained him and one or two others to send us messages. Then in summer 1943 we got word that he was on his way home in a German submarine. We expected him to land somewhere on the coast of Clare.He never reached here. A great many submarines were sunk at that time, if you remember. Radar had been discovered, and the Germans didn't know it. After the war, some of the others came home and it was they who told us about his work there, when he left and so on. As I said, I always felt specially responsible for him. He had a great sense of fun, like Pamela. In fact, he was very like her in temperament as well as in appearance.' Now there was no escaping his gaze. 'You did know about his death?'

I felt that my breath had almost stopped, but I managed to say quietly: 'Only that it happened. No details. I got a printed card through Mrs. Sanders' lawyers. She was dead by then.'

'I see. Aren't you going to go to London to see Pamela?'

'She has taken great trouble to avoid me. I doubt if it would be a success.'

'Won't you at least try?'

'What about you? Have you ever attempted to see her?'

He said, quite casually: 'It was out of the question for me to see her ever again. I've told you how I felt about that.'

'Did she know you were the authority that had ordered her out of the country?'

'Did I say I was? Well, I suppose you read between the lines. No, she didn't know. Apart from that, as I said, I understood – I sympathised with her – I might have seen her again. But when she married a British army officer, obviously we could never meet.'

'Still you thought it was all right to write to her?'

'After she married, I didn't answer her letters and she stopped writing too. Then, as I told you, she wrote again, and Paul turned up soon after her letter, expecting a welcome. It would have been brutal to turn him away. And there was his heredity. I've always felt badly about my part in his father's death. I can't say I was not responsible. In fact, I know I did it deliberately. I've carried that load on my conscience all these years – what's the matter? More water –'

'No. It's nothing. I'm all right. Go on.'

Watching me, he went on slowly: 'You remember that man Horgan, who was in the Four Courts and in the hotels with us? He was killed in an assassination attempt.'

'Yes, of course.'

'A rough man, but very patriotic. I remember your saying once that he and some of the others were not leader types. Well, it was obvious that he was the father of Pamela's child. You could tell by the way he talked about her to the others, always defending her – I already knew he was crazy about her. I sent him out that night, knowing that his chances of escaping were almost nothing. And he didn't escape.'

'Why did you do it?'

'The scandal. I felt that the Republicans couldn't afford any scandals. The Staters were disgracing themselves. Our best hope was to prove that we were carrying the torch for the nation – that's how I saw it.'

I realised that I was shaking. I even thought I was about to faint, as Bill Webber had warned me might

248

happen. The gun – I had waited a long time for this moment when I would take revenge for the ruin he had made of my life. Now I found that I couldn't do it. You must be in practice to take revenge. The idea suddenly seemed pointless and silly. From his own mouth I had learned that he had injured me even more than I had known, and still I couldn't bring myself to kill him. Our conversation had proved that his obsession was at least the match of mine.

But there was a still stronger reason which hadn't occurred to me until now. In killing Dunne I would put myself in his power more surely than I had ever been when I was young. I would never be rid of him. Even as it was, I knew that his comments and questions would haunt me for the rest of my life. Why had I not gone to find Pamela; why had I stayed all those years away from Ireland? Inevitably I had asked myself the final question: why had I so easily abandoned my son? All that had happened was as much my doing as Dunne's. There was no longer any point in killing him.

I stood up with difficulty, letting him take my arm.

He said: 'Are you sure you'll be all right? It's quite a long drive back to Dublin. Where are you staying?'

'Buswell's hotel, beside the Dáil. I'll be all right. I'm used to taking care of myself.'

'It brought back the old times – I'm grateful for your visit. Can you come again?'

'I doubt it. I'm lucky to have been able to come this once.'

He looked puzzled and uncertain as he escorted me to the door, as if there were still some questions he would like to have asked. At the very moment of leaving him, some devil took hold of me and I said: 'By the way, Pamela's child was mine. Paul was my son.'

I walked quickly down the rocky little path, risking my neck at every step and glad of the light from the high-sailing, wintry moon. When I reached my car I climbed in and drove away, with one backward glance at the cottage. The door was closed.

A week later, I crawled down to the hotel bar for a drink at six o'clock. John MacDonagh saw me at once and came over to my table. He put his glass down beside mine, looking worried, and said: 'Where have you been? We missed you.'

'Got a touch of some bug. I've been sleeping it off. They got me a doctor – he gave me something for it.'

'I've been thinking about you all day,' he said. 'Remember asking me about Paul Dunne? Did you ever track him down?'

'Indeed I did. I went to see him last week; spent an evening with him.'

'You were just in time. He was found dead in that cottage today. I read it in the paper at the office. He had been dead about a week, it seems. A heart attack. His nearest neighbour realised he hadn't seen him around and went to investigate. He was one of the old stock. There will be a military funeral. The President will be there, an oration over the grave, a volley – the whole works.'

'Was he so well thought of?'

'He was a minor figure, of course, but there are so few of his generation left. They must get a good send-off. Don't forget, without them we wouldn't be sitting here, looking across at our own parliament house. They bred great men in those days, great men.'

Yes, I went to the funeral and was escorted to the front seat in the church as an old comrade. With no relatives to speak for him, it must have been assumed he was a Catholic. At the consecration of the Mass an army trumpeter marched up the aisle, accompanied by a standard bearer with the Tricolour, and played the Last Post. I shook hands with the President, a gentle man of about fifty, the age my son would have been, if he had lived.